Paul D. Carter was born in Melbour
going to Collingwood football matches ......
Marcus.

He completed a PhD while writing his first novel, *Eleven Seasons*, which allowed him to combine his own experience of growing up in Melbourne in the 1980s with his keen interest in modern Australian history. Paul currently teaches English and creative writing to secondary students in the western suburbs of Melbourne, as part of the Teach for Australia Programme.

eleven seasons

PAUL D. CARTER

ALLEN&UNWIN
SYDNEY·MELBOURNE·AUCKLAND·LONDON

Allen & Unwin
Sydney, Melbourne, Auckland, London

83 Alexander Street
Crows Nest NSW 2065
Australia
Phone: (61 2) 8425 0100
Fax: (61 2) 9906 2218
Email: info@allenandunwin.com
Web: www.allenandunwin.com

Cataloguing-in-Publication details are available
from the National Library of Australia
www.trove.nla.gov.au

ISBN 978 1 74237 971 5

Internal design by Lisa White
Set in 12/17 pt Adobe Garamond by Post Pre-press Group, Australia
Printed and bound in Australia by Griffin Press
10 9 8 7 6 5 4 3 2 1

part one
home 1985–1989

1. promise

All ten of the 1985 Hawthorn VFL swap cards are arranged in two rows on Jason Dalton's bedspread. Most of them are creased and rain damaged. Brand new they cost fifty cents a pack from Arthur's milk bar around the corner, but Jason had to win them playing flicks at school. Two players flick their cards against the wall, and the first player to land his card on top of another wins the other's cards. It took him only two days to collect the Hawthorn set. Afterwards, the other kids in Year Seven wouldn't play him. 'No way, mate—you're a freak,' they said.

Michael Tuck, the Hawthorn ruck-rover, is card ninety. He has a long-sleeve guernsey, a taut, wiry body and a teacher's brown beard. Jason wonders if his dad had a beard like that. Probably not. He might have looked like back-pocket Gary Ayres, though: tall and broad with black hair swimming around his collar. Card ninety-eight—last card in the Hawthorn set.

His overdue maths homework sits on the fold-out desk in the corner, forgotten. His textbook still looks unused, and it's June, almost the end of second term. Jason has problems focusing in class, his teachers say in notes to his mother. A tendency to drift off. He needs to spend more time listening and more time contributing to class discussions. Please check his homework when you can. He needs to be pushed.

He looks at the Casio on his wrist—11.16 pm—and pushes a button on its side to set the alarm. His mum will finish her overnight shift at the St Vincent's in six and a half hours, come home, sleep for two hours, check his work, then drive him to school. He needs a good excuse for why he hasn't done it. He decides to wait and see if she remembers to ask.

Above him, Flat Nine is already in bed, snoring as usual. Another neighbour is unlatching their metal letterbox at the front of the driveway, one floor down. Every night, the building's plumbing system groans and shakes whenever someone upstairs uses the shower. These are sounds he's lived with for so long he wakes in his sleep when it gets too quiet.

'Just another couple of years,' he says in his mum's voice. He says it again, making a face this time. She's still pulling double shifts, collapsing into bed and leaving rissoles in the fridge for when he gets home from school.

He wraps an elastic band twice around his set of cards and makes sure his favourite player, Lethal, is on top: Leigh Matthews, card ninety-four, the toughest man in the league. In the photo, Lethal is going prematurely grey and is so muscular he looks short. Jason wonders if his dad had a moustache like Lethal. Plenty of guys do—even his maths teacher, Mr Cyril. Or maybe his dad had a convict's moustache, like the Hawthorn wingman Robert DiPierdomenico—the Dipper, card eighty-nine.

Cars hiss through the rain outside. A lonely sound. He thinks of his mum at work, wheeling someone down a hospital corridor.

After packing his swap cards into the shoebox in his cupboard he shuts his blinds, and then checks the lounge room to make sure the column heater beside the kitchen is turned off. He checks the screen door and front door to make sure they're locked. He writes his mum a note so she can get some milk before he wakes up in the morning. Just as she told him to. He's a good boy, she tells his teachers. You should see how well he looks after himself.

He turns off his bedroom light and climbs under his fading *Star Wars* bedspread. He closes his eyes, rolls over, and sandwiches his head between his pillows to block out the world. He can see himself on one of the cards: a freeze-frame of him in mid-kick, an out-of-focus Essendon player lunging at him from behind. Jason Dalton, Hawthorn, card ninety-five. He tries to turn the rain hitting his window into the crowd. Instead, it sends him to sleep.

. . .

June Saturdays, July Saturdays. Winter has crept over Melbourne, a crisp chill, the sun high and faint above swampy grey clouds. At midday, he sits on his hands on the brown brick fence in front of his block of flats. His brown hair is longer, now a bowl over his ears and brow. He wears the green woollen jumper he got as a birthday present from his mum. She's asleep inside, recharging on her day off. In his backpack he's carrying the last two chocolate honeycomb muffins she baked. At school, he can trade them for homework answers, and on Fridays, hot sausage rolls from the tuckshop. The muffins are the greatest snack in the world.

Here comes his ride now—Hayden Bennett, his best friend since the Hawks' 1983 premiership. The black four-wheel drive glides into a space opposite. Hayden reclines in the front passenger seat, one arm hanging out the window, and he's wearing his father's sunglasses. He's heavy, barrel-chested and short, with clear skin and curly blond hair that can't be brushed. They're past waving at each other.

Jason climbs into the car, careful not to upset the golf bag behind

Hayden's seat. A sweet smell of aftershave hangs in the air. He looks into the rear-view mirror. 'Morning, Mr Bennett.' He's been best friends with Hayden for three years but still can't get used to calling Dean Bennett by his first name. Something in the way he dresses. Look at him now: expensive white shirt, black denim jacket, long tight jeans. Short, neat hair, blond like his son's, combed in a designer swirl that never loses its shape. He always looks like he's making money, Jason thinks. Even on his way to the football.

'What's news, Jase?' Dean says into the rear-view mirror. He turns down the volume on Radio National so he can hear Jason's reply.

'I'm good thanks, Mr Bennett.'

Nodding, Dean wheels the Range Rover into a smooth three-point turn and heads up to the main road. 'How's Christine?'

'She's okay. Asleep.'

Hayden unbuckles his seatbelt, turns onto his knees and eyes Jason from above the headrest. He pushes the sunglasses back up his nose and his face goes expressionless, like a cop in one of his comic books. 'What did you get for the maths test?'

'Uh, twelve out of twenty.'

'I got eleven. What about the science test? And don't bullshit. I got sixty-four.'

'I got sixty-six.'

Disappointment flashes across Hayden's face. He resettles in his seat and punches his seatbelt into place. 'He's talking shit, Dad.'

'No, I'm smart,' Jason says to his window. 'I just keep it secret.'

As they coast down Johnston Street to Princes Park, the Hawks' home ground, the streetscape changes from houses with fenced gardens to warehouses and locksmiths, hardware suppliers and second-hand clothing stores. Shopfronts stencilled with Vietnamese characters seem to pile on top of each other. The side streets shrink and become jammed with old cars. Traffic slows to a grind at the Collingwood end. Magpie supporters stream around the cars in tides and funnel towards Victoria Park. Hayden shakes his brown-and-gold scarf at them. It's no good. Even this year, when the Magpies might not make the finals, they out-number the Hawks' supporters three to one.

For a while the boys talk football. Same thoughts, different week. Who's a better player—Phil or Jim Krakouer? How much of a poof is Warwick Capper? When are we going to a night game at the MCG? Or they chat about school, hot girls in the senior years, movies. 'Let's get *The Terminator* on video again,' Jason says. He's already seen it four times.

Hayden says, 'Here's what I think.' He pushes his palms against his mouth and makes a farting sound.

They park on Drummond Street, half a kilometre from Princes Park, in what Dean calls 'the secret spot'—a disused parking bay behind housing commission flats. Walking to the stadium, across Lygon Street and down the pebbled track alongside Carlton cemetery's spiked fence, Hayden takes out his football and the two boys handball it to one another. Jason can catch it behind his back and kick with both feet. Hayden copies him but keeps fumbling the ball into the gutter.

Wind shakes the trees. Hundreds of feet scuff the pavement. Once they're inside the parklands the smell of mud and torn grass rises around them. Loud teenagers are selling the *Record* for eighty cents and Jason buys one so he can study the player statistics on the middle pages. Ahead, they can hear turnstiles revolving—tic-tic-tic-tic—as hundreds step into the arena.

At the ticket office Dean unfurls ten dollars from his clip, hands it to the ticket seller and ushers the boys past him.

Jason digs into the pocket of his jeans for a five-dollar note.

'It's on me, mate,' Dean says. 'Give that money back to your mum.'

Jason nods, but it's not his mum's money, it's his. He gets ten bucks a week for doing his chores but doesn't say so—who needs to know? 'Thanks, Mr Bennett.'

Across June and July they see Hawthorn play St Kilda, Geelong and Sydney. The Hawks win each game easily. They can beat every team, except Essendon, the invincible premiers. The Hawks have Peter Knights at full-forward and the best defence in the league: Gary Ayres, Chris Langford, Rod Lester-Smith, Russell Greene and Rodney Eade. Hard, no-frills men led by Lethal Leigh. Lethal's kicked more goals and won more best-and-fairests than any Hawthorn player in history. When he doesn't play, Jason feels slighted, as though Lethal has stood him up.

At half-time they watch the Little Leaguers running up and down the centre of the ground. Hayden shakes his head. 'If the Falcons were out there, we'd smash them.' The way Hayden talks about his team, the Hawthorn City Falcons, makes them sound like an elite army unit. Every Tuesday and Thursday at recess, Jason hears about their work-outs, their increasing endurance levels, their knock-on style of play. But he has seen them at their home ground and they're not much better than Little Hawthorn. No way would the Hawks bother sending scouts to watch them.

He unwraps his chocolate honeycomb muffins. When Hayden sees them he holds out his hands and whines like a hungry dog.

'What do you say?' Jason asks.

'Please.'

'And?'

Hayden makes a face. 'Okay. You get half my chips.'

'That's right.'

After the game they jump the fence and play kick-to-kick on the wing. They test each other in close with stab passes and gradually work backwards until they're launching torpedo punts at each other from thirty-five metres. Jason practises kicking with his wrong foot, watching the ball onto his sneaker just as the training manuals say. Tim Watson, Essendon's champion ruck-rover, started senior football when he was fifteen. Jason bets he could play in the seniors before he finishes school, too. He can see himself swaggering into school on Monday morning after playing at Princes Park on Saturday. Younger kids would crowd around him at recess. Girls would look at him.

Seeing Dean watching from behind the fence, five rows back, he kicks a low torpedo at Hayden's head and watches Hayden stumble backwards to retrieve it. Too easy, he thinks. When he looks over the fence again, Dean waves.

The game is his gift, he knows. Some guys are good at school and telling jokes, or, like Hayden, they have the latest stuff. Others are cricketers and basketball players: they can do things with the ball that make their classmates talk about them when they're not around. His thing is football. He becomes the centre of whichever team he plays for: he becomes the advantage. Students in the years above him know it, too. There's that Dalton kid, they say. You should see him kick. Inside the game he stands out.

. . .

He decides to ask his mum about the Falcons again on her next day off, a Tuesday in the middle of July. When he arrives home from school she's propped on the sagging cloth couch in front of the television, two pillows supporting her back and a copy of *New Idea* open in her lap. Her long legs extend to the armrest. She's still in her pyjamas and there is sleep in her voice when she speaks.

'I don't think it's a good idea.'

'But Mum . . .' he starts.

'They're too rough.'

'Hayden's dad says it's okay if Hayden plays.'

'Am I Hayden's dad?'

'No.'

She pushes her toes forward until her ankles crack. After running her hand through her hair she rubs her thumb and middle finger together and frowns at them, then resumes reading her magazine.

He hates the way she does this. As though the argument's settled. He says, 'It's not too rough. I'm a good player. I don't get hurt.'

'I suppose those players you see on the weekend, they're good players too. The ones with blood all over their faces.'

'This is different. You don't get hurt in the Under-Thirteens.'

She shakes her head. 'Every week I see another boy on the ward with a broken wrist. All it takes is a second.'

'I'm not them,' he says. 'I don't get hurt.'

'No.'

'Mum! That's not fair!'

She drops the magazine into her lap. 'I'm not arguing about this. I don't want you playing football. End of story.'

'But why?'

'End of story. I'm trying to rest. You have homework, don't you?'

He retreats to his room and kicks his schoolbag halfway up the wall. She might as well be deaf. He lies on his bed with the pillow over his head and tries not to listen to her magazine pages turning. It's the same each time. He could argue, he could give her the silent treatment, he could drag Dean in by the arm and get him to plead with her, but it would still do no good. It's part of the zone she disappears into in her time off from work. And at dinnertime, she'll act as if nothing's happened.

Having a dad around would change things for them. His dad would understand in a way she doesn't; he'd know what it's like to be a boy. The risk of getting hurt isn't as important as the feeling of being in the middle of a game and then getting to talk about it with your mates afterwards. Having a dad around would make it easier for her, too. She wouldn't have to be two people instead of one.

It seems she's been tired all his life. Tired is how he always sees her in his mind. Her long wavy black hair tangling around her shoulders, unwound from the bun she fixes it in for work, the sound of her heavy feet on their kitchen floor as she cooks him a special breakfast, then her fine oval face drooping slightly above the steering wheel as she drives him to school. Her joints cracking, her telltale sighs. The way she works to raise a smile when he looks at her in stray moments, her eyes softening above the faint concave lines on her cheeks: it's all right. Everything's all right.

She wants a house with a back porch where she can read, she says. Away from the traffic, nestled among the trees. Somewhere further east, Ashwood or Ringwood, where she can drive to the Dandenong Ranges on weekends and share Devonshire teas with him. The house will have a fireplace and a lounge room where she can fall asleep on a long sofa in front of movies. There will be bookcases in the hallway and bedrooms. They will have a kitchen filled with natural light where she can bake the blueberry cheesecakes she doesn't have time for right now.

'The wages we nurses get,' she tells him with an empty laugh. 'You'd think we were replaceable. A strike is on the cards. The government had better wake up to reality. Professionals would never suffer these conditions.'

When she gets like this, he finds it easier just to nod and eat his food.

She wants to know about his life at school. But how do you explain Year Seven to your mum? Girls in his classes have started wearing make-up. They talk about *Countdown* and listen to Top Forty songs he's never heard. The cool guys wear gel in their hair and roll up their shirtsleeves. They throw rude notes at the girls they like. The girls write put-downs and throw them back. You have to be the star of your own show. You need to be someone identifiable—Smart-Arse, Cool Dude, Crazy Man, Big Stud—otherwise you fade into the background and the girls don't see you.

'I hope you're keeping up in class,' she says. 'I wish I could be around more to help you out. Do you get mad at me for not being here?'

'No, Mum, it's okay—I'm used to it.'

'But the extra money for the night shifts makes a difference.'

He washes his dishes. He vacuums his room. He makes his bed and leaves his dirty sheets in the laundry hamper. He takes the washing down from the Hills hoist at the rear of the building when it rains. He ticks his chores off the list beside the phone and adds new ones, too, so she knows he does more than he has to.

Sometimes he comes home from school and a gift is sitting on his pillow-case: a Game & Watch, or a *Garfield* book, or Starlight Zone stickers. She attaches notes to them, thanking him for his patience and understanding.

He feels indignant when he sees his richer classmates showing off the Walkmans they got for their birthdays and talking about the family holidays they're going on at Christmas. They won't ever know how much tougher he is than they are, surviving as he and his mum do. They expect to have whatever they want. When his mum buys a house and the two of them finally move out, he'll remember how it used to be. He won't be like the others, like Hayden, and think the world owes him something.

. . .

On the first Wednesday afternoon in August the phone rings while he's studying his cards in the lounge room. It's Hayden, home after train-ing, and his voice is hoarse from running around breathing hard. 'Hey, mate. Listen—did you do that geography assignment?'

Jason climbs onto one of the kitchen stools. 'The one she gave us on Monday?'

'That's the one.' Hayden hacks into the mouthpiece. 'I haven't done it. If I don't hand it in tomorrow, I'm screwed.'

'Yeah?'

'Have you got it with you?'

'I got the first half of it from Reardon. Zac's giving me the rest before class tomorrow.'

'Give us what Reards gave you.'

Jason presses his forehead against the cool concrete wall above the phone. 'Nah, give Fawkner a call. Dobney'll know if we've all got the same answers. She's a hard-arse.'

'I won't copy it straight off. Just give us an idea. What's the topic again?'

'Ethiopia and Australia.'

'Why we've got it good and all that?'

'Hang on a minute.' Jason drops the phone on the kitchen bench and saunters into his bedroom to collect the assignment from his folder. He returns with two loose-leaf sheets stapled together, scrawled over in a shorthand that he can no longer read. He picks up the phone. 'Seriously. If we cop it, I'll kill you.'

'I know. I suck. I'm a stupid bastard.'

'Yeah.'

'Hey listen—you spoke to your mum about playing footy?'

'Nah. She's got this thing about it. The same shit I told you.'

'Dad told me last night he'll get you some gear. Boots and socks and that.'

'Yeah?'

'Tell her it won't cost her anything. Maybe she'll come around.'

'I doubt it.'

Hayden hacks into the mouthpiece again. 'Why's she being such a Jew?'

'Do you want the notes or not?'

'Hang on. Let me get a piece of paper.'

Hayden's phone calls shouldn't bug him anymore. They're part of

going to the footy together and backing each other up against Year
Eights. But Hayden's right when he says he's an arsehole. He's a baby,
he's up himself, he's full of shit. He's the one with the home tutor. It
should be him running around getting the answers. When Jason listens
to this voice in his head, anger sours his stomach and he has to lie down
for an hour, as if he's just thrown up. To relax he grabs his football from
beneath his bed and goes outside.

On the rear wall of their block of flats he has drawn a target with
blue chalk he steals from the blackboard ledges at school every few
weeks. The target is made of two circles, one inside the other. The outer
circle is the width of his shoulders. He practises kicking into the centre
of the target on the afternoons his mum is at work. He kicks with his
left foot, then his right, dodging from one tenant's vacant parking space
to the next, until the tenants with cars arrive home. The other tenants
keep their distance, except Flat Four, who drives a light truck and likes
to handpass the ball back to Jason on his way to his front door. Jason's
never learned his name—he's never bothered to ask.

He keeps a tally of his hits and misses. His all-time best is fifteen in a
row. He doesn't let himself go inside until he hits at least eight with his
right foot and five with his left. Training is about discipline and routine.
The rhythmic slap of ball against brick centres him as he pounces from
side to side.

His body thinking for him, his mind is free to drift back through the
course of his day. There's a girl in his home room, Abigail Taylor, who sits
two rows in front of him. She has tanned skin, red hair. She wears odd
socks in winter. One of her lower teeth is missing. He wants to kiss her
and put his hands inside her school dress. He muses on this as he kicks
his football into the target and marks it. He decides he will speak to her—
just stroll up to her after lunch and ask her how she's been going.

When he stops playing the world intrudes. He remembers he hasn't
spoken to her since their first class of the year. If he tried to start a

conversation with her she would probably just laugh at him. Then the other guys would rag him out and call him soft. People would find out he liked her and he would look like an idiot.

Finally, he goes inside, resigned to doing his homework, but most days his schoolbooks remain unopened on his desk. It's more fun to sort through his card collections and remember the different football boots he has tried on at the local school clothing store. Or he works on the flipbook cartoon he's developing in the upper right-hand corner of each page of his maths textbook—a man being shot, his head flying off, blood everywhere.

Disappearing into Year Seven at Burnley Secondary is easy. As long as he looks as if he's writing, as long as his homework is half done, most of his teachers pass over him, preserving their energy for his louder class-mates angling for attention in the back rows. With one ear he listens to the girls in the front rows who have answers, their books first-hand.

On the nights she's not home his mum leaves meals in the fridge and cooking instructions on the notepad beside the phone. He eats rissoles and beans, steak and onions, chicken fillets with homemade gravy. He knows how to mash potato and sprinkle it with garlic and pepper. He can tell the difference between rosemary, oregano and basil. The closest she will let him get to fast food is fish fingers but even this is a treat, in her reckoning. Cardboard food, she calls it.

. . .

They eat together on the Saturday night after he sees Hawthorn beat Carlton at Princes Park to move into third place, a week from the finals. It's a fresh round of her spaghetti bolognese. Normally he eats it with one eye on the remaining meat sauce on the stove, looking forward to seconds. This time he pushes the spaghetti away from the rim of his bowl and leaves it piled in the centre like compost.

'What's wrong?' she says.

'Nothing.'

'You can tell me.'

'Nothing. Never mind.'

'You have that look.' She reaches across the kitchen bench and runs her free hand through his fringe. She has an old blue napkin wedged in the collar of her white blouse.

Jason shakes his head, stabbing his food.

'What is it? Tell me.'

He takes a mouthful of spaghetti and chews it to mush.

'Is it the football?' She places her cutlery on either side of her plate and wipes her mouth. Two lines appear at her temples. 'I just don't want you to get hurt,' she says. 'You don't know what I've seen happen.'

'Yeah,' he says into his pile of food.

'Jason?'

'What?'

'Please don't be upset with me.'

He drops his fork into his bowl and it bounces, dirtying the bench top with orange oil. 'I never get anything,' he croaks. 'I do everything you tell me to and you never give me anything. All I want to do is play footy and you won't even let me do that.' He stands up. 'I do everything you want me to, and you don't give a shit.'

'Jason—'

'You don't.' He dodges her hand and stomps into his bedroom. There's no lock but he knows if he closes it she won't come in. He crouches against it and puts his head on his knees.

'Jason!'

In response, he thumps the back of his head into the door and it rattles against his shoulders. He pushes his face into the darkness below his knees, tunnelling away from his room and into the small tight place where no-one else can go, the cave he keeps inside himself.

All she thinks about is her own life: her job, the place she wants to live, her future. He's in the way, that's all. She doesn't play sport. She doesn't know what it's like to be good at something and be able to claim it, to have something that makes you stand out. She just works all the time, like a robot. Anyone's life outside of hers doesn't matter. Black rage spirals inside him. One day he'll run away, he decides. He'll take the burden off her completely, if that's what she wants.

The following morning, she has his breakfast waiting for him on the kitchen bench. He eats it moodily, embarrassed by his tantrum, though admitting to what he'd been like would only make him feel more childish. Afterwards he rinses their breakfast dishes and turns on *World of Sport*, settling once more into their usual Sunday routine. But two days later, when he gets home from school, he finds a note on his bed. She has cleared up and smoothed his blankets and propped the note on his pillow. In her large friendly hand, it runs three-quarters of a page:

Jason,

I'm sorry we fought on Saturday night. It's okay if you want to play football. I talked to Dean Bennett from work last night and he said it had done a lot of good for Hayden. You've been so good looking after yourself. I understand if you get mad at me sometimes, because you do so well and it's my fault I don't tell you enough. We'll get you a mouthguard next week. Is there something footballers can wear on their head? I'll find out. I'm still worried you'll get hurt. You MUST wear the mouthguard when you play.

I'm working today, Wed-night and Thurs-night. I'll leave some chicken and fish in the fridge. Eat the chicken for dinner and the fish tomorrow night. I'll be home by 7.30. I love you very much.

He reads the letter again, then a third time, captivated by the thought of her writing it earlier in the day.

I love you very much.

He reads the letter one last time then folds it into the back pocket of his grey school trousers. He reaches under his bed and draws out his football. He spins it in his hands, the cracked leather worn smooth, the Sherrin logo on its side now faded to almost nothing, the ball's greying seams fuzzy where the leather has chipped away. Just turning it in his hands relaxes him.

He drops the ball to his heel and guides it back under his bed. Not today, he thinks. He has homework waiting for him in his schoolbag. He should finish it so that he can show it to her when she gets home.

• • •

His first game with the Hawthorn City Falcons is at Victoria Reserve at nine the following Saturday morning, a five-minute walk from their flat. It's on the rich side of Hawthorn where the kids from private schools live. The streets are broad and quiet and the houses look like the Neighbourhood Safety icons he's seen on posters at school. The reserve's football ground is huge, with a sanded-over cricket pitch in the middle and practice nets on the far side. The sky is low and threatening, and the misty air has tinged the ground's uneven grass with frost: classic football weather.

Hayden has loaned him his old boots for the game. They fit more like hard gloves than shoes and their worn-down studs force him to walk lopsidedly. He also has Hayden's baggy black shorts and black football socks, and a spare guernsey Hayden scrounged from the Falcons' laundry bag. It's purple with a yellow sash, hangs down to his thighs and smells of mildew. Then there's his helmet—half a dozen black bands of hard rubber crisscrossing his hair and held tight to his skull by a strap running under his chin. A mouthguard, too—bonewhite, squishy and cumbersome. He looks poor, unfortunate, like a foreign kid who doesn't know the rules.

He jogs with Hayden into the centre of the ground. Jumping on the spot, toughening himself to the cold, he tries to ignore the opposition players looking at him and grinning. 'Nice helmet,' the opposition ruckman says. 'Yeah—don't hurt yourself, mate,' says the rover. The Burwood Wolves.

'Hey, mate,' Hayden says to the ruckman. 'Tell your boyfriend to shut up.'

Jason scans the crowd—twenty or so parents, Dean Bennett standing at the back in his fleecy bomber jacket, looking over their heads. No sign of his mum yet. She said she'd do her best. He hurries to the half-back flank where the coach—Frank or Garry or something—has decided to start him.

Two halves, twenty minutes each. That's how long he's got to show everyone what he can do.

The umpire meets them in the centre of the ground. He's young, maybe twenty-five, with a skinny upper body and taut powerful legs. They look as if they belong on a different person. 'Grouse,' he says. 'Let's get this show on the road.' He blows his silver whistle and hurls the ball into the air. The two ruckmen launch themselves at each other, the ball topples from their fists and the six players around them fight for it in the mud.

The opposition rover kicks the ball into the Wolves' forward line without looking. Jason anticipates the kick and is underneath it when it lands. His hands sting when he marks it and his first kick is like kicking cement, but the ball reaches his teammate on the wing. The crowd claps and his confidence surges. He crosses the centreline and hovers in the middle of the ground, remembering how Lethal does it, so that when the ball comes back he's there for the next contest. He marks again and kicks to Hayden, who follows up with a pass to the full-forward. A kick later, the Falcons are on the board.

Soon Jason's teammates begin passing to him. Where he runs, the ball follows. He slips into the forward line, anticipating a reversal of play as the ball floats out to the wing. Here it comes. He's on his own, in space, ten metres from his nearest opponent. He takes a bounce and roosts the ball into the vacant goal square. As it tumbles between the goalposts and over the railing on the other side he feels relieved, complete. It's the kick he spent all night thinking about. He's just as good in a real game as he is at recess, maybe stronger: inside the boundary line, the game is the only thing he has to think about.

Hayden runs across the goal face and rests his hand on Jason's shoulder. 'Centre it next time. I was in the middle.'

'All right,' Jason says. 'Sorry, mate.'

'Next time, okay?'

'Yeah.'

At half-time they stop for ten minutes to suck sliced oranges and compare the steam rising strangely from their hands. Jason knows he's got his teammates' respect now—they slap him on the back on their way to the coach's huddle.

The coach is wearing a tracksuit and has a clipboard with the team statistics on it. He gathers the boys around him and points to each goal face. 'Clear the forward line,' he says. 'Who's looking for the handpass? Let your mates know where you are.' As the players jog back into position he motions Jason towards him. 'Keep back a bit this half, mate,' he says. 'Give the forwards a go.'

Jason nods and jogs into the back pocket. 'That's Jason Dalton,' he imagines the parents on the boundary saying. 'The new kid.' When the siren sounds he bolts into the centre square and out the other side with the ball. The backline can get stuffed. It's the last game of the season. He won't have the chance to play in one again for six months.

At game's end he sits on the white concrete steps outside the change rooms with the Bennetts. He claps Hayden's old boots together, spraying mud and grass on the steps below. Two goals, twelve kicks, almost best-on-ground in his first game. Everything he thought he could do, he did. His teammates even had a nickname for him by the end of the second half—'Helmet'.

Dean leans towards him. 'I guess she got held up.'

'Yeah, I guess,' Jason says. 'Don't worry—it doesn't matter.'

Hayden says, 'Hope the boots were all right. I was going to throw them out, otherwise.'

'Yeah, they were fine.' He passes back the old boots and peels off his black socks. 'I'll get Mum to wash these for you.'

Dean takes them from him. 'Your mum's got enough on her plate already.'

'Thanks, Mr Bennett.'

They drop him off outside his block of flats. Hayden presses his mouth in a blowfish against the passenger window and the Range Rover growls away. Jason turns to face his building. It's become a still day. The narrow crooked street has emptied out, disturbed only by the faint sound of a lawnmower buzzing somewhere. He hobbles up the driveway. His feet burn from the boots and the mud on his legs has set to plaster. Before his shower, though, he grabs his football from beneath his bed and takes it downstairs to his practice target.

The game is still humming inside him. He bounces the ball and leaps for marks. Every kick into the centre of the target is another goal he has woven through the Wolves' backline, every one-handed gather off the concrete another possession. The crowd of parents he remembers on the boundary railing swells in his imagination to include his classmates, everyone in his year, his teachers. He weaves around the parked cars and snaps impossible goals from outside the Hills hoist. A scout from the Hawks is watching and taking down his name: Jason Dalton, the youngest Hawthorn recruit of all time.

The following afternoon, under a cloudless August sky, his mum drives with him an hour and a half east to the lookout at the top of Mount Dandenong. Her Corolla climbs the tourist trail slowly enough for her to take in the forest on either side of the road. 'See how high the trees have to grow to get to the sunlight?' she tells him. 'They're mountain ash. They'd be some of the tallest in the world. And the ferns around them, they're shaped that way so they can catch the water that runs off.'

The gravel car park at the top of the trail is quiet and still. Through the lookout binocular he can see the Rialto and the MCG. When he steps away from it, the hazy cityscape is the height of his thumb, and Hawthorn is impossible to tell apart from the flat gridded plains of suburbs reaching to the bottom of the mountain. 'Is this still Melbourne?' he asks.

'To the other side of the mountain, it is.'

She wanders along the lookout fence, cricking her back and stretching her body out of its driving shape. Her smile is real. She opens herself to the air. This is what the silence is like in Echuca, she's told him, when you get outside of the town.

The Corolla's bonnet is a heater for their dinner: fish 'n' chips from the general store in Emerald. Leaning on the windshield and licking the vinegar from her fingers, she has a looseness that will leave her when they get home. 'I wonder what sort of birds you'd get up here?' To stop her neck from seizing up in the mountain coldness, she layers it in the scarf that one of her patients had knitted for her. 'In Echuca some nights, down by the Murray, I used to sit on the riverbank with a book and listen to the rosellas.'

Two-storey houses with decks and sliding-glass doors peek out from behind trees along the mountain's corkscrewing roads. Peering down from the lookout fence, he compares them. They look so safe, cushioned from their neighbours on all sides by the forest. Some have slanted roofs and storybook windows. They must be the kinds of places she has in mind when she goes to bed at night.

'I'd live in the wooden one over there, on stilts,' he says.

She points to a house with a chimney at the edge of the cloud shadow. 'I like the cottage.'

'Was your house in Echuca like these ones?'

'No, these ones are very nice. We had an old weatherboard, same as everyone else. Corrugated roofing. You could hear the possums fighting on it. They were unreal.'

'A possum died in the roof above the art room this term. The smell was so bad, we had to have class in the quadrangle.'

'I think we got used to the smell. I don't remember it.'

'Where was your school?'

'Across the road.'

'No way.'

She winks like a thief. 'Me and my girlfriends used to sneak back to my bedroom at lunchtime and listen to records.'

'Were you a rebel, Mum?'

'No, I was a good girl.' Her smile says maybe she wasn't. 'If I even looked at a teacher the wrong way, all they had to do was shout out the window and my mum would be there in five seconds flat.' She laughs with her whole body.

They stay until the sun is gone and the suburban grid blooms into light. The night sky is deeper than it is in Hawthorn, revealing stars behind the clouds. 'On a clear night up in the country, you can just about read by starlight. You can even see Mars.' She tries to tilt the lookout binocular, but its hinge is set. 'But you can't down here. It's the city. There's too much light pollution.'

On the drive home he uses her scarf as a pillow. Term three will be over in a week, and Hayden leaves for the Gold Coast on Sunday. The Hawks are only one more win from their third grand final in a row. Who would he support if he'd been born in Echuca, with a house like she described, four hours from Melbourne? Still the Hawks, he decides. Being a Hawks supporter is a part of himself that he likes best.

His mum turns on 3UZ. He watches the suburbs crowding around them again and listens to her sing as they drive past the petrol stations and the hospital on the hill. Soon they're back in the world he knows.

2. the boundary

On the last Saturday in September, Jason sits on the couch in his lounge room, alone, with his ten Hawthorn swap cards and a 'Go Hawks' poster from the *Sun*. It's a Hawthorn–Essendon grand final, same as the previous two years, except this year the Bombers are unbeatable and everyone says so, including the commentators in their pre-match forecast. The Bombers have Madden, Watson, Van Der Haar, Merrett, Daniher, Ezard. They have the equal-record number of wins for the season. They have Salmon at full-forward standing half a foot above Mew's head. They have Sheeds in the box and last year's premiership in their pocket. Everyone at school has told him the same thing: No way the Hawks, not this year, not after the last one. Wake up, Dalton, you're a goner.

It shits him that they're right.

By the end of the final quarter he has slid to the floor. His cards are stacked forgotten on the couch's armrest. He'd used them to charm the Hawks through the semi-final, but today they're not enough. They were never going to be, not with Hayden and Dean on the Gold Coast for the third-term holidays and their circle broken. Each time Essendon kicks another goal and the players mob each other he feels as if one of their supporters is stepping on him. Essendon have turned the game into a parade. He has seen the Bombers do this to teams during the season—finish games off and then put the boot in for the fans—but never in a grand final and not so every one of his classmates, even the ones who don't follow the game, will know the Hawks got smashed. This loss makes the whole season feel like a delusion.

Do they even get the football up there? he wonders. Are they even watching this? He can picture Hayden listening to the game beside a hotel pool, in Dean's sunglasses. Hayden's postcard from Sea World had arrived the day before. Every sentence finished with an exclamation mark. Jason had slid it under his bed, hoping he would forget about it.

The final siren sounds before the Bombers can kick another goal. Their seventy-eight-point victory is almost another record. The commentators are in awe. That's back-to-back flags now. As the TV cameras circle the Hawks the players look exhausted and stunned, like people on the news who've lost their homes. 'Come on, boys,' Jason says through his hands.

Supporters clamber down onto the ground as the Hawthorn players raise Lethal to their shoulders. It's Lethal's final curtain. After three hundred and thirty-two games and nine hundred and fifteen goals, he's entering the players' race for the final time. He sobs into his armpit, sagging forwards. The cameras stay focused on him, but Jason doesn't want to watch. It's a cruel joke, watching a player like Lethal cry during his last moments on field. This isn't how he should be remembered.

He turns off the TV when the Bombers begin their victory lap of the 'G. The blank screen crackles against his hand. The rest of the day returns to the room. He looks at the carpet and the closed windows and the stove's clock flashing HE:LP. His mum is doing another double shift and won't be home till eleven.

Next year, she has told him, we'll go to New South Wales, stay on the east coast. I want us to see Australia, eventually, once the money sorts itself out. Give it time, sweetie. We'll get there.

He rolls his football from beneath his bed and changes into the shorts and socks he'd worn playing with the Falcons. Wearing them, and bouncing the ball down the driveway, fills some of the emptiness the Hawks have left in him. When he gets to Victoria Reserve he is alone except for the people walking home from the train station across the road. He jogs the boundary line for a lap, just as the Falcons had before the match, and stretches his legs on the railing behind the goal-posts. He feels pride in being the committed one, still serious about his game at the end of the season when other players are packing away their boots. To practise his marking he kicks the ball as high as the elms behind him. The Hawks haven't won, but he still can. By March, he'll be a season's training ahead of every other player on the team.

On Monday morning, three of his classmates put on their Essendon jumpers for kick-to-kick at recess. Each time they get the ball they re-enact moments from the game: Salmon over Mew, Madden over everybody. 'Matthews—no!' they shout whenever Jason goes for the ball. As they work the ball around the pack to one another they laugh at him as if he's one of the migrant kids.

'Why don't you kiss each other, you poofters?' he says.

It's two weeks before they stop being the enemy, but he can't forget the way they looked at him. That's what life at school would be like if he wasn't good at sport. Copping shit in the hallways, on the train, at the tuckshop. Ignoring them wouldn't work. He's seen the migrant kids try but in the end they always snap, and when they do they look even more pathetic. Once they've got you, you're gone.

• • •

The term soon dissolves into his anticipation of the coming summer. Lessons pass over his head like clouds. He reaches the final page in his maths textbook—there's nowhere left to draw. After class his teachers pull him aside and say the same things. 'Jason, you're drifting. You need to spend more time listening. You have to push yourself.' But the only place he finds he can push himself is at Arthur's in front of the Galaga arcade machine.

When the bell for home time rings on the last day of the school year his body seems to fill with sunlight. Summer sleepovers at Hayden's are a holiday up the road: days of cricket in the backyard, nights of Atari in the den upstairs, and the Rivoli Cinema is only ten minutes' walk down the hill to Camberwell Junction. Living like Hayden, he can do what he wants, though it makes him feel weirdly guilty watching Hayden's mum making lunch and dinner and cleaning the house by herself every day.

'I hope you're nice to Hayden's parents,' his mum tells him. 'It's hard enough having one boy in the house.'

'Yeah, Mum. I know.'

'No, listen to me. Your behaviour reflects on me. I don't want them to think I'm a bad mum.'

'His dad thinks you're great.'

'I don't want them feeling sorry for me, either,' she says. 'Make sure you wash your hands and look decent before you sit down with them.'

'Stress less, Mum.'

'Don't talk to me in that voice.'

'What voice?'

'The one that makes me feel old.'

On the days she does double shifts, two and three times a week, she drops him off at Hayden's front gate and comes back to collect him the following afternoon. Hayden's home in Camberwell is a vintage brick two-storey house hidden from the street by giant trees. The front rooms on the ground floor have polished cabinets and furnishings he is afraid to touch. The kitchen is the size of his lounge room and the entire wall behind the dinner table is a window. When he walks through these rooms and upstairs he keeps his hands in his pockets to prevent himself from accidentally breaking things.

Hayden's den on the second storey has no proper furniture, just some corduroy beanbags and a set of furry couch seats strewn around the television. Its messiness feels more like Hayden than the expensive stuff downstairs. They spend most of their time playing *Ms Pac-Man* and *1947* and eating junk food. But there are days when it's more fun to climb onto the tiled, mossy roof outside Hayden's bedroom window and sunbake. From here they can see as far as the tennis court three doors down. Two older girls play tennis there, sometimes, in singlet tops and bike shorts, never with boys. According to Hayden they're both lesbians, and with this image in mind Jason has guiltily fantasised about them at night, sweating in his sleeping bag in the spare bedroom.

The Christmas tree in Hayden's lounge room is real and almost reaches the roof. Jason helps Hayden and his parents to decorate it on the Monday before Christmas. Hayden's presents appear beneath it in the days following, and also presents for Hayden's aunts and uncles. Hayden has family in Horsham and this year it's the Bennetts' turn to host them. The bogan brigade, Hayden calls them. 'Trust me, mate,' he says. 'You're lucky. Rellos are just a pain in the arse.'

When Hayden sulks at having to clean the den in time for Christmas Day, it occurs to Jason how satisfying it would be to force Hayden to swap lives with him for a week. He imagines Hayden up to his elbows in dishwater and burning his dinner because he forgot to set the timer. He imagines him unable to sleep at night with the building's pipes groaning and shuddering in his bedroom ceiling. After a few days, he'd be in tears. Before the week was through he'd run back to his house, too soft to handle reality.

At home Jason has helped his mum set up the miniature plastic Christmas tree in the corner beside the television. It's looped with red and gold tinsel and has a silver star on top. Many of the plastic leaves have fallen off over the years so he has turned the barer side to face the wall. It's a success; from a distance, the tree looks perfect. The two presents beneath it are wrapped in the same paper, but it's obvious whose are whose: the present his mum wrapped is seamless, while his present for her is a raggedy bandage of sticky-tape and twisted paper.

Before lunch on Christmas Day they stand together on either side of the tree and wait for the timer on her camera to beep. It's a photo she's been taking since before he can remember. The previous ones are in a photo album under her bed, including the ones of him as a baby. Afterwards they kneel together in front of their presents. 'Go for it,' she says. 'I'm waiting.'

He already knows his present is a shoebox—he'd inspected it the previous night. He lifts the lid and inside is a new white and black pair of shoes with Velcro straps. 'Hey!' he exclaims, trying to sound surprised. 'These are unreal!' He tries them on. 'I've been wanting a pair of these for ages.' He walks around the room in them, showing them off for her, conscious of her anxiety. He jumps up and down and rips the straps off and on again. 'Yeah, they're perfect.'

She carefully unsticks the mounds of tape from each corner of her present and the wrapping starts to unfold itself. Inside is a gift voucher from the homewares shop near the Rivoli. 'Dear Mum,' she reads from the card, 'Merry Christmas and thanks for everything this year.'

'You can get something for when we move out,' he says. 'Maybe some cooking stuff or something.'

They move the card table from his room and set it up beside the kitchen bench. Once the beef has finished roasting she serves their meals onto plates while he sets the table and opens her bottle of white wine. She passes him a bottle of Solo from the fridge. He makes sure her seat is facing the lounge room, so she can keep her eye on the clock above the phone.

They sit down to eat. 'Cheers,' they both say, tapping their plastic flutes together.

Her food is fantastic. The beef Wellington is tender and juicy, and the roast vegetables are layered with half a dozen spices. He eats slowly, savouring each mouthful, though she always makes so much food there are leftovers until New Year's Day.

'What are you going to buy with the voucher?' he asks.

'I'll have to see what I need.'

'Get something for the new kitchen. For cooking.'

'This is delicious, isn't it? I can't wait to get the time to do more. Then I can teach you, too.'

She leaves for work at two-thirty. He rolls his football from beneath his bed. Outside, the leaves in the driveway are turning in spirals. Another Christmas storm is coming. No cars are on the roads, though the hotel across the road from Arthur's milk bar is crowded to the windows. At Victoria Reserve, a family as big as a cricket team is fielding; the two girls batting don't know how to run and hold their bats at the same time. Hayden's family will be playing at their local ground by now, he realises. It's a family tradition of theirs. Jason's mum must have had traditions like that too, at some point. She'd mentioned them once or twice before: bush Christmases by the Murray when her parents were still alive. If his dad hadn't run off, they could be doing the same. The thought robs him of the will to practise. He sits on the clubhouse steps with the ball in his lap, a spectator.

. . .

The January heat spreads everywhere in Hayden's house—into the boys' conversation, their clothes, their sleep. Even when playing Atari, they sweat like racehorses. There's only one place left to go where it's fun to move around—the swimming pool, as often as they can.

Hayden's mum drops them off at the Harold Holt Centre in Malvern. They hurry through the chlorinated dampness surrounding the indoor pool to the grassy outdoors and the staggered diving towers near the back fence. There's a five-metre, a seven-metre and a ten-metre platform, their silver ladders dripping above the sound of wet feet. Puddled kids mill in lines at their bases. Songs from sunbathers' stereos float from the stands alongside the diving pool. There are always plenty of sunbathing girls to ogle, their oiled skin catching the sun whenever they roll over.

From the ten-metre platform they dive together, arms spinning as if they want to fly away. They each strike the water with one knee clutched to their chests and shower the sunbathers. Below the surface is a rumbling dreamscape. Jason touches the slimy bottom of the pool and shoots upwards, ignoring the pulse of pain in his ears. When they wade to the edge of the pool and hoist themselves onto the concrete they already know what's coming: the pool's sandy-haired lifeguard, all zinc and sunglasses, telling them what they can't do and why.

• • •

Returning to school at the beginning of February is horrible. The thought of spending another eleven months in the same holding pen makes Jason fold his head into his arms. This is where it stays for most of his classes. When he does look up his gaze soon drifts out his home-room window to the football ground on the opposite side of the road where he imagines the marks he will take and the goals he will kick in the new season for the Falcons.

'Where are you, Dalton?' his English teacher asks him after class one day. 'You're always a million miles away. This is Year Eight, mate, not Grade Five. You ought to take a look at yourself.'

He does this every night after he showers. He's not happy with what he sees. His nose is pointy. His eyebrows aren't thick enough. The only part of his face he needs to shave is the thin moss of hair on his upper lip. There are two blackheads on his right cheek and the possible beginnings of a third on his left. He has freckles. His shoulders are too skinny. Even his earlobes, it seems, are too red. At least his teeth are good—but do girls even care about teeth?

'We should go and see Halley's Comet,' his mum tells him as she drives him to school. 'We should drive up to the Dandenong lookout again and use the telescopes. We can have dinner in one of the restaurants up there beforehand. Wouldn't that be great? As long as you're happy to hang out with an oldie like me.'

By his calculations she was his age in 1965. She would have been at high school in Echuca. There must have been nothing going on up there. So maybe it makes sense that she feels old all the time, even though she's younger than the other mums he sees dropping their kids off at school.

In the last weeks of first term his home-room teacher, Mr Eaglesby, shifts him to the other side of the class. It means he no longer has a view of the football ground, and even when his teachers are facing the blackboard they can see what he's doing. His only company is the new kid, Darren Jackson.

Darren, he soon realises, is the kind of guy who is so smart he doesn't have to bother trying. Instead, Darren fills his time drawing pictures—grinning skulls on fire, motorbikes, antique guitars. He draws scenes of a boy riding a skateboard, each frame zooming in and out, like stills from a movie. With a slash of his pencil a weird collection of circles and squiggles suddenly becomes a teacher's face. He speeds through their maths exercises as if he's ticking boxes. Most days he even gets the homework finished early, and Jason is able to scribble the answers into the back of his school diary before they leave.

'So what footy team do you go for?' he asks.

'North Melbourne,' Darren says. 'You?'

'Hawthorn.'

'You for real, or are you one of those pussies who only go for them because they win premierships?'

'Get stuffed. I know every player.'

'Name the backline.'

'Last year? Langford, Ayres, Greene, Morris, Mew, Schwab.'

'You for real, mate?'

'I go to all the games.'

'Why?'

'Why do you draw so much?'

'Dunno.' For the first time Darren seems to need a moment. 'Guess it's my brain. There's a word for it.'

'Retarded?'

'Yeah. You're copying your homework off the retarded kid.'

When they count their tuckshop money at lunchtime, Darren's pockets are always full. He tosses two-dollar and five-dollar notes onto his desk at random. The packet of Winfields he keeps in his sock is never empty. He's got cool stuff, too, like a Swatch with a transparent face that shows the cogs turning the clock's hands.

'How'd you get so loaded?' Jason asks him.

'I work in my old man's restaurant,' Darren replies. 'You like pasta?'

'Where is it?'

'Abbotsford, off Johnston Street. You should come down with your old lady. We'll give you a discount.'

'Nah, my old lady works all the time.'

'I hear that. What's she do?'

'She's a nurse.'

'Nurses are hot,' Darren says. He raises his eyebrows. 'Nah, I'm just breaking your balls, J.D. Where's your dad?'

'No dad,' Jason says. 'He ran off when I was born.'

'Jesus, man, that sucks. So you're on your own most of the time? Shit.'

'Yeah, but that's how it's always been.' He shrugs. 'It doesn't bother me.'

No-one has ever called him 'J.D.' before. Just 'Jase' or 'Dalts'. 'J.D.' though—there's something mysterious about a guy referred to by his initials. He starts carving them into things: his desk, his ruler, the vinyl underside of his bag. On a toilet break from maths class he works them into the wooden boards behind the toilet roller. They make him some-one different from boring old Jason.

After school, he follows Darren to the bluestone alleyways, a block from the train station, where the Year Nines and Tens go to smoke. Dead leaves crackle under their feet. The smokers stub out their butts on the barbed-wire factory fences and drop them in the drains. The girls sit on their schoolbags and the guys circle around them. Jason watches them flirt with one another, bait each other, and play dumb. He watches Darren light a silver zippo with a smooth snap of his wrist. Then Darren throws it to him and he practises the manoeuvre.

It amazes him how normal Darren seems to think his life is: earn-ing a wage, being an adult already. He can dress however he wants, he can talk to guys in older years like equals. School, for Darren, is just a dumb necessity between the parties he goes to and his shifts at work. His parents treat him like an employee. That seems a fairer deal than having chores expected of you and getting pocket money as if you're still in primary school.

. . .

At the beginning of the Falcons' 1986 football season Dean Bennett buys Jason a new pair of football boots. They're Pumas, size five, black with a white strip flowing across the stitching from the ankle to the instep. Each boot has six screw-in stops that he threads into the soles with a butterfly-shaped plug. There's a thumbnail of room in the toes and the laces are so long he has to circle them once under each boot to tie them properly. They cost forty bucks. He checks this in the store one night after school, just to make sure he knows how much money he needs to save to pay Dean back.

He writes the club initials on the tongue of each shoe in case his mum sees them. If she asks, they were provided free. He figures Dean won't say anything either. Whenever his mum and Dean speak, she gets the same tone in her voice as she does when the bank calls.

Each Monday and Wednesday night after training he sits on the cold concrete stairwell outside the flat and cleans them. He uses a kitchen knife to unwedge dried mud from the stops and an old pyjama singlet as a washrag to clean the surrounding leather. It's a superstitious habit—wearing clean boots onto the ground is a good-luck charm, he feels. He washes his helmet in a bucket of hot water, wipes it down, and leaves it to dry on the coat hook behind his bedroom door. It's part of his on-field identity now. It gets him more of the ball. The other Falcons recognise him in the packs and so do the umpires. He likes the way the opposition players sneer when he circles the ruckmen at the centre bounce. Who's the kid in the helmet? they're thinking. Why does he need it? The helmet tricks them into underestimating him.

He starts as a half-back flank. After finishing in the top three in his first two games the coach shifts him to ruck-rover. He's faster than every other player on the ground and can pass with both feet. Whenever his teammates are in trouble, they look for him. He can find room to kick even when he's being tackled. He protects his teammates when they have the ball and always tells them where he is. At training, the coach points out the way he plays and tells his teammates to use him as a role model.

He looks for Hayden at full-forward when he's kicking into attack. If he passes to someone else Hayden makes a face and spits his mouthguard onto the grass. 'I'm the full-forward,' Hayden says. 'Do your job.'

'I can't kick to you if you're covered.'

'I wasn't covered. He was behind me.'

'Whatever you reckon.'

The coach is right: Hayden waits for the ball. When he comes off a lead he slows down before he jumps. He's got weak wrists, no recovery. He's got no left foot. He doesn't do the one-percenters. That makes him dead weight, Jason reckons, no matter how much Dean claps for him.

The Falcons win four of their first eight games, but they lose three of them by ten goals. These are games when the ball spends most of its time in the Falcons' defensive half, and when Jason looks up to the forward line he sees Hayden skulking there, hands on his hips. There are players on their team who don't know how to handball or shepherd— they just dive at marks and kick the ball without looking. Why won't they commit? When he sees them joking with the opposition backmen he glares at them and spits on the ground. They're disrespecting the game. They should be taken off.

Between quarters he looks for his mum's face in the crowd. She says she wants to make it along and see him play. 'This weekend, Jase, I'll try and wake up early and drive down,' she says. 'Where did you say you were playing? You'll have to get me directions from Hayden's father.' But she's never there, and when he gets home after games he finds she's still in bed, the back of her dark head just visible in the dim bedroom, submerged in her sheets and pillows.

He finds her notes on the kitchen bench. It's the Friday night graveyard shift she needs to recover from, or she's coming down with something, or she had to do their weekend shopping before she went back to work. Jason crumples these notes in his fist and throws them in the bin.

. . .

By the halfway point of the 1986 VFL season, Hawthorn are on top of the ladder, with a bigger percentage than Sydney and three wins more than Essendon. With Lethal gone, he thought they'd fall, but they have a new weapon from South Australia to replace him: the Rat, John Platten, the best rover in the country. They're a force now, as the commentators say. Even when they're down, they find a way to win.

Only ten thousand supporters come to watch them play Melbourne at Princes Park, the smallest crowd of round eleven. But anyone who says they're boring is just pissed off because they win so much. For Jason, their eighty-five-point victory is predictable in the best way—Brereton roaming half-forward like a bull, Dipper rough and tough on the wing, Platten terrorising the packs, Ayres and Langford chopping down everything up back. He counts the steps Buckenara takes lining up for goal. He flexes his arms whenever Brereton flies for a mark.

Having a kick on the ground after the Hawks have played is always a rush. It rains footballs. The sound of them being kicked—whump, whump-whump—is as good as any during the game. Standing on the wing, he can see moments in the match as the players would have. This is the spot where Wallace kicked it fifty metres, over there is where Dipper marked and took a bounce. He keeps losing Hayden among the hundreds of other supporters and has to pull back from his kicks.

Trailing one of Hayden's floating drop punts along the wing, he collides head-first with another supporter. Dean buys him a packet of frozen peas on Johnston Street to hold against his brow on the way home. He ducks his head to inspect the swelling in the rear-vision mirror; it looks worse than it is. To get his story right he replays what he can remember of the hit: leaping for a mark, tasting mud, opening his eyes to find the fat kid in the Dire Straits tee-shirt standing over him looking worried. Could have happened to anyone.

She's home—he can see light in their flat from the driveway. As soon as he comes through the front door she drops her magazine on the ground. 'Jesus, Jason!'

'Don't get up.' He watches her rush to the bathroom. 'It's nothing.'

She has iodine, white hospital tape, band-aids, cotton wool, a flannel and a pen-sized torch. She presses him onto a stool at the kitchen bench and takes the packet of frozen peas from him. 'Hold still.' After inspecting his eye and the graze on his cheek with her torch, she dabs a swab of cotton in her bottle of iodine and holds his face. 'Tell me how it happened.'

'We were having a kick after the game. I was going for a mark and I hit a guy.'

'He ran into you.'

'We ran into each other.'

She grabs his jaw and turns his head as if she's scrubbing an old shoe. 'It's bound to happen, isn't it? A thousand people playing on a ground together, a hundred footballs, little kids running around.'

'I'm thirteen, Mum.'

'And how old was he?' she says.

'You've never been to a football match. You don't know what it's like.'

'Yeah, I bet.' She drops the flannel on the bench. The freezer door opens and he can hear her searching among the frozen containers for her ice packs.

'Happy?' he says, but she doesn't answer. He leans sideways to the TV and turns the black knob to the 'on' position to check the Saturday night replay.

She slams the freezer door shut and crosses in front of him to switch the television off.

'What's your problem?'

'You've got homework to do.'

'I'm doing it tomorrow.'

'You're doing it tonight. You're not leaving your room till it's finished.'

'Jesus, Mum.'

'I got a phone call from the vice-principal this week.' Her arms fold like doors. 'She called me at work. How do you think that made me feel? Having her in my ear while I was doing my rounds?'

He can't think of anything to say.

'That's right, we had a nice long chat. Because apparently you don't do your work anymore. You just copy everyone else's.'

He looks at her left sneaker, then up. 'The teachers hate me.'

'Really? Well, maybe they wouldn't hate you so much if you put in some effort.' She lifts his chin. 'I don't work fifty-five hours a week so you can doze.'

'You want me to do my homework? Fine. See you later.' He stomps five paces to his room and shuts himself inside.

'Get back here, Jason!'

'You can't come in.'

'Jason!'

'It's my room.'

She goes silent. From his bed he hears one of her joints crack. She's still standing there, outside the door. When she speaks again, her voice is resigned. 'Fine. Act like a baby. Run away.'

He crouches on the seat in front of his desk, his fists at his sides. He flexes his fingers and runs his hands over his head. Act like a baby. Run away. Just six words, and he's been undone. She can do that. He drops his head on his arms. His own words just came out, and if she'd kept at him he would have said more. They'd felt good, too—powerful. But the thought of scaring her brings tears to his eyes. This is who he's becoming: a brat like Hayden, a failure at school.

...

Following Darren and his circle of smokers into the toilets at lunchtime becomes a daily ritual. Jason's silver zippo from the Aussie Disposals in Camberwell Junction costs him three weeks' pocket money. Darren's hip flask has his initials on it, D.J., in a curling design he says he made himself, and his dad's Jack Daniels stays on their breath all afternoon.

'Top three hottest chicks in our year?' Darren asks him between drags.

'First to last? Abigail Taylor, Robyn O'Loughlin, Nikki Marini.'

'Marini stinks.'

'Tits, though.'

Darren swigs from his hip flask. 'Not as good as your mum's.'

The other guys cackle.

Jason flicks his zippo. Whenever Darren cuts him down, a cautiousness settles over him. Without Darren's approval, he'd be back playing basketball at lunchtime, among his primary school friends. Nikki Marini has a boyfriend from another school now. Robyn O'Loughlin is dating a basketballer in Year Nine. And Abigail Taylor is in class 8C, across the hallway. He's seen Darren sneak sketches of girls into their schoolbags. He's heard their thrilled howls of dismay when they discover themselves shaded in pencil and ink. As Darren says, confidence is everything. It's as simple as that, and as hard.

Home and school fall away from him inside the boundary line wherever the Falcons play. The best feeling is when momentum shifts in a match and, for whole quarters, he and his Falcons teammates are one force. How good they are as players doesn't matter. What matters is the group. They will each other to take marks, to kick straighter, to work harder. Goals flow from the confidence they inspire in one another. Together, they're conquerors.

With one round to go, the Falcons have won five of their last six games. They know each other now. They won't finish on top, but the difference between who they were last year and this year is clear. They're getting serious now. But listening to Hayden bragging to Dean on the way home after each match, he feels wistful for someone else's recognition. Dean's compliments—'I reckon that bloke you were on was tagging you by the end of the game, Jase'—feel like charity. Other dads record the games and tally their sons' stats. He thinks of his mum and frustration smoulders in him. She can't see it, how much he pushes himself. From what she knows of him at home and at school, who he is on field might as well be someone else.

· · ·

The Falcons' end-of-season presentation is after their final game, a grinding seventeen-point win against the Ashburton Swans. His wish has come true. Jason Dalton, Under-Fourteens best and fairest for the Hawthorn City Falcons in his debut season. At the ceremony inside the club rooms the club president gives him a trophy, thirty centimetres high. It's a sculpture of a golden footballer taking a mark over his opponent's back, set on a burgundy tower of enamelled wood, and beneath the tower, carved onto a plaque:

HAWTHORN CITY

U/14 BEST AND FAIREST

JASON DALTON

1986

The golden footballer gleams in the midday light.

Dean has organised the end-of-season barbeque. The players and their parents are gathered on the far side of Victoria Reserve, between the cricket nets and the metal swings. Dean stands over the slanted metal grill wearing sunglasses and a black denim shirt, forking and turning the meat, shaking hands with mums and dads as they approach him with their white cardboard plates. It's a clear day, spring arriving early, and everyone is happy to be outside in the bright chill air. Several of the players have brought footballs and are now playing kick-to-kick across the ground's nearest wing, bread and sausage in one hand as they contest for marks.

Hayden is standing beside his father, sullen, eating a beef burger. Beside him, on the greasy ledge adjoining the barbeque, he has left his own trophy: Most Consistent. It's the same model as Jason's trophy, only silver and smaller. When Jason ducks beneath the boundary railing within earshot, Hayden says, 'Where's your mum?' His voice is cold.

'She said she'd be here at twelve.' Jason looks across the park to the main road.

'It's twelve-thirty now. Everyone's about to leave.'

'I know.'

Dean Bennett's tanned face is shadowy and difficult to read behind his sunglasses. 'I'm sure she's got a good reason, mate.' He throws a stick of charcoal-crusted meat onto a nearby paper plate and passes it to him. 'Here, take the last sausage. Hayden, help me clean this up, would you?'

Jason watches the players on the ground. He looks at the mums standing together, relaxed. One woman has her hand in her husband's coat pocket. Another is patting her parka in search of cigarettes. Most of them are in their forties. He has seen them picking up their sons from training and dropping them off at games. He figures that, like Hayden's mum, they probably don't work. They probably cook dinner every night and clean their kids' rooms for them. They probably have a lot of time on their hands.

Still no sign of her car.

Hayden slings a plastic-wrapped loaf of bread against his chest. 'Help pack for once,' he says. 'I always do everything.' He slouches away from the barbeque and onto the football ground to join the other players.

Jason helps Dean put the used plates and napkins into the metal rubbish bin beside the boundary fence. Dean slaps him on the back. 'Those footy boots we got you must've had rockets in them.'

'Thanks again for that, Mr Bennett.'

'Pleasure's mine, sport.'

'I want to pay you back.'

'No way.' Dean winks at him easily. 'You've earned them.'

At no particular signal, the party starts to separate. The parents tramp along the pebbled walking track around the ground to the reserve's exit and the main road. There are football games to go to, gardens to mow, Saturday newspapers to read, parents to visit, other kids to pick up and drop off. Ordinary life must resume. The parents shake hands good-bye and summon their sons from the field. Thommo, Derek, Hayden, Shane—time to go.

A shout. 'Jason!' Here she is, heading towards him from the main road. She's in jeans, an old sweatshirt, white sneakers. She hasn't brushed her hair and half of it is hanging in front of her ears. As if she's forgotten how to jog she alternates running with walking. She reaches him, panting, her cheeks pink in the cold air. 'What's happening? I thought you said twelve-thirty.'

'No.' He closes his eyes. 'Eleven-thirty.'

'Oh.'

'I wrote it on the pad in the kitchen.'

'I'm so sorry.' There are creases on her face from where she's been sleeping. 'I should've checked. I thought it was twelve-thirty.'

'Well.' He raises his eyebrows and scratches the back of his head, looking down. He remembers what he's holding in his hand. 'Here, look. I won best and fairest.' He passes her the trophy and starts walking in the direction she came from.

'What's this?' She brings it closer to her eyes. 'Hey, you won best and fairest!'

He stops, but doesn't turn around. He sniffs, clears his throat and holds his hands against his sides.

'Hey, that's fantastic.' Her voice struggles to find the right note. 'Wow! Congratulations.'

'Yeah.'

She walks up beside him, holding the trophy like a vase. 'I wish I'd been here when you got this. I'm sorry.'

'Where's the car?'

'I'm sorry, Jason.'

'Okay.' He sniffs and clears his throat again. 'Where's the car?'

'It's on the next street along,' she says. 'You must be so proud.'

3. the up-and-comer

Darren's place is not what he expected—he thought Darren's parents would be richer than this. They're close enough to Richmond station to hear the trains. The house is just a faded weatherboard with no driveway and a small front yard. He could kick a drop punt from the front gate and clear the back fence without a problem.

At half-time of the grand final he takes a break on their front verandah. His cigarette is making him dizzy. He looks at his can of VB, holds the can over the verandah's edge and waters the bushes with it until there's only a sip left. He takes another drag of his cigarette and watches the smoke stream in a flat line from his mouth. Darren says that's how you can tell if you're inhaling properly—the way the smoke comes out.

The flyscreen door swings open behind him. It's Darren's cousin, Fish, scratching his belly beneath his Hawthorn jumper. 'Hey, mate,' he says. He swigs from his can of VB like it's water.

Jason says, 'Reckon it's in the bag?'

'It's in the bag,' Fish says. 'Show was over at quarter time. Carlton are cactus.'

'What about Bucky? Four goals.'

'Bucky's a champion.'

'Yeah.'

'Pass us your durry?'

'Huh?' Jason looks at his cigarette. 'Oh yeah, here.' He makes a mental note of the slang.

Fish pinches the cigarette between his thumb and forefinger when he smokes, his spare tucked tradie-like behind his ear. He's lost one of the fingernails on his right hand, but he seems as if he wouldn't care about a missing fingernail. 'Daz said you won best and fairest.'

'Yeah. Most of the side's shithouse, though. You play?'

'Used to. Then I fucked up my hand.' He makes a fist and shows Jason his knuckles. The first joints of his index and middle fingers are disfigured and stick out like busted screws. 'I can't close it anymore.'

'Shit. What happened?'

'Ah, I went for a mark, pack fell on top of me.'

Darren calls to them from inside. 'Oi, dickheads! Second half's starting!'

Fish takes a final drag of the cigarette and flicks it into the bushes. Jason follows him inside, tipping the last of his beer into his mouth. When he swallows it he has to shut his eyes and hold his breath to keep from throwing up.

They sit in the two vinyl chairs beside Darren in the lounge room. The draftbook sketches on the coffee table and the spanners on the floor make it feel more like Darren's bedroom. The silver TV they're watching is balancing on a tower of yellow pages, and each time the wind rumbles outside a wave of ash crosses the screen. The image cuts from Brereton niggling Dorotich at half-forward, to Bob Hawke in a Superbox beside the members, to the open ecstatic faces of Hawks' supporters on their feet and draped in brown and gold.

'Carn the Hawks!' Jason shouts. The Hawks are up by twenty-one points. His hands tingle when the umpire steps into the centre circle to bounce the ball and start the second half.

Darren is using a six-pack of VB as a footrest. He sits forward and clears another can from the middle of it. 'Hey, J.D.—heads up.' He lobs the can at Jason, aiming for his chest.

Jason catches the can before it hits him. 'Yeah, cheers,' he mutters. The beer from his last can is still churning in his stomach. He places the new one beside the leg of his chair and leans towards the TV. It's going to be their fourth premiership in ten years. Lethal might not be there but they've got the Rat in the centre now and Bucky, Brereton and Dunstall are on fire. Fish is right—the Blues are nowhere, they're going to get smashed. Serves them right, the rich bastards.

'Two players each,' Darren commands. 'They touch it, you drink.'

'Let's do it,' Jason says.

Fish burps like a giant. 'Ready when you are, ladies.'

They drink when Langford or Buckenara get a kick, when Platten or Dunstall touch it, when Brereton or Dear take a mark. They drink when the score flashes on the bottom of the screen or a supporter appears in close-up. Darren staggers to the fridge for fresh supplies and comes back with a fourth can for each of them. They drink whenever the umpire touches the ball.

Jason sinks onto the floor and rubs the smile on his face with one hand. It feels good to be somebody—to know he's finally living in the world, not watching it happen around him.

In the spring darkness after the Hawks' premiership presentation he weaves slowly back to Richmond station. There's beer in his hair, on his tee-shirt, on his jeans. Outside the station entrance he quietly vomits into the gutter between two parked cars. He finds his feet twenty minutes later. He can't walk straight but the feeling of victory is dazzling. The Hawks have won! The Hawks have won! The whole city knows.

• • •

Hayden has his grand-final autographed football in his schoolbag on Monday morning. Dean's tickets had put the two of them in the northern stand above the Hawthorn change rooms. Almost all of the best players have signed it: Brereton, Tuck, Dunstall, Ayres, Dipper, Wallace, Langford. He'd shaken hands with each of them. 'Dad got my picture holding the premiership cup with Dipper,' Hayden tells him. 'We're getting it blown up so I can put it on my wall. There were heaps of supporters there. You could walk around and meet everyone.' He offers Jason his rolled-up copy of the grand-final *Record*. Gary Ayres has signed the front cover. 'Here. You can have this if you want.'

At home Jason files the *Record* in the same box as his football cards. Jealousy prods him each time he opens it. He'd been with Hayden and Dean to eight games during the season. How much would another ticket have cost them? Somehow it was just like Hayden to brag and to offer his cast-offs. Look what you missed, he was saying. You're not as cool as you think you are, Jase.

Before meeting Darren and the crew on Friday nights he spends twenty minutes in the bathroom adjusting his black jeans and Dunlop sneakers, tucking in his polo shirt to make it tighter against his body. He brushes his hair back, messes it forwards, drops it over his ears. He turns up the collar on his jacket and puts a cigarette in his mouth. Examining his face, he wishes his eyebrows were darker, his lips thinner.

He meets them outside South Yarra station. They shake hands like older men, light each other's cigarettes and check things out. It's the hip side of town. As the night goes on, it gathers energy around them. Restaurants, hotel bars, glamour. Drivers in Toranas whistle at women in high heels crossing their headlights. The boys trade looks. Did you see that arse? Those tits? She was bad.

They swagger down the Toorak Road hill to the corner of Chapel Street. Jason hooks his thumbs into his jeans, copying Darren. Somehow

Darren knows how to stand, how to dress. He seems so relaxed, as if style and fashion mean nothing—they're just his life.

They climb the rampway into the Fun Factory skating rink on the corner. The rink's disco lights play along the wall opposite the ticket counter—pink, blue, yellow, green. The ticket seller's an older girl with glitter in her hair and crucifix earrings. They pass her their money to get change for the pool table and she stamps their hands with a red star. Her voice is a monotone. 'Skate hire's five bucks. That's what's left.' She chucks a thumb at the tiered shelves behind her.

They keep ashtrays on the tables alongside the machines and pass cigarettes behind their backs, keeping a lookout for management. There are girls on the rink wearing denim shorts and loose singlets. There are girls whose bikini tops are visible through their tee-shirts and whose chests swell when they toss their hair over their shoulders. The disco ball spins points of light across them as they roll past. The best of them can twirl and backskate in time to the top forty pounding from the speakers: Run DMC, Bruce Springsteen, Bon Jovi.

Darren motions at girls on the rink and makes a composite girl-friend from them. 'Her tits,' he says. 'That chick's arse. That chick's face. Her legs.' He points out their faults as if he's shopping for a car. 'What about you, J.D.?' he says. 'You got a chick?'

'Bloke on the footy team's sister,' he lies.

'You score?'

'Yeah. She was all right.'

Girls from school on the rink come over to the railing to say hi and steal drags from their cigarettes. Darren always talks to them as though he finds them funny in a secret way. His conversation is mostly bullshit but they seem to like it, and they seem to like it even more when he ignores them. So this is what he must do, Jason realises, if he wants girls to pay attention to him. Tease them, keep them guessing. Don't ever let them know what you're thinking. Once they've figured you out, they get bored.

Sitting in his room afterwards, he imagines what it would be like if a girl like Abigail Taylor or Nikki Marini saw his flat, if she came into his room. Do either of them live in places like this? He feels certain they don't. Both of them would have houses like Hayden, two parents, and go on holidays interstate. In here, they'd feel as if something was missing. They'd have to be polite, hearing the pipes in the ceiling while his mum used the bathroom before work.

He consults the player profiles in his grand-final *Record*. Brereton and Greene are both from Frankston, the roughest suburb in Melbourne. Dipper must have been the only Italian kid on his team in North Kew. When did they know they were going to be footballers? When did everybody else?

· · ·

His birthday is on the sixth of December, a Saturday, less than a fortnight after his mum's. When he gets up he finds her already cooking his birthday lunch in the kitchen, and his present is waiting for him on the kitchen bench. It's so much bigger than normal it takes him a moment to guess what it could be. She stands beside him as he tears the wrapping down the middle, revealing the black and white picture on the side of the box: a twin cassette stereo. He'd seen them in the window of the Brashs in Camberwell Junction but never thought he'd own one.

Her face is already glowing before he kisses her on the cheek. The basil on her hands leaves its aroma on his skin.

'This is the greatest present of my life,' he says, and means it.

'Give your mum another hug then.'

'Can we play a tape?'

'If it's something I know the words to.'

He places the stereo on the carpet in front of the television and plugs it into the wall. When he turns on the radio and holds his hand over one speaker he can feel the sound pulsing into his palm.

'Wait here.' She stands slowly and disappears into her room. She's wearing her slippers, the ancient ones with coffee stains on the insteps. When he's older, he decides, he'll make sure he gets her what she doesn't have now: new furniture, a good TV, a holiday.

She returns a few minutes later, grinning, with her old shirtsleeves now rolled up to her elbows. 'Got it.' She lobs a white cassette to him. 'I hope it still works. It must be ten years old.'

Neil Diamond. He purses his lips. But when Diamond's voice rises over a clean acoustic guitar the mix sounds awesome. His Aerosmith tape is going to rattle the windows.

'Lovely.' She claps her hands together and checks the oven. 'Lamb's nearly done.'

'Cool—I'm onto it.'

By midday everything is ready: the card table, the cutlery, the coasters, the plastic flutes, her bottle of red wine, his bottle of Solo, the braised lamb, the Moroccan salad. She adjusts her camera on the back of the couch and takes a photo of them sitting at their meal, glasses raised. He waits for her to start eating. 'Cheers,' she says, tapping her glass with his. They listen to Diamond's voice glide over his backing group and she hums, sometimes, the choruses escaping on her breath.

'And how's Hayden?' she says.

'I think he's good.'

She frowns, hearing something in his tone. 'Are you still friends?'

'I dunno. It's different, now.'

'Hayden and your other friend—Danny. Do they get along?'

'Darren.' He hesitates. 'We do different stuff. Hayden's got other mates, too. It's no biggie.'

'Do you and Darren go out with girls?'

'Huh?'

'Girls,' she says.

'Yeah. We talk to girls sometimes.'

'Make sure you treat them well.'

He can feel his ears turning red. 'What do you mean?'

'Treat girls with respect.' She takes her napkin from her lap and folds it, watching him. 'Most guys don't.'

'I do. I always do.'

'Boys don't know how girls feel.'

'What do you mean?'

She thinks for a moment. 'Girls do things just to feel wanted, sometimes. To feel that the boys think they're special. So you go along with them. You do what they do—things you wouldn't do normally.'

'Well—like what?'

She dabs her mouth with her napkin and holds it there, against her lips, thinking. She stays like this, her elbows on the table, looking at some unfocused point beyond him. She blinks. 'I don't know. Nothing. Sorry.'

'I don't get you.'

'Never mind. Forget about it.' She shakes her head and reaches across the table for the salt. 'Here, do you want some . . . ?' As she leans forward her arm knocks her glass of wine and it falls sideways on the table. Jason pushes back in his chair. The wine pools and spreads around his plate and runs over the table's edge. It drips onto the carpet where it sinks and expands, inches from his shoes.

'Shit!' She stands up, staring at the wine. Her hands make fists.

'It's okay.' He hurries to grab a washcloth from the kitchen sink. 'I'll clean it.'

'Shit.' She shuts her eyes, gripping the table. 'I'm so stupid!'

'Mum, it's okay. It's just some wine. Sit down.' He wipes the tabletop and starts soaking the stain from the carpet. He can sense the tension radiating from her.

'I'm sorry.' She drops into her chair and peers through her fingers at the mess. 'How is it?'

'It's fine. It hasn't stained.' He rinses the rag and squeezes it out in the kitchen sink. Now he's caught her unease—his stomach feels hard, as if he's been winded. He takes a dishtowel from the stove and wipes his hands on it. Then he sits down at the table, picks up his fork and shovels lamb into his mouth.

For some time the only voices in the room come from the cassette.

She pours herself another glass of wine and looks at him. She clears her throat and says, 'This meat really is good, isn't it?'

'Yeah, it is.' He wipes his mouth. 'We've done well this year.'

After lunch, when she's left for work, he rolls his football from beneath his bed and goes jogging with it to Victoria Reserve. The Hawthorn City cricketers are playing. He follows the boundary railing to the elms on the ground's homeward side. As he jogs he counts ten paces on the crunchy grass and bounces the ball, counts and bounces, alternating hands, until the tightness in his stomach passes. He remembers the strangeness in her voice. He loses count of his laps and his hands begin to tingle in the heat.

• • •

A week later he helps her put the photos she has taken into the family album she keeps in her wardrobe. The pages are almost full now. It's strange to see the years rolling through them. He gets bigger while she doesn't. Her clothes hardly change—her jeans and old shirts and dresses, her work uniforms. There's always a lone candle in the centre of her birthday cakes and she doesn't label her age on these photos as she does his. Whenever she's alone in a picture, her smile isn't her good one.

Over summer, when he doesn't have to stay at Hayden's house, he trains in his room. He draws up a timetable and sticks it on his wall:

exercises along the top, days along the side. Push-ups, sit-ups, jogging, chin-ups, squats, jumps, kicking and marking practice. Each time he completes an exercise he ticks the corresponding box. There's something about filling in the sheet every day; he can shape himself to it, he can see where he's going.

He looks at his body before he showers and weighs himself on the scales beside the toilet. He gains a kilogram, but where it's gone he can't tell. He looks at his swap card of Chris Langford, the Hawthorn fullback, fixated on the sculpted arms and thighs. Langford has a body like an action hero—perfect proportion, no fat. His muscles are mesmerising.

When Jason goes to Hayden's place he brings his Metallica cassette. They listen to it while they play Hayden's new Nintendo. Jason headbangs to the music. The thundering guitars and James Hetfield's roar channel a dark energy inside him that he didn't know was there. Every day he needs another fix. At night, before his mum comes home, he sets his stereo on the kitchen bench and leaps around the room, barking the lyrics, playing air guitar atop the armrests of the couch.

Around Hayden, he can feel himself holding back. The Bennetts are so sheltered, he decides. Hayden could be going to a private school like the other kids on his street. He needs permission to catch the bus to Chadstone, and when they go to the movies together he stands away from Darren and the rest of the crew so he doesn't get smoke in his clothes. Hayden is soft inside, Jason knows, and won't keep up—especially not in Year Nine at Burnley Secondary.

Training for the Under-Sixteens starts at Victoria Reserve in January. They have to drill around the uncovered cricket pitch and the balls bounce high on the baked grass. Some of his older teammates, the Year Tens, have hairy chests and chiselled limbs like the labourers he's seen toiling at the end of his street. The tempo is stern, unsmiling. The days of kick-to-kick during warm-ups are gone. Now it's push-ups, lunges, wind-sprints.

Arnie Singer, his new coach, stands in the centre of the ground with his arms folded across his team guernsey, watching the squad pace to the end of their final lap. A rumour has circled among the players that he once played for Preston in the VFA. 'Bring it in!' he barks. He doesn't bother with a whistle.

Once the squad has surrounded him he waits for them to finish dousing themselves with water bottles. 'Right.' He points to the star shape he has measured with witches hats across centre-half forward. 'Star-drill, no passengers. Anyone drops it, they hit the turf and give me twenty. Go!'

Jason wipes his sweaty hands on his shorts. The drill begins, loud and fast. He shoots diagonal to Blakey as Blakey accepts a handpass from Lex. Blakey's handball floats but Jason's good enough to take it in midair and peel it off to Corbs in one motion. It's a slick move, balletic and fierce, that raises the intensity of the drill another degree. He rounds off behind the nearest cone and tightens his helmet strap. After the cardio work it's great to get at a contest.

Five minutes later Arnie calls an end to it. 'Some of you blokes are strolling through.' He pauses to let the sentence fall on their heads. 'You're stopping once you've given the ball off. Why? What did I say, Nichols?'

'Sharp and clean!' Nichols shouts.

'Bullshit, Nichols. What did I say, Dalton?'

'Train like you play!' Jason shouts.

'That's bloody right. You think the Hawks do anything at half-pace? This isn't the bloody playground. You run through, you take the ball, you hit your target, you keep running flat chat. Take it back ten metres and do it again.'

They drill from one end of the ground to the other. One player marks and handpasses, one shepherds, two lead, two chase. They have to swerve to avoid knocking each other down. The principles are simple,

Arnie has told them, maximum intensity, maximum teamwork. Talent will get you to the door, but only hard work will open it.

They train until the sun has set behind the reserve's willows and the practice footies are yellow smudges in the air. Arnie walks among them as they limber down. He holds his arms behind his back, shoulder muscles bulging, and studies the sunset. 'New season starts Saturday week. Are we ready for it?'

'Yeah,' the squad says.

'C'mon, then—are we ready or what?'

'Yeah!' they shout.

'We'd better be. And if we're not, pretty soon we're gonna find out. It's up to you blokes. Don't let me down.'

It's a good feeling to sit in the cool, unlit change room and listen to his teammates yapping at one another and stirring the guys in the showers. The smell of their deodorant surrounds him. Exhaustion brings a buzzing to his ears and stills his mind until he notices the rhythm of his breathing. He listens through the doorway to Arnie's friendly growl as another teammate says goodbye to him.

'Big things, Dalts,' Arnie tells him. 'You're a talent. Make the most of yourself out there.'

. . .

Year Nine is about choices, his home-room teacher Mr Shields tells them on the first day back at school. For homework he has them identify their year's study goals and their chosen career in ten years' time. 'Eyes to the front, Dalton. Who are you going to be? What do you want to achieve?'

At home that night he sits at his desk and gazes at his best-and-fairest trophy. Ten years into the future will be 1996, just four years off *Beyond 2000*. He'll be older than his mum was when he was born. Will he have a kid by then? The thought appals him.

'Be someone who sees the world,' his mum tells him at dinner. 'Take it from me. You don't want to get stuck doing shifts.'

'I put down ambulance driver and renovator.' He waits for her approval. 'I thought, you know, helping people.'

'You're the active type, aren't you?'

'I don't really know.' He lets her scrape the remains of the couscous onto his plate. 'What did you want to be?'

'A doctor. Or a physiotherapist.'

'Could you have done that?'

'I had the grades.' She looks away from him.

'Mum?'

'Yes?'

'Thanks for dinner.'

Her smile returns. 'It's a new recipe. You can taste the African spices.'

He lies on his bed afterwards with his football on his chest. Who would she have been if she hadn't met his dad? Feelings of unease and resentment creep over him. She would have been a happier person, probably, without having a kid tied to her. His earliest memories are stark—being bathed in the sink and unpacking the groceries from the Salvos—though she was always there. Maybe that's what his dad had run from and why she won't talk about him. His dad had chosen himself over both of them.

He turns off his light without opening his schoolbooks. Mr Shields is wrong. Year Nine is a continuation. People like his mum are going to keep battling, and people like Darren are going to get straight As and be successful, and people like Hayden are going to be rich no matter what they do. Everyone has a place.

The following Thursday night the phone rings and disrupts his final set of push-ups. Bare-chested and pink, he staggers into the lounge room and gathers the phone from its cradle. He expects to hear his mum's voice on the other end, telling him she'll be home late from work again. But it's Hayden, calling him for the first time since the start of pre-season training. Hayden's newly broken voice is becoming Dean's. 'Jase, how are you?'

'Hey.' He lowers himself to a seat beside the kitchen bench. With his free hand he caresses his contracted chest muscles. 'What's up?'

'Long time no speak.'

'Sorry about that. Uh—I've been caught up with other shit, you know?'

'How's footy training?'

'We're starting to look good. Shame you quit.'

Hayden's voice falters, then resumes in a more definite key. 'Well, it wasn't fun anymore. I just wanted to kick goals and shit.'

'Yeah.'

'All that training was a pain in the arse.'

'Sure.'

Hayden makes a smirking sound. 'You probably think I'm a pussy, huh?'

Jason scans the wall above the phone as though the words he needs to say are written there. 'No, no, no way. If you're not having fun, mate—fuck it, don't do it.'

'That's what I thought.'

'It's your life, mate.'

'Yeah. So—' Hayden inhales as if he's about to dive underwater. 'You want to come to the Panasonic Cup? We're up against the Tigers at Waverley.'

'I can't. I'm, uh, going to the game with Darren.'

'Oh.'

He listens to Hayden thinking, and adds, 'Maybe we can meet up at the end, or something?'

'I'm going with Dad.'

'Oh. How is your old man?'

'He's selling the business.' The smirk in Hayden's voice falls away. 'He asks about you.'

'Really? Well, say hi to him for me.'

'I'll do that.'

'Well—' Jason stands up and leans against the kitchen bench, closer to the phone. He starts hitting himself on the hip with his fist. 'Guess I'll see you at school tomorrow.'

'Okay. See you then.'

He replaces the phone and holds it on its stand for a moment. 'Jesus,' he says to himself. His ears burn when he thinks of Hayden alone at the other end of the line. Mates are supposed to look out for each other, aren't they? When he goes back to his room he turns up his music until Metallica buries his thoughts.

The numbers on his fitness tables are stepping upwards. When he adds together the columns of push-ups, sit-ups and squats the totals are in the thousands. Instead of doing his homework he makes graphs from them and tapes them to his wall. They're cool to look at, the mountain ranges he's scaled in his body.

In the school toilets he watches himself drawing on a cigarette in the graffitied glass. He's different now. It must be true because when he sees Hayden in the corridors, Hayden looks different, too—a bit taller, less tubby, with acne on the left side of his face where his stubble should be. He remembers to say hi when they pass.

. . .

The 1987 football season starts autumn bright. Fresh chalk speckles the Sherrin during the Falcons' warm-up laps. Arnie has their match plan on the blackboard in the Victoria Reserve dressing rooms. It's a new style of play for them: sharp kicks to moving targets, lots of handball, keep it in the corridor. Jason and the onballers are to drop back into the hole. Grunt work, Arnie has told him. That's where you can grow as a footballer.

Wherever he crosses the white line—in Burwood, at Punt Road, in Fawkner Park, at home—the effect is the same. A buzz prickles up his shoulders and down to his fingers. His feet lose weight. His mind goes. Before the opening whistle he grabs the ball and lets it dance over his fingers. He kicks it to himself, once either foot. He shakes his opponent's hand. From the exact left corner of the centre square he watches the umpire raise the ball to the sky, and the opening whistle runs like a charge through starter cables clipped to his toes.

Arnie starts him each game on the half-back flank. He plays on fast kids like himself, goal kickers who'll run with the ball as soon as they can. But they can't kick with both feet as he can and they don't have his mongrel in close. They'll wait for the handpass instead, or seek space in the pockets when they should be waiting at the fall of the forwards. It makes them easy to run off. They're taller, sure, and their tackles usually come with a jab to the ribs, but he can tell what they're going to do as if they've got keys in their backs.

By the midpoint of the season the Falcons have won twice as many as they have lost. It puts them fourth on the ladder. Two of their victories were twelve-goal blowouts but one of their losses was by fifty-three points to the East Richmond Tigers, the undefeated league leaders. Getting thumped was a good thing, Arnie tells them. It showed us where we bleed.

Matches are scheduled each Saturday between ten and one. Jason keeps the schedule taped to his bedroom wall, beside his poster of the Hawthorn 1986 premiers. When the Falcons aren't playing at home they play as far away as Glen Waverley. He has to map out his journey using the directory in his mum's car. There are line changes to calculate, distances to walk. To get there half an hour before the game, as Arnie instructs, he has to leave before his mum wakes up.

'Where are you all the time?' she asks. 'I don't see you.'

'Just out.'

'Just out?'

'I'm here. You're the one who's gone.'

'To work,' she says. 'Where do you go? Football doesn't take that long, does it?'

'I've got a life, Mum. Deal with it.'

Maybe she's as tired as she says she is, and still expecting her to show up when he plays is unfair. The empty boxes of sleeping tablets in the medicine cabinet back up her story. But if she's tired all the time, how can she keep going back to work? Why does she keep filling in for people? Anger hardens in his stomach when he thinks about her, and not even Metallica can force it out.

When he wakes in the early morning he turns on the light and thinks about playing. At the same time he tosses his football at the ceiling and marks it on his chest. He counts twenty marks, then thirty, then forty. He looks at the escalating exercise graphs on his wall. If he turns off his light and the building is too quiet he takes his mouthguard from the shoebox in his closet and wears it to sleep.

Following the second-last game of the season, a rematch against the Cannons at home, he sits on the change room's soothing concrete floor, his back against the wall, and watches his teammates dress and leave. It looks as if they've carried most of the centre square's mud with them indoors. Their shorthand speech echoes against the low ceilings. Teddy, their bloodnut ruckman, turns to him while he's combing his hair behind his ears. 'Coming to Waverley, Dalts? Should be a corker.'

He waves Teddy away, shaking his head. The Hawks are playing Essendon and he's due to meet Darren and the crew outside light tower three at quarter time. But first he has to find the strength to get off the floor. After a full game as the changing ruck-rover, he can feel his joints rusting into place.

'Soft cock.' Teddy stoops to gather his gear, whistling the Essendon theme song.

'Ranga.'

'Skinner.'

'See you, Teddy,' Jason says.

'Dalts.'

He showers in his shorts once the other players have finished. He scrubs the cracked mud from his legs, lost in time. As the steam rises around him it strikes him how quickly the season fades now that it's almost finished. Everyone just moves forward, as if it means nothing.

He changes into his jeans and bomber jacket and heads out the door. Outside, two amateur clubs are jogging a warm-up lap of the ground before their game. He scans the crowd for his mum but she's not there. He starts walking, his backpack heavy on his shoulder, and wonders if she'll be there when he gets home. He hopes he can slide in and out of the flat without having to face her.

'Dalton!'

He turns around. Arnie is striding towards him, a sports bag in each hand. His tanned, creased face is hard but friendly. 'Where you off to?'

Jason waits for Arnie to fall in stride with him. 'Home. I don't live too far.'

'Got time to give us a hand?'

'Sure.'

Arnie passes one of the sports bags to him and points to his blue Kingswood station wagon parked near the edge of the reserve. 'I got some stuff in the car needs unloading. I'd appreciate it.'

'No worries, Arnie.'

The Kingswood is so dirty the windshield wipers have shaped half-moons on the glass. Between the trunk and the front seats lie half a dozen toolboxes and enough cans of paint to fill a bathtub. Jason has to wedge himself in the passenger seat between four wooden planks that are stacked from the rear window to either side of his headrest. Beyond his knees, he can see a tangle of red and yellow dashboard wiring. He moves to wind down the window, then realises the handle is missing.

Arnie starts the engine and the Kingswood shudders to life. 'Excuse the mess. I'm renovating.'

'Where do you live?'

'Up here.' He guns the station wagon onto the main road and past Arthur's milk bar. 'Sorry, Dalts—it'll only take a minute. You got plans this arvo?'

'Just the footy.'

'Likewise. We'll make it snappy, then.'

A minute later they turn off the main road into a shaded, dead-end street ten minutes' walk from his flat. The houses here are like the houses his mum has imagined: hidden, simple, safe, unchanging. Arnie pulls into the driveway of a peeling weatherboard and parks halfway down behind a ute. His house has shingles and potted plants hanging above the front door and seems broader than it is long. Jason untangles himself from the passenger seat and climbs out of the car. He swerves to avoid the dead rosebush that greets him on the side fence.

'Thanks for this, Dalts.' Arnie pulls open the trunk and starts sliding the planks out of the car. 'Just stick 'em in the garage at the end there.'

As they unload the contents of the car they chat about the Hawks and the teams that are likely to trouble them in the finals. Melbourne's defence look good, Carlton's got the star imports, Capper and the Sydney Swans are fun to watch but that's as far as it goes. Lockett should win the Brownlow and the Bears are doomed.

Jason frowns at the clutter of boarding and hardware now stacked around the garage's murky walls, between ladders and tarps and corrugated sheeting. 'Big job,' he says.

'Yeah. With a bit of luck I'll be done by Christmas.'

'Need a hand?'

'Should be right.' Arnie walks back to the car and Jason follows him. As he's about to step into the driver's seat Arnie looks at his overgrown front yard and says, 'Come to think of it—what're you like at gardening?'

Jason edges around the rosebush and opens the passenger door. 'Dunno.'

'Well—can you work a lawnmower?'

'Yeah.'

'Can you tell a weed from a flower?'

'Yeah.'

'Then you can do gardening. God knows I'll never do it. I've got all the gear, you just need to turn up.'

'Cool.' Jason nods, convincing himself. 'I'll give it a shot.'

'Sensational.' Arnie lowers himself into the driver's seat and jingles through his crammed ring of keys until he finds the right one. 'You live round the corner, you said.'

'Yeah, near the milk bar, about a k or so.'

'Come see us next weekend, then. We'll get you started.'

'Awesome. Thanks very much, Arnie.'

'No thanks necessary.' Arnie revs the engine and reverses at dangerous speed onto the street. 'Good to have you on board.'

Arnie drops him outside his block of flats just after one o'clock. Jason races upstairs. He's only got an hour to get to Waverley, and he still needs to get changed and eat lunch before he leaves. For the moment, though, none of this worries him. Finally, a paid job, and one he might actually like. Finally he'll be able to live his life on the weekends without being dependent on his mum. He can't wait to tell her about it.

When he checks her bedroom she's not there. He checks the kitchen bench, but she hasn't left a note saying where she is. For a moment he's confused and disappointed. Where could she be? He writes her a note, an eighteen-word scribble that he folds and stands on the bench before dashing into his room:

Got job gardening. More later.
Am staying at Darren's place. Home tomorrow.
Speak then. Don't work too hard. J

4. finding space

Arnie's front and back yards are about the same size as one of the class-rooms at school. They've been neglected for so long that when Jason starts work on them he can hardly see the dirt through the weeds. But he enjoys the job as he's never enjoyed schoolwork. Turning the soil and ripping out weeds feels good. It's got a point and a system to it. It's not like class, where his mind keeps drifting away from the endless exercises and towards Abigail Taylor, or Darren, or the Falcons missing the finals. The weeds and the dirt are real things. He can sit on his heels, slip Arnie's gardening gloves into one hand, wipe the sweat from his face and see the difference he's made.

He works for three hours on the first two Sundays in September, from two until five, and Arnie pays him twenty-five bucks a session. It's a good wage, compared to the five bucks an hour his classmates are making at Safeway. And he's got rock music, too, from Arnie's old transistor. It crackles on the window ledge behind him while Arnie paints the inside rooms. Between tasks Arnie pours them each a glass of beer and they chat about results from the VFL finals. Can the Hawks stop the Demons? Will Brereton be a hero again? Are

Carlton better than they were in '86? Will Platten get the Brownlow he deserves?

'Like your work,' Arnie tells him as he inspects the yard. 'You say you've never done this before?'

'Nope.'

'Tell you what—wash the car and sweep the driveway, I'll give you another ten.'

'Will do.'

'Outdoors type, aren't you?'

'I reckon.'

'Same here. I couldn't stand classrooms.'

As Jason scrubs and shammies the Kingswood he learns about Arnie's removals business in Richmond: his two trucks, his partner from high school, the early shifts, the tomcat employees he'd fire if it weren't for the union. How he started off as a twenty-seven-year-old driving a dual-axle Kenworth truck he bought from a mate's dad for fifteen grand. Nine years later, he's got his own house and a shack in Rye on the south coast. 'Live life, mate,' Arnie tells him. 'Don't let life live you. That's my attitude.'

At five o'clock on the following Sunday afternoon, Arnie invites him inside to watch a tape of the semi-final replay. They settle on the adjustable leather couches in Arnie's lounge room to relive the game's conclusion. In twenty-four hours, the final minute has become legend. Jason holds his head for the second time when Bucky takes his free kick on the Hawks' fifty-metre line. The siren sounds. Would Bucky have got onto one and made the distance? His gut says no, he wouldn't, not from that pocket at Waverley, not when the Hawks didn't—he has to admit—deserve to win.

Somewhere off screen Jim Stynes, the Melbourne ruckman, steps across the mark and gives away a fifteen-metre penalty. What could he have been thinking?

At the umpire's signal, Bucky walks fifteen metres closer to goal, still looking calm, somehow, and changes his grip to a drop punt.

'If he kicks this goal, Hawthorn are in the 1987 grand final,' says the commentator. 'If he misses, Melbourne are in.'

From thirty-five metres, Bucky's kick sails between the top of the goalposts.

'It's a goal! It's a goal!' screams the commentator. 'Hawthorn have won with a kick after the siren!'

Jason looks at Arnie and they laugh at themselves hovering above the edge of their seats, back inside the moment when every Hawks supporter leaped a foot from the ground with their arms in the air.

Later, as he walks home in the murky spring light, he studies the twenty-five dollars in his wallet and savours the feeling it gives him, the light, clear memory of the afternoon he's just shared. It's more than money. It's an accomplishment. It'll be there next week, too. The predictability is comforting.

With the extra money he's earned he buys a fake ID from a Year Twelve Darren knows. His new name is Anthony Kilpatrick, and he was born on the seventeenth of September, 1969. The card's laminated photo fools the bottle-shop owner near Darren's house and he can buy whatever alcohol he likes there. 'How's Tony?' Darren asks Jason, and soon it becomes their running joke. 'Tony got so pissed on the weekend he passed out in his own vomit,' they say. 'That Tony can't control himself—he should see somebody.'

His unattempted assignments spread up the walls of his school locker like fungi: an essay on apartheid, an essay on fossil fuels, a hydro-physics prac, another hydro-physics prac, an assignment on parabolas, an assignment on algebraic fractions, an assignment on local geology. He feels he knows the score. He'll never succeed at anything that involves sitting behind a desk, he concludes. He must have been born to be something else.

But what? Beyond football his vision of the future is weak. Getting through school is hard enough. Images of himself as a carpenter or a fireman remain toy-like in his mind, jobs his adult self will assume over the horizon when he has money, a car, and a life of his own. Maybe he could figure it out faster, he tells himself, if everyone would just trust him and leave him alone.

'You've made one big step,' his mum tells him over dinner. 'Now you've got this job, the rest might fall into place.'

'It will, Mum. I'll make a big effort next year.'

'It's great you've found something you like.'

'Yeah, I like it a lot.' He taps his fingers on the kitchen bench. 'Can I tell you something?'

'What?'

'I really don't want to stay at Hayden's this summer. Me and Hayden, we're both . . . We don't see much of each other anymore.'

'You're not friends?'

Hearing the words out loud for the first time is difficult. 'No,' he says. He wants to add more, an apology of some kind.

'I see.'

'I can look after myself here, though. I can do everything you need me to. Chores and stuff. Same as usual.'

'It's not the chores I'm worried about.'

'Right.'

'Can I trust you?'

'I'll do everything, I promise.'

She points at him with her fork. 'Don't make me regret it.'

At Victoria Reserve each night after school he kicks his football as high as he can and shoots at goal from wherever it lands. Calmness fills him as he tracks the ball's silent arc and puts a divot in the ground where it lands. The longer he trains, the further the world behind the boundary line retreats. He has time, he remembers. He and his mum have been able to look after themselves so far. It occurs to him that he could start another job and build from there. Other guys at school no smarter than him are grocery clerks and packers. He could do what Arnie has done and become his own boss. But walking home, his inspiration fades into the roaring traffic. Those guys got jobs because they knew people, he reminds himself. If he had a family business to go into, like Darren or Hayden, his problems would be solved.

. . .

On weekends across November and December he journeys six stations to meet Darren and Fish at the skate park opposite the government housing towers in Prahran.

The vert ramp alongside the park's bitumen basketball court is the size of a house. Its gleaming surface is shadowed with graffiti. Skaters crouch on the mottled grass behind the court, eating fast food and smoking. Others sprawl shirtless beneath the ramp and watch their friends practising tricks. He knows it's not his space, it's theirs, and he's careful not to look them in the eye.

They drop their boards and push off. Fish takes the vert ramp, Darren takes the basin behind it, and Jason spins at the top of the staircase, practising his moves. He uses Darren's old skateboard, an '85-model Tracker. It's a health hazard; the nose and tail are chipped from years of being smacked against the ground, the grip is flaking, there's friction in the wheels' trucks and when he speeds up the board shakes. But it's his deck, his membership card in the park. He knows his mum would crack the shits if she ever saw him using it. Part of him feels guilty at being less responsible than she expects him to be—she hasn't got anyone else to trust. But a part of him soars on the board. When he reaches top speed the air turns to wind on his skin, and the onrushing world puts him in the moment in the same way as when he has the ball in his hands during a Falcons game.

Later, when the buzz of the park has faded, the three of them catch the train back to Burnley station. They swagger to the end of the platform and jump onto the tracks. Darren has four cans of spray-paint he keeps hidden in his knapsack. He leads Jason and Fish through the weeds and rubble to the sites he has in mind. Along the way he points out the graffiti he recognises. 'See that one—Strangler—that's an Abbotsford crew. I know this chef at work, Trent, he used to run with them.' He stands in front of tags and shapes each letter in the air, working backwards to figure them out.

They tag their names on stained brick walls, on the railway's utility boxes, on fences, on abandoned steel bridges overlooking one-way streets. They take turns standing guard. It's broad daylight and there's every chance they'll be seen, but this is part of the point. If there was no risk it wouldn't be worth it. As Jason sprays his initials onto the concrete, the steel and the brick he feels a cross between nerves and excitement he hasn't known before. The skateboarding, the graffiti, the beer they will drink later at Darren's house. Everything is speeding up.

At home, he showers the aerosol smell from his body and keeps his clothes in a separate bag to his regular laundry. By the time his mum is up he is once more the person she knows, in the shorts she'd bought him for his birthday, cooking dinner according to her instructions.

Was his dad as responsible as she is? He couldn't have been, Jason decides. Otherwise, he wouldn't have run away. At night, gazing up at his fading Starlight Zone stickers, he imagines his dad as someone like Dermott Brereton or Dipper. Tough, risk-taking, living fast. He tries to put his mum in the picture, flying through the night next to his dad in a sportscar like the one Dipper owns. Is that what she was like when she was young?

She seems much older now than when he was in primary school, and duller. Worry lines have formed around her eyes and mouth and the roots of her hair are greying. She rises later on the weekends and moves about the flat as if her spine is made of glass. Who is she, away from here? he wonders. What's it like working with her? He only knows her co-workers, her friends, by the voices they leave on the answering machine: Lori, Brenda, Jamila. Is she different with them? Do they know something about her that he doesn't? Around the phone she leaves traces of her real-estate research. There are unsealed envelopes from agents in Ringwood and Belgrave. She writes other numbers and names on the backs of them. The words 'Cardigan Road, Mooroolbark' appear three times, once circled. Mooroolbark is in the Dandenong Ranges section of the street directory, he discovers, beyond the city train service. There are more gridlines on the Mooroolbark page than roads.

The October sharemarket crash was good, she tells him. House prices will come down. So will the interest rates. Sit tight. Let's wait and see. After hearing her out, he has to train at Victoria Reserve to calm down. Anger stirs in him at the thought that she would uproot his life now. She doesn't know what it means to finally have the Falcons and Darren's crew, to be part of their strength. But her words are empty as well: she won't change her routine. He runs until her voice is no longer vibrating inside him and the sadness he can sense behind it has washed out with his sweat.

The second-last day of the year is a scorcher. By six in the evening it's still thirty-eight degrees and the air inside their flat is a blanket. He sprawls against the arm of the couch, stripped to his shorts, holding a block of ice to his throat. Each time he moves, the couch sticks to his back.

She has put on her John Lennon album while she gets changed in her bedroom. He knows every bar of it now. There was that month way back in primary school, after Lennon got shot, when she'd played it every night. The sameness of it maddens him. He drums his feet and cracks his knuckles, pissed off at being stricken by the heat.

Her voice comes through the wall. 'Can you put the lasagne on, thanks?'

'Next commercial break.'

'I have to leave soon.'

'Commercial, Mum.'

'Please, Jason, turn it off and cook the dinner.'

He crawls to the TV and increases the volume. Then he goes into the kitchen, lights the oven, and bundles their lasagne onto the lowest shelf. She strides out of her room in fresh work clothes, pours coffee beans into the grinder and plugs it into the wall. 'Where are you going tonight?'

'Darren's.'

'Will his parents be home?'

'Later on—once they've shut the restaurant.'

'Are you going out?'

'Dunno.'

'It's not too hot to speak in full sentences. If you're going out, I want Darren's phone number. And what's the name of his parents' restaurant?'

'You can't call them, Mum. They're at work.'

'So am I.'

'Here.' He writes Darren's number onto one of the envelopes beside the phone, where Cardigan Road is still nagging at him. 'Fish 'n' chips and a video is ten bucks. I did the vacuuming last night, and the laundry.'

Her voice rises above the clacking of the coffee grinder. 'I thought you said you didn't know what you were doing.'

'It's ten bucks.' He looks through the serving hatch at the TV. Australia are still surviving New Zealand's final overs of the third Test. If only he were at the MCG, and not here. 'Hayden doesn't have to do housework and he gets twenty bucks a week from his parents. They just give it to him.'

'Your reasoning being that how Hayden lives is how you should live.

Not considering what it does for Hayden's understanding of the real world, giving him money just for being himself.'

'I want a life, Mum. That's all.'

'I want you to have your independence too, Jason. I know you're stuck here all day. I know you do a lot of work, and I appreciate it. But maybe you'd be happier if you found a job that paid more.'

'On top of school, on top of chores, on top of training.'

'Maybe if you didn't train so much.'

'It's a football thing again, isn't it?'

'It's not a football thing. It's a grown-up thing.'

'You told me you saved fifteen hundred bucks last month.'

'I'm not a credit card for you and your mates.' She steps into the kitchen doorway. For a moment, he's shocked: they're the same height.

He says, 'You don't even know them.'

'I don't know them at all. Every Friday and Saturday, you just disappear.'

'What, you want to keep tabs on me? You want to call a babysitter?'

'Don't talk to me like that.'

'Like what?'

'As if I'm not worth your time.'

He steps around her, seeking space. But the lounge room is so small. Everything looks like a corner. 'You hate my life. You just want me to do everything you never did.'

'I don't hate your life.'

'What do you want me to say?'

'I don't want you to say anything. I just don't want you to throw it away with these—' She stops short. 'Whoever they are. Footballers.'

Something inside him bursts. 'Come off it, Mum. It's just a bloody game. What's wrong with that? The one thing I'm good at and you don't give a shit. You never have.'

'Jason—'

She's too late. He grabs the front door and sends it into the skirting board. No shoes and no shirt, but he doesn't care, it hardly registers. He sharks across the balcony, down the staircase and onto the driveway, slapping the walls and spitting words into the concrete.

The way she looked at him, as if playing football is a crime.

He hits the kerb at the end of his street and turns with no idea where he's going. He continues past Arthur's milk bar and crosses the road. He reaches Victoria Reserve. The Hawthorn City cricket team is finishing another cricket match. There are spectators, a dozen or so, and he can smell the fried kiosk food as he passes the clubrooms. He circles the oval to the far corner of the reserve, the dry grass prickling his feet, and sits on a wooden bench beneath an elm tree glittering in the twilight. The way she'd looked when he shouted, her eyes shocked and fearful. He'd brought that on in her. Self-disgust pulls him forward; his head bent over his knees. He doesn't stand up until the cricketers have left the field and the horizon is mauve.

He skulks back into their flat and sits on the end of his bed. His room and who he feels like now don't match anymore. His *Star Wars* doona cover belongs to a child, and his desk still has the gold stars he stuck on it when he was in primary school. But who he was then wouldn't have said what he did or slammed the door in her face. He has caused her so much pain, he knows. But he can't explain even to himself the hardness that overcomes him. He holds his head in remorse.

On stray nights in January, after he's finished shopping for groceries at the Glenferrie supermarket one train station away, he sits in the empty brick stand on the city side of Glenferrie Oval and watches the Hawks train. Their squad jogs the boundary line in front of him: Dunstall, Brereton, Ayres, Langford, Bucky, Tuck, the Rat. Their voices dart through the sky as they sprint past the grey gum trees that sit like a cordon at the railway side of the ground. As dusk settles, the players' shadows multiply under the ground's floodlights. He cranes forward, using his grocery bags as armrests. His hands are restless at the thought of joining them.

He thinks about his old football cards, counting them on his pillow at night before he went to sleep. He had always thought his dad might resemble one of the players. Where could his dad be now? Where do men go when they do a runner? The question scratches at his mind. Maybe he's in some mining town up north. Maybe he's gone to England and changed his name. Would he recognise his dad if he saw him?

He watches the Hawks' squad drill with crash bags and admires the cut of their bodies. The best players work harder, he realises. They're never satisfied. Sweat plus sacrifice equals success, as Arnie says. If he can stick with it, if he keeps to his routine, he'll get biceps like Brereton and legs like Platten. He imagines stretching with them, grappling, contesting loose balls. He's certain he can do everything they can. He just needs time.

. . .

Another year at Burnley Secondary dawns at the end of the month. There are guys in Year Ten who have shot upwards over summer and now lope down the staircases like the older brothers of themselves. At recess he sees them thumping across the basketball courts and doing slam-dunks. There are Year Eights who were playing with tennis balls in the quadrangle three months before, now smoking in the toilets. Girls he hadn't noticed the previous year have blossomed dangerously. Their breasts and hips fill the corridors like neon signs. He blushes when they look at him, certain they know what he's thinking.

On the days his assignments are due he meets Darren in the laneway before school and copies down the answers while Darren smokes. It seems this will be the Year of Darren. Other guys in their class have started wearing white socks with their school shoes as he does.

'So what's your girl situation, J.D.?' Darren asks him.

'I don't have one.'

'Dude—you've just gotta go in there and talk.'

'I'm not you, mate. You've got the gift.'

'Seriously. Just crack some jokes and shit. You're a funny guy.'

'I can't do jokes. I can't go, "Hey, here's this funny story." It's lame.'

'Think about it this way. What's more dangerous—you running backwards into a pack of five blokes when you're playing for the Falcons, or some girl standing there?'

After school Jason catches the train home from Burnley station, spying his own graffiti through the plexiglass windows. He watches his classmates flirting on the train. They throw their arms over each other, listen to Walkmans together and write their phone numbers onto each other's wrists. He's heard stories on the platforms and in the smokers' laneway: they're having sex—at parties, at summer shacks. Guys are getting jerked off in their bedrooms and carrying condoms in their wallets. Every weekend someone scores, or is about to score. Even Hayden, from what he's heard.

At night he imagines himself in a backyard as big as Hayden's was, and Abigail Taylor gazing up at him from the grass. When he takes off his school shirt he has arms like Dermott Brereton. Underneath her school dress she's not wearing underwear, and when he pushes himself inside her she makes a face like Madonna. He fucks her hard, making her dirty. Afterwards he holds her until she falls asleep, in the twilight before his mum gets home.

• • •

By the end of March, two games into the Falcons' 1988 season, he's struggling to fit into his clothes. Each of his tee-shirts has become a brace, and he can no longer button his school shirts to the neck. The only jumper he owns that doesn't ride up his arms is his guernsey.

'You're not wearing that around the house,' his mum tells him when he sits down to dinner. 'This isn't a locker room.'

'Nothing else fits me.'

'Fine. We'll go to Chadstone tomorrow night and get you some proper clothes. But you're to take it off now.'

'What else am I supposed to wear?'

'Put your pyjamas on.'

At Chadstone Shopping Centre the following night she leads him past Myer and the streetwear outlets to a narrow store off the main concourse. A 'closing sale' sign has been taped to its window. The man behind the counter shows them the two racks of business shirts remaining and goes back to his calculator.

Jason stands like a scarecrow while his mum holds one shirt after another against his chest for size. 'I need clothes I can wear, Mum. Not shirts.'

'You'll need them if you go to job interviews.'

'I'm not going to interviews. I have a job gardening at Arnie's.'

'You can't mow lawns forever.' She lets the man behind the counter step between them with his tape measure. 'We'll get a belt with the pants, too. Give him some growing room.'

The store's one change room has no mirror. Jason closes the curtain and sighs out of his clothes. The business shirts she has chosen drape his hips, and the pants look like something his teachers would wear. In his underwear, he leans against the change room's cool wall until the knot of frustration in his throat unravels. Let her have this one. Keep the peace.

. . .

By eleven pm on the night of his sixteenth, Darren's concreted backyard is as crowded as a pub. There are almost as many girls as guys.

Jason stands near the back fence, swaying, and tries to make people out in the half-darkness. Gatecrashers in torn jeans keep striding through the back door. Girls from other schools are swivelling on the couches inside the lounge-room windows. More of them are babbling in the hallway. He hears the muffled thump and slap of Darren's drum kit in his bedroom. Noise in the yard dips at the sound of a breaking bottle: a hip flask of vodka, in pieces beneath the yard's stone bird bath. Jeers swarm in its wake.

A girl is sauntering towards him. She's tall and thin as a crane, with a foot-long ponytail. Sneakers, frilled skirt, leather jacket. She could be fifteen, she could be seventeen—it's difficult to tell.

'Hey.' Her half-smile shows gums. 'You got another cigarette?'

He offers her the packet.

She takes it from him and taps a cigarette loose. He watches his lighter follow her cigarette to her mouth. Leaning over it, she almost topples into him.

'What's your name?'

'Chantelle.'

He loosens his fist and offers her his open hand. 'I'm Jason.'

'Is this your place?'

'No, it's Darren's. A mate of mine.' He nods at the door. 'Playing drums inside.'

'He's pretty shit.' She slips his beer from his hand and lifts it slowly to her mouth. 'You both musos?'

He shrugs, watching her swallow.

An INXS song opens loud through the weatherboard wall. Someone inside has turned up the stereo. It's a single he recognises from a video clip: Michael Hutchence doing it for the girls, not really his style. But Chantelle reaches towards the lounge-room stereo as if she's going to embrace it. 'Oh, I love this. We have to dance.'

'I don't—'

She finds both of his hands. 'Come on.'

He follows her hips into the house. Near the back door he hears a word, 'bongs' or 'cops', and a guy clutching Darren's cordless phone wants to know whose place it is. Four of Jason's classmates watch him from the lounge-room wall. In the corner, Darren's silver hi-fi stereo sits behind empty cans and packets of potato chips. Girls are dancing in front of it, their tee-shirts slipping from their shoulders. At the chorus they freeze and point at each other, joining in, singing loudly.

Chantelle drops his hands and dances away with her arms above her head and her hair swinging. He moves his hips and feet. There's a beat in the song he tries to concentrate on but keeps missing. He can feel people's eyes on him, other guys from school and girls he doesn't know, holding their hands to their faces and laughing: look at this guy.

The song ends, and in the hiss of empty tape he looks at his revolving feet. 'What's—what's your favourite band?'

'I saw these guys in concert.'

'Oh—cool.'

When the next song begins she holds his shoulders. Piano chords bounce. Hutchence sings come-ons while the band snap their fingers. Jason holds her waist and forces himself to look her in the eye without looking away. She has sweat on her eyebrows, freckles on her forehead. Soon there's nothing between them, just a wash of sound. Her hips stop moving.

'I like your eyes,' he hears himself say.

'Come here.'

When he kisses her his ears buzz and he almost trips on her feet. He feels her breath and her body pressing against his. Her mouth tastes of champagne and cigarette smoke. He's afraid of shutting his eyes in case she stops. But just when she seems to be drawing away she closes her eyes and grabs him again.

They surface when the cassette changes. Some Michael Jackson fan has taken over the stereo. Jason holds Chantelle's arm for support. The couches and the floor slide together. What time is it? He brings his wrist against his nose, blinking. It doesn't matter. He could stay awake all night now.

She regards him for a moment, rocking slightly. 'You're glowing.'

'Am I?'

'Help me find my friends.'

His classmates on the wall are still looking at him, their smirks rigid. Nugget, Bolton, McCaffery, Baird. They nod and raise their beers when he passes. He adjusts his fringe and tries to make his smile less obvious.

Hours later, crashed out alone on Darren's lounge-room floor, he can still feel her breath in his mouth and her body's warm shelter. A happiness fills him unlike anything he's experienced before. Chantelle. Thinking her name draws her closer. He drifts into sleep, the memory of her touch flowing through him.

'She was pretty good,' he tells a classmate on Monday. 'Tall blonde chick with a tan.'

'What was her name?'

'Chantelle. She showed up about eleven, her and a bunch of mates. Usual story.'

'And you rocked over and picked her up?'

'Yeah. I figured, what the hell?'

'Nice one.'

'It was a huge night. You should've been there.'

At home he lies on his bed and tries to recapture the sensation of being with her. He burrows into the memory of her skin against his, of being inside the softness of her arms. The closeness of her body had been almost scary. But her confidence had passed into him. For the rest of the night, what people thought of him hadn't mattered.

. . .

Through the first month of winter he marks his height and weighs himself every Wednesday night. He feels certain that she's done something to him. The escalating pencil marks on his bedroom door are proof: one hundred and seventy-four centimetres, sixty-four kilograms, and counting. He's a different player to what he was the previous season.

'My God, you've grown,' his mum tells him, reaching up to place her hand atop his head.

'Three centimetres since April,' he says.

'Let me look at you.' She holds him away from her like a dress.

'What?'

'I don't know.' She lets him go. 'It's just a shock, that's all. Here—have some more dinner.'

At training his guernsey is tight as rubber against his chest and his feet blister in his boots. He can outmark teammates who used to be able to monster him in one-on-ones. 'Jesus, Dalton,' they say during their stretches. 'You taking steroids or something?' They grip his arms and tell him to flex, whistling at the granite feel of his biceps.

He asks Arnie for a wage advance to buy new boots. It feels good to be borrowing money from him instead of his mum. Using the advance he buys size nine Pumas with fluorescent stripes, like Dermott Brereton's boots, and a sleeveless Hawthorn guernsey. At training he gives Arnie the receipt for eighty-one dollars and promises to work it off over the next two Sundays—wash his windows, clear his gutters, whatever he needs.

Arnie nods and folds the receipt into his sock. 'You know what a performance-based contract is?'

'I think so.'

'Good. Here's the deal—the better you play, the less you pay me.' He holds out his battered right hand. 'Agreed?'

'Yeah, agreed. Thanks, Arnie.'

'Don't make me regret it.'

Each game, the Falcons come onto the ground as one, lock arms and form a circle. They do it in the centre so every player on the other team can see and hear them when they start shouting. If there are kids from school on the other team he takes the time to shake their hand at either end of the match. But between sirens he hits them as hard as any of their teammates. He's a Falcon and if they can't cop it, they're pretenders.

After each game Arnie drives him back to his house to work on the garden and clean the garage. He's building a pool-room extension into the backyard where the previous owner's shed used to be. His drawing of it is stuck to his kitchen fridge. Other people would give in and hire someone else, Jason reckons, but not Arnie—his belief in himself is amazing.

Work experience week is the second-last of third term. He signs on with Arnie over the phone. It isn't supposed to be a holiday, the careers counsellor has told them. But it sounds much better than school. No desks, no bells, no homework. Daily travel and lunch in the pub. The thought of being Arnie's right-hand man fills him with pride.

Arnie's company logo is printed on both of the three-tonne trucks in the lot behind his West Richmond office, in the same black font as a Sherrin football: 'Premiership Removals—Number One for Your Possessions'. In the gloomy pre-dawn Jason circles them, tapping the tyres with one foot and peering through the windows. For the full week he'll be paid one hundred and fifty dollars, one hundred and twenty-five more than Darren's getting for his week at a film production company in the city. It's enough to buy a Walkman. It's enough to redecorate his room.

They warm up in front of the trucks— him, Arnie and Arnie's two employees, Doyle and Shane. Jason wears his Hawthorn guernsey and jeans. Seeing his reflection in Arnie's tinted office windows, he reminds himself of the guys he sees on the building site near his school, and allows himself a small smirk.

Their first morning job takes them to an empty two-bedroom cottage in Canterbury, and their second to a third-storey flat in Elsternwick. A job following lunch is at a starter home in Brunswick that shares walls with the neighbours on either side, and this is followed by a job at a terrace in East Melbourne. Walking into strangers' homes, carrying out their things and putting them together in new places gives him a funny feeling. People hold on to so much: magazines, plastic cups and bowls, broken lampshades and light fittings, shoes, bathroom supplies, vinyl collections. From the outside, it looks worthless. His mum's room is just the same. She doesn't let go.

'Be careful with that money you get,' she tells him. 'You should put it away. One of these days you'll have to live off a budget. It's a skill. Get used to it now and it'll be easier later on.'

'How about you? What about the house?'

'Another six months or so.'

'Another six months.'

'Jason.'

'That's what you said at the start of the year.'

'Please don't.'

'I'm just saying.'

'Then stop saying it.'

She starts her graveyard shifts at ten. Before she leaves she plays music in her room. It's loud enough to wake him. Her floorboards creak to the rhythm of her feet. He could ask her to turn it off, point out he needs his sleep, that she's not the only one working. But that might only stir up the other stuff as well.

Another six months. Thinking of her words pulls a trigger in him and, agitated, he gets out of bed. It's the flat. Pacing from room to room once she's left, he can't escape the way her life has turned out. Her tiredness is in the couch, her bad back is in the lower cupboards, her years of night shifts are in the notes stuck by flower magnets to the fridge.

He puts his stereo on the kitchen bench and turns up the volume, but even James Hetfield's primal roar can't stave off his thoughts. One day he'll be older, and she'll be old, and they'll still be here, pretending that it's different.

'Where's your mum from?' Arnie asks him the following day.

'Echuca.'

'You go up there much?'

'My grandparents died before I was born. She doesn't have any brothers or sisters.'

'And you were born down here.'

'St Vinnie's, I think.'

'Mum ever dated?'

'No.'

'You can tell me to shut up if you want.'

'It's fine,' Jason says. 'There's not much to tell. She's a bit crazy, that's all.'

'Jase, everyone's parents are crazy when you're fifteen.'

Putting life in the apartment with her into actual words makes him feel heavy. 'She's started locking herself in her bedroom inside the flat. It gets so I hardly see her some days. When I do, she's at me about who my friends are and how I'm spending too much time playing football. But I'm not ten anymore.' He notices Arnie watching him. 'I hate it. It's like she can't deal with me getting older, or something.'

'Being a single mum's hard, mate. It's one of the hardest gigs there is.'

Out the window of the truck is a stream of bigger and bigger houses, some pocketed among trees. 'She likes the Dandenongs.'

'Yeah?'

'That's where we'll move when she gets the money. We go up there sometimes, on her birthday and stuff.' The shuddering of the truck felt through his seat and the greasy smell of the cabin is an escape from himself. This is Arnie's world, not his. 'She's cool up there. Both of us. We can talk, you know? Away from it. Like we used to when I was a kid.'

The next house is in Mitcham, half an hour from his block of flats, hidden in a crosshatch of streets where most of the homes have citrus trees in their front yards. This is where she could be. Climbing up and down the house's front steps with lampshades and coffee tables against his chest, he can see her kneeling in the front yard, in a sun hat, a wheelbarrow beside her for the weeds, her back strong again, and her face an older version of how it used to look when he was in primary school, mapped in lines that show when she smiles. The vision lifts the sadness from him, sending it out into the weekday street.

5. the outer

After four hours and three quarters it's still hard to believe he's really there—the 1988 VFL grand final, the Hawks' sixth in a row.

As the umpires run the ball into the centre following another Dermott Brereton goal Jason turns again to absorb the crowd. It's colossal: ninety-five thousand people divided into columns forty metres high, tickertape shimmering above the middle tiers. He looks at the supporters around him—the jokers in capes and tinted glasses, the kids with dyed hair and face-paint, the well-dressed men rosy with alcohol. There's so much to remember. And the brawling sound of them all, unrepeatable in the world outside.

Why hadn't he done this before? All it took was a night queuing outside the MCG ticket office. Thirty bucks a seat—or a day and a half's work at Arnie's. He should've risked it. He should've packed his sleeping bag and worried about his mum later. But he didn't have Darren and Fish back then—he had Hayden. If only he'd known.

A thunderstorm in the first half has left the MCG scarred with mud. The ball is waterlogged and soapy. But this hasn't stopped the Hawks from kicking sixty-two points clear of the Demons and there's still twenty-five minutes to go. Dunstall has five goals, Brereton has four, and the Hawks' backline is impregnable. Three-quarters of the crowd are Melbourne supporters and their dejection is so bare-skinned he almost feels for them. They haven't won a flag in twenty-four years. And the way the Hawks are going, Melbourne has no chance.

Beside him, Fish stands astride his bucket seat and sings with the other Hawthorn supporters jammed into the terrace. With each brass beat in the club anthem he punches the air with his team scarf, his voice tuned to a single bellowing note.

James Morrissey, the Hawthorn goal sneak, snatches the ball on the far wing and loops a handpass to Russell Greene on the forward flank. Greene casually guides the ball to Brereton, who is somehow five metres clear of his opponent and just a lazy kick from goal. 'Morrissey!' Jason shouts. 'Greene! Brereton again!' The afternoon's barracking has scraped his voice to a bark.

'Jesus,' Darren says beside him, raising his eyes to the roiling sky. In his North Melbourne guernsey and glittering top hat he resembles a cartoon character. 'How'd this game get so shit?'

'Shut up and barrack for us,' Jason says.

'This is the worst grand final in history.'

Jason starts counting off his fingers in front of Darren's eyes. 'Six grand finals straight. Two Brownlow winners. The night premiership. The Coleman medallist. The best rover in the league. The best centre-half forward . . .'

'Hey, J.D.? I've got something for you.' Darren puts his hand in his pocket and pulls it out with his middle finger raised.

Fish steps down from his seat, still holding his scarf, and charges along their row to high-five every Hawthorn supporter in reach. They hug him, they laugh at him, they roar in his face. He borrows a gold-and-brown flag from a stunned child and parades up and down the aisle with it. Darren screams at him and points to the city scoreboard:

'Check it out, dude.' There Fish is, five metres tall, looking in the wrong direction.

Eighteen minutes later, after the Hawks have kicked seven more goals and broken the record-winning margin, the final siren sounds. Jason is standing on his seat when it happens and the crowd reaction almost lifts him into the sky. He raises his arms to God, his voice a static hiss. Victory. He bear-hugs Fish and gapes at Darren with no more sound in his throat. Somewhere beyond the streamers and tickertape and thumping flags the players are converging on each other to link arms. They're the greatest Hawthorn side of all time, no question, and he's with them.

. . .

Each Saturday night, he catches the train to North Richmond station to meet the crew on Victoria Street. It's a hard neighbourhood, mangy and dimly lit, the Vietnamese shopfronts crammed together under webs of powerlines. Sev, Richie, Blain, Darren, Fish, Darcy, Crow, Hatto and himself. They're a good unit. Everyone's got cash. It's funny, the way old people cross the street thirty metres in front of them, as if they're carrying knives or something.

The Queen Margaret Hotel is two blocks away, a squat brick pub with a blue façade and a chalkboard mounted on its street-side wall. Inside, the pub is a barn. The carpet sticks to their feet. Every breath is like another drag on a cigarette. It's so noisy they can hardly hear the songs on the jukebox.

Darren's new girlfriend for the summer is Robyn O'Loughlin. She seems to think so, anyway. She circles Darren like a moth, drinking rounds of girly vodkas through a straw. She's got her own crew, smokers from school, but compared to them she looks like she could be in her twenties. When she bends over the pool table to make the easy shots

Darren gives her every guy in the room watches, including the bouncers who should be kicking them out.

'Who's your girl, J.D.?' she asks him.

'Don't have one yet.'

'There's always one. Who do you like?'

'Nah.'

When she tilts her head and smiles at him a nameless feeling rises in him, not love exactly but something else, warm and white at the edges. 'Abigail Taylor,' he says.

'Join the club.'

'What do you mean?'

'She's gorgeous.'

'You want to go with her?'

'No.' She pokes him, and it hurts. 'I just want to be her.'

On his way to the bathroom he stops in front of the Collingwood football portraits decorating the wall next to the bar. There are team photos, action stills, a guernsey signed by the members of the 1981 grand final side. There's a caricature of Peter Daicos, their uncanny centreman and goalsneak, his broken smile wide above a body with as many arms as a Hindu god.

In the mirror he studies the fuzz forming around his jaw and below his nose. Is it the same colour as his dad's? Guys in faded singlets and stonewashed jeans scowl at him when they stagger in but he pretends not to see them. His dad could look as they do, he realises, but he leaves before the thought can take hold. They look so ordinary.

When the band finishes they keep drinking. Jugs of VB, tequila shots, so many cigarettes they lose count. Robyn's friends get louder but they talk in scribbly lines that don't make sense and whenever he opens his mouth their expressions change, as if he's slowing them down. He drinks until his cheeks hurt from smiling so much. When the pub's lights come on he has to follow the wall to find the door.

Clean air hits him and the rest of the night fragments: a taxi, finding coins in his wallet, leftover pizza, dark spinning floor space in Darren's lounge room.

On Sunday afternoons he crawls along the edge of Arnie's backyard, searching for weeds and trying not to throw up. Sweat trickles down his cheeks. He pushes his head into the cool dirt and tries to muster spit in his mouth. Never again. Never, ever again.

Arnie's never fooled. 'Jesus, Dalts—what happened to you last night?'

'I'm right.'

'Bullshit. Get inside and drink some water, you goose.'

'Sorry, Arnie.'

• • •

The fourth term of Year Ten is ragged without the weekly rhythm of the Falcons to follow. In class he sits in the shadow of his end-of-year exams, trying not to be consumed by his classmates' talk of the parties they've been to, or are going to, or will have as soon as their parents go away for the weekend. He can see what will happen in the exam room when the day comes: the supervisor will call them to begin, the white page will glare up at him and he'll freeze as he always does. If only he could make himself feel as he does in a game: loose, ready, positive.

Maybe school isn't the answer, he thinks. Other guys in the Falcons are starting apprenticeships in the new year. He could talk to his mum about dropping out and working for someone like Arnie. He'd be his own man. Except that's not what the real world is like, he reminds himself. The real world without an HSC or money behind you is being hammered by shiftwork and scrimping and saving. It's being forced to live a life you don't get to choose. School is opportunity, as his mum says. The alternative is what she has to do every day.

Detention on the third-last Friday of term is in his old Year Eight home room. When he arrives it's already crowded with students—the same glum guys as always, plus a few virgins. His old geography teacher, Mrs Dobney, is correcting assignments by the window. Jason drops his pencil case on a desk by the door, flops into the seat and takes his English assignment from his folder—'Barriers to Communication: The Berlin Wall'. Due three days ago.

'Hey,' says the girl diagonal to him. 'Got a pen?'

'Sure.'

He spends most of the next hour looking at her. Catalina Anderson—one of the newer faces in Year Ten. Has she got a boyfriend? He hasn't heard. Below the hem of her skirt he can see a spider web penned across her thigh. Occasionally she leans back, pushes both hands through her blonde boy's haircut and stares at the ceiling, dropping his biro into her mouth like a lollipop. She turns once to look at him as if to say: hey, take a photo while you're at it.

At four, Mrs Dobney closes her manila folder and raps it with her knuckles. 'Right—we're done.'

Jason watches Catalina merge with the crowd bottlenecking at the doorway. Her school dress clings to her back and hips and he can see the outline of her bra. He follows her into the corridor. As she descends the staircase he says, 'Hey—you catching the train, Cat?'

She pauses, three steps from the bottom, and looks up at him. 'Yep.'

'Cool.'

She walks fast, with the strides of a taller girl, and he has to hurry to catch her. 'So, where do you live?' he says.

'Richmond.'

'You know the Marg?'

She smirks. 'Do I know the Marg? Yeah, I know the Marg.'

'I'm down there every Saturday night.'

'So am I.'

'I've never seen you.'

'I've never seen you, either.'

They reach the school's front gates. There are no parked cars left on the street, just peak-hour traffic bypassing the main road. A gardener is mowing the nature strip. Catalina looks at him, just a few fingertips away. A familiar nervousness reaches up his stomach like a tentacle.

He says, 'Maybe you look different when you're not in your school uniform.'

'Bullshit.'

'Yeah, sure—you'd pass for eighteen, wouldn't you?'

She considers him. 'Speak for yourself.' There's something in her voice, a sliding sarcasm that reminds him of the way his teammates talk. 'So where you from, Jason?'

'Hawthorn.'

'You'd know the Governess Hotel, then.'

'No.'

'You don't know the Guv?'

'We stick to Richmond.'

'Who's we?'

'Mates of mine. You know Darren Jackson?'

'Oh God.' She looks at the sky as if seeking divine help.

'Nah, he's cool.'

'It's like, woah, you know? I forgot you run the world.'

The street finishes at the main road a block from Burnley station and they stop at the traffic lights. Jason looks at his shoes, then down the road. There's got to be something more to talk about. The red man flicks to green and they cross. He looks at her again, her thumbs under the straps of her backpack, her chest out, sunburn lines visible on her upper arms.

She says, 'So what did you get a detention for?'

'I skipped a class. You?'

'Graffiti in the toilets.'

'Who caught you?'

'I don't know. Some old bitch. Red hair, glasses.'

He nods, looking at the footpath. 'We used to do a bit of that. You should see the guys' toilets.'

'It's just dicks and naked girls, isn't it?'

'How did you know?'

She laughs, a genuine sound, big and close. 'In the girls', when someone's got a crush on a guy, they write it on the door.'

'Yeah? My name up there?'

'Maybe.'

'So whose name were you writing, then?'

'Nobody's. I was scratching mine out.'

Just before they reach Burnley station the bell clangs and the boom gates drop across the main road. To their left the city-bound train is accelerating towards them, its yellow rimmed face sharpening in the pale distance.

'That's me,' she says.

He watches her go. 'Hey, I'll look for you next time I'm at the Marg.'

'If you recognise me.'

'Yeah, if I recognise you.'

She boards the train three carriages from the rear and he watches it pull away. He says her name to himself and kicks the footpath lightly, just to feel the concrete rasp against the sole of his shoe. He crosses platforms and boards a city-bound train to be out of the flat for a while longer and watch people—the office workers lurching home, the uni students at their fat textbooks, the lone schoolkids listening to Walkmans.

. . .

When he gets home from the gym the following Monday night and nudges into his room, something's wrong. The three towers of tapes beside his stereo are as straight as buildings. Both of his closet doors are shut. He hears his mum's soft work shoes shifting on the kitchen floor and finds her drinking coffee there, one hand on her back.

'So what did you find?' he says.

'What?'

'You've been in my room. What did you find?'

When she turns around the look on her face makes him strike the doorframe.

In his bedroom he pulls down his shoebox of football cards from his wardrobe shelf and strides back to the lounge room. He sends the lid spinning onto the couch and overturns the box on the kitchen bench. 'Footy cards,' he says. 'Here, a mouthguard. What are you looking for?'

'Jesus, Jason.'

'Why don't you call the cops? Bring them in and get them to search me.'

She pushes against the sink as if she's about to wrench it from the bench. When she looks at him her eyes are red. 'I've had enough of this.' She walks past him and upends the laundry basket onto the floor. 'You want me to look through your things? I'll look through your things.' She digs between wrinkled linen and her work blouses and pulls out one of his old black tee-shirts. She grabs it by the shoulder and thrusts it into his face. 'See this? Look at this. Explain it.'

There's a streak of fluorescent green spray-paint along the shoulder's seam. Not much, but it's unmistakable: an old graffiti tee-shirt. He must have forgotten to keep it separate from his usual laundry. For a moment he hesitates. Then he slaps the tee-shirt onto the floor and retreats to the corner of the lounge room. 'Fuck off.'

'Spray-paint.' He can hear her ragged breath. 'You bloody vandal.'

'You went through my room.'

'Every bloody weekend the same thing. Booze and graffiti. You and those mates of yours. You're grounded.'

'You can't ground me. You're never home.'

'I said you're grounded.'

'You can't do shit.'

'Stop talking to me like that.'

'That's my room.'

'Where do you go with them? The bloody pub?'

'Out.'

'Oh, out. I see.'

'I'm here. You're the one who's gone.'

'Who are they?'

He kicks the couch. 'Just go to work already.'

'Tell me, you bloody . . . Tell me!'

He slams his bedroom door on her and folds himself against its base. The empty space between his knees is a shroud. He presses his hands tight against his ears and the trapped air sounds like his own blood roaring. He sees himself carrying his schoolbag full of clothes to Flinders Street station. How much would it cost to leave for a week? Food, a train ticket out of the city, a camping ground some-place. He could make it ten days, even a month. Long enough for her to send out a search party anyway, and know what life would be like without him.

Remembering their argument the next morning is like trying to remember being drunk with Darren and the crew at the Marg. The words run together, and what evidence remains of his rage is leaden in his stomach. He searches his face with trepidation in the train window on the way to school. He sees the anger in his eyes, unsure of where it comes from.

• • •

Robyn O'Loughlin's birthday party is on Christmas Eve at her two-storey house in Burnley. He arrives with Darren and the crew just as it's beginning to jump. Cigarette tips are glowing outside the second-storey windows and they can hear Robyn's hi-fi system from the street. A band of girls in tinsel wigs are welcoming everyone at the front gate with hugs and kisses.

'This is the night,' Darren says to him. 'Robyn, upstairs.'

'Solid.'

'You got a chick, or what?'

'Might have. We'll see.'

'Man of mystery, are we?'

'Ask me tomorrow. I'll tell you then.'

After skolling from a cask of wine in the front yard he circles his way indoors and into the kitchen. Catalina is there. Her breasts look bigger in her baby tee-shirt than they do in her school dress. Her hair is spiked over her forehead, Roxette-style, the flipside of her look at school. She's necking a long bottle of beer, one elbow on the sink. 'Recognise me?'

'No,' he says. 'Who are you?'

'Friend of the birthday girl.'

'You look older.'

'That a problem?'

'Hey, I'm nineteen.' For once, the words are easy.

'So what are you doing here?' she says.

'Friend of the birthday girl.'

She passes him her beer and frowns. 'Could've sworn I saw you someplace else.'

'You always hang out with high school kids?'

'Some of the boys are cute.'

Heat pulses through him. 'You want a cigarette?'

'Sure,' she says.

Three beers later, with his arm around her waist, he leads her through the hallway to the spare room at the top of the staircase. The party wheels around them, drunk and firing. It seems most of Year Ten is there. Some of them are watching. They can see what he's doing and soon everyone will know: she wants him. It's real.

They leave the spare room's light off and close the door.

'Hey,' he says.

She moves into his arms. It takes him a moment to find her mouth, then her hand is holding the back of his head and her lips unlock. Her breath is fierce, brushing like a blade against his lower lip. He slides his hands down her back and up her sides.

She leans back. 'Slow down,' she says.

He presses her against the wall and runs his fingers down her arms to her stomach and up inside the soft cotton of her tee-shirt. He senses her press back, responding to him. He pulls up her bra in one motion and gropes her breasts.

'No.'

He licks her neck, tasting the metal in her silver chain, and pushes his tongue back into her mouth, still holding her breasts. Alcohol rings in his head.

'No. No, don't.' Shoving him off.

'What?'

She pulls her tee-shirt down over her chest. 'You're too horny.'

'What did I do?'

'Forget it.'

He grips her shoulders and chases her mouth.

'No,' she says, louder.

'I don't get you. What?'

'I don't want this.'

'You came here with me,' he says. 'What?'

Her stare is freezing. 'You arsehole.' She steps out of his reach and grapples for the door handle.

'Hey—'

'Fuck you.' She draws the door shut behind her.

In the darkness he looks at the empty space on the wall where they'd been kissing and goes over the muddle in his head. He can still feel her breasts on his hands. What happened? Feet tumble on the staircase outside—probably her. She's gone. And she's not coming back. He leans into the door, supporting his weight with his arms.

Later that night he finds Catalina and her friends cooking nachos in Robyn's kitchen. They don't look at him while he helps clear the used stubbies from the benches nor when he says goodbye. He carries the commentary of their silence home, as heavy as iron.

'Robyn's pretty wild, man,' Darren tells him over the phone on Boxing Day. 'She's trouble, definitely. I'm not the first guy she's been with.'

'How's that?'

'The way she moves.' Darren raises his eyebrows. 'I got three fingers up her.'

'Really?'

'Yeah, man. I don't know. She's a loose bitch. I think I'm gonna dump her.'

'Yeah?'

'Or just keep it casual. Relationships are bullshit.'

There are times when he wants to punch Darren. There are times when he wants to throw something at him, screaming, 'All right, I get it! I'm not as cool as you! Congratulations!' There are times when he fantasises about embarrassing Darren in front of their entire school year, somehow, so that all the girls will finally laugh at him.

• • •

At home over the holidays he continues exercising. He does squats in his room, building the muscles in his thighs, keeping his knees unlocked as the trainer at the gym instructed. But girls never seem to notice. They still look at him as they always have: that guy, Jason, the sporto meathead footballer. What he'd done with Catalina would have only made them more certain of it.

The bus for the Falcons' training camp at Anglesea leaves from Victoria Reserve on the morning of January ninth. He packs his bathers, his sneakers, his training singlets and his Metallica cassettes. Twenty-three of the squad board the bus with him. All roar when its engine starts. As Hawthorn disappears behind them he feels renewed, as though freed from its grasp. For the next four days, all that matters is the team.

By one o'clock, Anglesea Beach is sparkling in the sun. Their new Under-Seventeens coach, John 'Jaffa' Mackay, is a generation older than Arnie, but just as fit. In his Speedos, singlet and duct-taped glasses, Jaffa looks as if he could run back to Melbourne if he needed to. 'What are we doing, Morto?'

'Out and round the buoy, hundred metres up to the flag, hundred back,' Morto says.

'Last five in give me forty. Marks, set . . .' Jaffa's brought his policeman's whistle. He blows it and they scamper for the water, all twenty-four of them, their hats and towels scattered on the sand behind.

The last five to reach the finish line drop to the sand beneath Jaffa and grunt out a set. He brings them all away from the shore to the soft sand beneath the cliffs and jams a marker into the ground. From fifteen metres they take turns, in pairs, racing to the marker and diving to swipe it. They slap together, they jostle, they hip-and-shoulder. They run heats, then finals, then tag teams. Soon the whole squad is grinning and shaking sand out of their hair.

The boys are looking fit. Some already have biceps and shoulders like magazine models.

Kayaking for an hour, then sit-ups on the beach, then sprints in and out of the water, then lugging rowboats up the hundreds of steps to the car park and back, then to the sand dunes to finish. Goddamn Jaffa. With his whistle and taunts—'Aw, princess, this doesn't hurt, does it?'—he's a bloody bastard. But he's been at the club eight years, according to Arnie, and his team has never finished lower than third.

'Most of you blokes've still got some soft-cock in you,' Jaffa tells them, grinning. 'I can see it in your faces. We're gonna rub it out.'

They sleep on the cots downstairs at the lifesaving club. Jason lies on the bunk above Critto with his Walkman in his ears, staring at the concrete roof and pushing his feet into it. He tries to summon the feeling Chantelle had given him on the dance floor at Darren's. But eight months have elapsed, and her face is a blurry canvas he can't focus on without turning her into someone else.

He looks ahead to Year Eleven and wishes he could stay where he is, far from Burnley Secondary and Hawthorn. Catalina haunts him. He could try talking to her, but mentioning again what had happened at Robyn's party would only make it more real. He could ask someone for her address, but they'd want to know why. He could put an apology letter in her bag, but she might pass it around. Figuring out what to do is like trying to see through a closed door.

• • •

Three mornings into Year Eleven, he knocks at the careers counsellor's office for his appointment. He finds her already seated in her padded chair. She smiles craggily at him. Mrs Irene Hewson. Behind her gold-rimmed glasses, one of her eyes is slightly bloodshot, and the rest of her face is sagging, except her famous silver hairdo—Bob Hawke, the yard calls her. 'Shut the door after you, John. Take a seat. It is John, isn't it? No, Jason. I've muddled you.'

He watches her leaf through manila folders, and nods when he has to. Twenty minutes later he shakes her hand and leaves her office for the heat outside. Hospitality studies, arts studies, agricultural development, trade apprenticeships, the armed forces, a guide to studying for the HSC—he shoves her suggestions and flyers into the back of his locker and closes the door before they can tumble out.

The Year Eleven corridor is empty. As he approaches the stairwell at the darkest end he can hear his English class through the brick wall alongside him. His teacher, Mr Parkes, is giving them another roasting: 'Get with the program, or get out.'

There are no teachers in sight, just a Year Twelve girl crouching by her bag and applying eye shadow. He walks through the yard to the shed behind the boys' toilets. Maybe a smoker will be there. Then what? Art class, Abigail Taylor, rissoles waiting for him in the fridge when he gets home.

One of the new girls in his year has already staked out the shed and is sitting against its side wall. She's tall, with washed-out skin; brown hair hangs over her eyes like a curtain. She's reading a worn paperback and every so often raises a cigarette to her mouth, inhaling, flicking ash and inhaling again without taking her eyes off the page.

'G'day,' he says. 'You got a smoke? I'm out.'

'On top of my bag,' she says. Her lips hardly move.

Her knapsack is on the ground by the shed. She's smoking Marlboros. He takes one, as well as her lighter, and stands beside her—but not too close. 'I'm Jason.'

She glances at him.

'Thanks,' he says, indicating the cigarette.

A few moments later she closes the paperback against her chest. 'I'm Daphne.'

'Good book?'

She smiles, her eyes going wide, as if he's caught her reading porn.

'No, seriously.'

'Beats chemistry,' she says. 'Where are you supposed to be?'

'I've just been in with Hewson. You seen her yet? Bob Hawke?'

'Who's she?'

'Careers lady.'

'No.'

He stops his knee jiggling. 'Know what you're going to be?'

'I hate that question.'

He crouches and looks at his hands. It wasn't so much what Hewson had said as the expression on her face when she said it—as if he was the fifth boy to mention football to her that day. Old bitch. Maybe it's true, though. Maybe he's no different from half the students she sees.

Daphne walks over to her bag. When she lifts it up to her shoulder he notices that her arm is skinnier than it should be. 'There a milk bar round here?'

'Yeah. Not far.'

She looks at him through her hair, though it feels more as if she's looking through him. She could give his mum a run for her money. 'If you show me where the milk bar is, you can have another smoke with me on the way.'

It's a five-minute walk to the milk bar. She doesn't say anything, just falls behind him, out of sight but not earshot. They pass his old graffiti at the bus shelter and on a stop sign but he doesn't point it out. That's the kind of thing a Year Nine would do.

When they reach the milk bar he opens the door and holds apart the plastic strips for her.

Inside, the store hums. For a while he moves among the racks of chips and chocolate bars, remembering his summers at Hayden's. The 1989 season's swap cards are for sale in the glass cabinet beneath the cash register. Then he remembers he's out of scourers at home. After finding a twin-pack he takes it to the counter and fishes two dollars out of his pocket for the Vietnamese owner. The footy cards would only end up forgotten in the bottom of his bag.

After Daphne has bought a pack of gum he lets her open the door and follows her outside. She looks at what he's purchased. 'Scourers. You're a good boy.'

'Tragic, aren't I?'

She passes him another of her cigarettes. He takes it, though he can still feel the last one in his chest. Again she follows the concrete behind his feet. It's strange, as if she's hiding—but if that's it, why did she invite him along? Once they've turned onto their school's street she says, 'Want these?'

He turns around. In her hand are four Mars bars. She's smoking another cigarette and her face is the same as before—closed, unimpressed.

'You didn't have to.'

She shrugs. 'It was fun.'

He slows down so they're walking side by side. She walks quickly and with her head lowered, but in half-strides. He watches her take a water bottle from her bag and swig heavily from it. It's an old bag, he sees. She's drawn the letter 'D' all over it. Some of the letters are fading. 'What school did you come from?' he asks.

'Interstate.'

'What state?'

'All of them, now.' She doesn't laugh.

'It's your folks, is it?'

'My dad,' she says. 'It's not a job thing.'

'Divorced?'

'It's a longer story than that.'

When they come in through the side entrance the corridors are vacant again. Someone's locker whines shut on the other side of the school and feet thump on the Year Eleven stairs. Class is already under-way. Mrs Garraty is going to give him her unsurprised, sarcastic look again, the one she keeps in reserve for him. He looks at the concrete. 'What have you got?'

'I have to check.'

'I can tell you where it is.'

'Yeah,' she says. 'Because I'd hate to be late.'

'Suit yourself. See you, Daphne.'

She doesn't reply. He watches her lope down the hall until she raises the back of one hand to him, quickly. She's all arms and legs, Arnie would say. It's hard not to look.

In the weeks that follow he looks out for her on his way to the quadrangle with Darren and the crew. She's always alone, flitting between groups of people as if she's under fire. There's something about her the yard has sniffed out. She's bulimic, some say. Others say she's a dyke. Overhearing his classmates' sniping, he wants to stand over them as he would an opponent when he's playing with the Falcons. They're wrong. He recalls Daphne striding from him with her old bag bobbing against her side. She'd trusted him with her silence. The way she'd palmed off the Mars bars as if stealing was a meaningless game, the same as school.

At home he moves the couch and vacuums the skirting boards. He pushes his bed to where his desk used to be and his desk to the other wall. He mouths Metallica into a roll of paper towel and cleans the dust off the windows. He scours the inside of the oven. He separates whites and darks, puts on a wash and later hangs it on the Hills hoist behind their building. The routine is soothing. Afterwards he flops onto the lounge-room floor, happy to know he's been useful.

After chores and homework, he doesn't get to bed until eleven. Including training twice a week, plus sessions in the gym, he figures he's on the go for twelve hours a day. That means he's doing sixty-hour weeks, as many as his mum.

'How's the saving going?' he asks her when she's home.

'Almost there,' she says. 'Another six months or so.'

'You said that a year ago.'

'Things have changed since then.'

'What's changed?'

'Don't take that tone with me.'

'Nothing ever changes.' He raises his voice loud enough for Flat Nine above them to hear. 'You work the same hours you did last year, saying the same shit. And we're still living in the same place.' How did fighting with her get so easy?

'That's right—we're in the same place. I work sixty hours a week doing a job that no-one gives a damn about and we're in the same bloody place. Thanks for reminding me.'

'Fuck this.' He leaves her bristling in the kitchen behind him.

Trains from the station leave every twenty minutes. The journey into the city at night's a lot different than coming home from school. The window shows nothing except his reflection. There are more weirdos on board, mostly men in track pants and tee-shirts. He compares them to the working men on their way home. Fathers, some of the men in suits must be, going home. Past Richmond the train descends into the city loop. The sudden roar of steel and air makes the train sound like a living thing. He slips his earphones to his neck to hear it.

The return trip from Flinders Street to Auburn station is the next five songs on the tape of *Appetite for Destruction* he'd copied from Fish the weekend before. He stays aboard until the end of the album, the tornado of Slash's guitar and Axl Rose's nasal scream an escape from the passing night. In the amber glow of Hartwell station he jumps the tracks to the city-bound platform, the tape whirring forwards in his pocket. But the wooden fences of the local houses and the willows along the embankments past the platform are too much like Hawthorn. Looking at them, he can still hear what he'd said to his mum, how he must have sounded. He hadn't even felt the frustration coming on this time.

. . .

On the first Thursday night of the new VFL football season Darren calls him while he's reheating some fried rice for dinner. 'Listen,' Darren says. 'I got a mate on the cleaning staff at the 'G—he says he can get us on the roster. Interested?'

'What's the pay?'

'Twelve an hour.'

'Mate.'

'Thought you'd be up for it.'

The following week, after yawning through the last quarter of the Richmond versus Footscray game, they join the squad in the old umpires' change rooms below the southern stand. The action stills on the walls and the workers' hardened voices make the room feel tough. By the time the maintenance manager clears his throat there are more than fifty people waiting to hear their names. Ticking his pen down the roster, he groups them a dozen to each patrol, and soon Jason and Darren are carrying brooms and garbage bags along the dripping roadway and into the arena.

They work from the front of each stand to the rear, one section at a time. Aluminium cans and plastic cups clatter along the concrete. The empty stadium seems to breathe. With square-head shovels they fill their bags and leave them by the roadway exits for an ancient yellow tractor to collect. Grime and spilled beer float into their clothes and skin—by the end of each shift their sweat reeks of it.

The best stand to clean, Jason decides, is the members' pavilion. On the other side of the boundary fence is the old tarp-covered bench for interchange players. He sweeps the front row as slowly as he can, absorbing the view. He imagines himself sitting there in a Hawthorn wind jacket, being handed the interchange phone and hearing Alan Joyce at the other end. The sound of the stand behind him while he sat there would be awesome.

'Wakey-wakey,' Darren tells him. 'You're not there yet, mate.'

Five hours a game, almost one hundred dollars a weekend. On Monday nights after school he and Darren swagger away from the MCG maintenance offices like dukes. He buys a Cindy Crawford poster, a Pantera cassette and a dancing Coke can for his room. After Falcons training he buys chips, cigarettes and soft drinks at Arthur's for his teammates. By Sunday night he's broke again but spending like this is worth it for the power alone.

'Put it in the bank,' his mum tells him. 'I'm not going to be buying things for you anymore.'

'You want me to be careful like you and not have things.'

'No, I don't. I want you to have opportunities. I'm a workhorse and I don't get paid what I'm worth.'

'You said the other day that you're saving.'

She looks at him as if he's an adult. 'That's not what I'm talking about. I mean when you've left school and you're out in the world. People out there won't look after you, kiddo. You have to be smart. Get a decent qualification, make opportunities, give yourself a chance to get away.'

A coffee-coloured stain is spreading from the corner of their lounge-room ceiling. She must know about it. The plaster there is beginning to crack. He can touch the red and black wires behind the room's light mount. The hot water tap in the kitchen drips no matter how hard he turns it.

'Your washer's gone bung,' Arnie tells him over the phone.

'What's that?'

'It's under the tap spindle. A little metal seal. You can pick one up from the hardware for about two cents.'

'My showerhead won't stand up, either.'

'Yeah, you'll need a shifting spanner for that. Look, when you come round on Sunday, I'll talk you through it.'

'Cheers, Arnie.'

Training for the Falcons without Arnie is less personal. He doesn't feel Jaffa's eyes on him in the same way. And none of his teammates ever did impersonations of Arnie's half-time speeches or the way he shouted at their opponents while they were playing. Somehow, Arnie had always been one of them, even when he was telling them what to do. He could see they were people, not just recruits. The time Jason gets to spend on Sunday afternoons gardening with him, chatting about the Hawks, is precious. A lot of his teammates, he reckons, would do the work for free.

Forward-pocket isn't where he thought he'd start the Falcons' season under Jaffa. He's faster than Morgs and Hoggsy and cleaner than them in the packs. But they're both in the centre, where the action is. It's as if Jaffa's stirring him. He watches each bounce from between the goal square and the boundary line, pacing.

Against the Burwood Wolves he kicks seven goals. The following week, against the Waverley Magpies, their backline double-teams him in the second half and he still kicks five. Flexing, it feels as if there's gunpowder in his arms and legs. There are times his winded opponents need help to stand up and the umpire has to warn him for unduly rough play.

Jaffa highlights his attitude in the huddle between quarters. 'Those bigger blokes know Dalts won't take a backward step and it scares them shitless. That's your reward for intensity. That's the respect you get for putting your body on the line.'

He gashes his side, he bruises his shoulders, he cuts open his knees. But after four games the Falcons are in the top two and his teammates know why. 'How many goals you kicking this week, Dalts?' they ask him. 'Give 'em a chance, for fuck's sake.'

Their fifth match, against the Canterbury Cannons at Victoria Reserve, happens under a downpour so heavy the umpire's whistle stops working. It suits Jason fine. The ball is a different thing in the wet. They

have to obey it, not the other way round. They have to protect it with
their bodies. Jaffa hollers at them from inside the railing, in boots and a
rainslicker, but he's hard to hear above the team's confused shouts. Jason
slides in on his knees and chest. He hoofs the ball off the ground and
slides after it again. When he catches breath the water pools fresh in his
mouth. He could play ten quarters in it, no worries.

The final siren sounds before he can kick his fourth and the Falcons'
eleventh. Eighty-three to fifty-one. He pulls his guernsey over his head
before he reaches the change rooms and wrings it out into the grass
at the edge of the concrete steps. A fresh bruise on his hip, the usual
niggle in his ankle. His calves are as sore as when they ran the dunes at
Anglesea.

'Hey, Jason.'

He turns around. It's Daphne, in a boy's duffel coat and thick scarf.
Her white umbrella is like a moon behind her shoulder.

'Shit. Daphne, hey.'

'Good game.'

He spreads his guernsey against his chest. 'What brings you here?'

'My brother plays for the Cannons. On the wing.'

'Okay.' He edges around her. 'Cool. I'll get changed.'

'Don't rush.'

Inside, most of his teammates are resting elbows on their knees and
looking at the puddles between their bare feet. It's Jaffa's review time.
What did you do right today? Where can you improve? What did you
learn about the team? Jaffa walks between them and murmurs, his rainslicker under his arm, his grey hair razored short around his bald patches.
Then he regards them, as one, from the corner. 'Righto,' he says. They
clap slowly and push a last, big sound out of themselves.

Jason doesn't bother showering. After running his gym towel over
his head he changes into his jeans and hoodie. Hanging out and drinking with the boys after the game can sometimes be too much. He slaps

hands with Teddy, Morgs and Corbs as he passes. He'll catch them at training, when they'll want the lowdown on the tall chick in the scarf.

Outside, it's coming down in diagonal sheets. The empty ground looks lonely. Daphne is standing in the rain, away from the players leaving with their parents and girlfriends. Her gumboots, long skirt and hood fill her out. Why hadn't he noticed her earlier?

'Hey, Daphne.' He steps into the rain. 'Where's your bro?'

'He's gone,' she says.

'Oh. Which one was he?'

She glances towards the road. 'He was one of the tall ones.'

'You live round here?'

'Near the tech school.'

'I live near there too.' He steps under her umbrella and waits for her to say something else after she lights her cigarette. But she doesn't. 'Let's go before we drown,' he says.

'Want one?'

'The coach might see me.'

They leave the ground through the side exit. The reserve's trees drool water into puddles and the torrent running in the street gutters almost swells onto the path. They walk carefully, watching the brim of her umbrella and each other.

At the main road he says, 'Bad day to come watch your brother.'

'I like walking in the rain, actually.'

Most of the cars coming their way have their lights on. He guides her away from the kerb. 'Didn't think you followed the game.'

'I'm a Hawthorn supporter.'

'Me too.'

She smiles. She has a nice mouth. 'I knew you would be.'

'Guess it's all over my face.'

'You play a bit like them. I was kind of surprised.'

'Yeah? Why?'

'I didn't think you'd be like that.'

They pass Arthur's milk bar and keep walking down his street. He thinks to ask her about school, the other ones she's been to, her dad. But it would feel fake, like when he asked her what she was going to be. Better to watch and listen to the rain instead.

They reach the driveway of his flat. 'This is me,' he says.

'I can walk you to your front door.'

'You don't have to.'

'Which one is it?'

'Over here. I'm number six.'

Most of the cars are still in their parking spaces and lit rooms chequer the side of the building. At the bottom of the stairwell she stops and lets him pass her.

'Thanks,' he says.

'You don't have to invite me in.' She doesn't look at him.

'If you want.'

'No.'

'A towel, or something.'

She says nothing.

'You're sure?'

'No. Bye.' She holds up her hand. Turning, she hunches her shoulders as if the rain might still hit her through the umbrella. Then she's gone.

He opens his front door. She'd had to ask him first. When you walk home with someone, you invite them in, you geek, he tells himself.

While his mum rests on the couch, her face masked behind her *New Idea*, he showers and lies on his bed to ease his shin soreness and the extra gravity that presses down on him at the end of every match. Daphne says she's moved a lot and that her parents have divorced. Other girls in their year wouldn't be so comfortable on their own. He dwells on his memory of her at the boundary railing, in her scarf and coat like a uni student, and tingles to think of her watching him play.

Fish Fingers, some of his classmates in the laneway call her. They say it with a grin because they know how stupid it is. That's what makes it funny. The girls make their groaning noises and hide their smiles in their hands.

'You know her, do you?' Darren asks him at work.

'Not really.'

'She asked me what footy team you play for.'

'Yeah? Why?'

'Dunno. Thought you would.'

'No.'

'You're not gonna hook up with her, are you?'

'I've had a smoke with her a couple of times. That's all.'

'She's mental, I reckon,' Darren says.

'Yeah?'

'Maybe she bats for both teams.'

She could be telling the truth when she says she has a brother who plays for the Cannons, but he hopes she isn't. At the Falcons' next two home games he looks for her among the spectators between quarters, but she doesn't appear. Maybe she had, though, and then left in secret. She's that type, he figures—a phantom. If she didn't want him to see her, he wouldn't.

. . .

On the first Tuesday night in June someone taps on the door while he's scanning his mum's magazines for naked girls. When he opens the door Daphne's standing against the far wall, still in her school uniform. He recognises her stooped posture from the sheds at school but there's something else about her as well, shrunken further.

She comes past him and into the lounge room faster than he expected and backs herself against the arm of the couch. He doesn't move from the door. When she looks up out of her hair the triangle of her face is bloodless. 'I wiped my feet outside.'

'Hey, Daphne.'

She drops her bag from her shoulder to her hand. He sees the quiver in her, now, at her knees and elbows. 'You were the nearest person.' Her control slips on the final syllable.

'Do you want to sit down?'

She looks around the room.

'Are you right?'

'No.'

'Here, I'll get you . . .'

'No. I don't need anything.'

He walks quickly to the bathroom, grabs the tissues from behind the mirror and takes them inside to her. She's sitting now, her expression remote, so he leaves the box on the arm of the couch.

She lowers her head and her elbows begin to tremble on her knee-caps. Then she lets go with a sound that seems too deep and hard for her to make and her elbows buckle. For some time he stands away from her, waiting for her to stop. He draws one of the chairs at the bench closer to her and sits down. She sighs, hard, as if she's pushing a wall. 'I'm okay,' she says finally.

'Should I call someone?'

'No.'

'You need to stay here?'

She lowers her hands to work at the buckle of her schoolbag. 'I've got ten bucks.'

'No way.'

'Here.' She holds out the note. 'Seriously.'

He shakes his head.

'Jason.'

'No, just chill out for a minute.' He throws his mum's magazines off the couch and passes her one of the pillows from the floor.

She looks at the couch, then walks in front of it and balls herself in the corner, facing the TV screen. He finds two glasses in the cupboard, trying to think what else his mum would do. After filling each glass with water he brings one of them to her. She places it on the floor before folding inward again. He waits for her to say something.

Eventually, she looks at him. Her ears are red, the same colour he knows he turns when he's embarrassed. 'Where are your folks?'

'Mum. She's doing a graveyard. She won't get home till morning.'

Daphne runs her hand over her nose. Her arms close around her ankles and hide the parts of her thighs her school dress can't.

'Some shit's gone down, has it?'

She nods.

'You don't have to tell me.' He looks around the room, at the magazines and the television, aware of his own burning ears. 'I can call someone.'

'I'm so sorry. My dad, he gets . . .' She deflates.

He tries to meet her eyes. 'I've got a sleeping bag. You can take my bed, I'll sleep on the floor. It's cool. I'll get it ready now. Just be cool, all right?'

He busies himself in the kitchen, nervously wiping down again what he'd wiped down an hour earlier. He glances at her through the serving hatch and tries to smile as his mum would. There's nothing wrong with her uniform or her face. She doesn't look as if she's hurt herself. But the glazed look that soon comes over her is bad, like she's asleep with her eyes open. Maybe Darren's right—she's a nut. He turns on the TV and throws the remote in her direction. 'If you need anything,' he says.

She nods intensely. Her eyes are welling but the rest of her face is expressionless.

'I'll be in my room. Milk and stuff're in the fridge, if you want them.'

He leaves his bedroom door open and unrolls his sleeping bag on the floor. After changing into boxer shorts and an old tee-shirt he wriggles inside it but doesn't close his eyes. It's possible she'll stay where she is on the couch all night and his mum will find her like that when she gets home. Great, another thing to fight about. Soon he hears her creaking across the lounge room and she steps over him, onto his bed. He looks up at the Starlight Zone stickers on his ceiling. It's strange, having someone else his age in his room. Together they're too big for it: the bed, the desk, the space between. The vibrations of the pipes in his ceiling carry through to the floor beneath his sleeping bag.

He looks through the gloom at her white forearm dangling against his bed base. 'Daphne.'

'Mmm?'

'Guess what?' It's easier to talk to her in the dark.

'What?' Her voice disappears in his mattress.

'You're the first person to sleep in that bed who wasn't me.'

Her head slides up on his pillow. 'It's got your smell on it, I think.'

'My pong, more like it.'

'Pong,' she says. She laughs—a throaty, drumming sound that breaks over him like a shower.

He lies awake long after her forearm becomes motionless and her breathing deepens. He props himself up on his elbows and looks at the slight swell of her curled body in his sheets, wondering. It wouldn't be hard, if he was Darren.

The thought of climbing under the sheets and holding her is a balm. He touches the base of the mattress, stepping his fingers up to her pillow and letting them drop. Pressing against her body would be enough. They could lie like that until morning, watching the slits of daylight appearing on his wall, her skin's warm charge better than sleep.

'I found some girl's bobby pin on the couch,' his mum says at dinner the following night. Her bed face, he's noticed, is becoming her daily face. The frizzy parts of her hair are spreading out from the grey in the middle. 'Who was she?'

'No-one. Never mind.'

'I'm not fussed if you have a girlfriend.'

'I didn't ask if you were.'

'Why are you being like this?'

'Because you're at me,' he says. 'It's always something. Then you're in my room or you're searching the couch.'

'I don't want to argue.'

'You don't trust me.'

She puts down her fork and holds her temple. It's her new thing, on top of her ankle-cracking and sighing. 'I'm not suggesting anything, Jason. I just wanted to know if you're having a girl over.'

'Okay, fine.' He pushes away from the bench. 'A messed-up girl at school I hardly know came over in tears and I let her crash. You weren't here. You were at work.'

Her hand drops. 'What's wrong with her?'

'Do you believe me? Or what? Or do you think we had sex on the couch?'

'I didn't say that.'

'It's all over your face, Mum.' He lets his knife fall on the carpet.

'Where are you going?'

'Like it matters.'

At Auburn station he sits against the wire fence at the city end of the platform, away from the other passengers. The city-bound express trains hurtle past. When a train stops he watches the doors shunt open and counts the passengers getting out—twelve from the first train, then eight from the next, then four. The train gasps forward and its tail grows faint as it curves into Camberwell. He listens to the passengers' feet echo down the rampway underneath him. Alone again, he pitches gravel from the other side of the fence onto the unseen tracks, thinking.

Two days later, at the start of recess, he finds a ten-dollar note wedged into the front pocket of his bag. Behind it, someone has tucked a folded piece of paper. It's a page from a school diary. Three words are printed in the middle, in lower case, the letters so tight they're almost touching: *please take it*.

When he sees her in the corridor she walks in flat steps, faster than everyone else. Her forehead has flared into pimples and she wears her hair over it like a bandage. He doesn't stop her. But at lunchtime he checks for her in the library, feeling like an intruder in the artificial silence. The librarian gives him a look.

'She's a major brain,' Robyn O'Loughlin tells him in the smokers' laneway. 'When she shows up, anyway, which is, like, every blue moon.'

'She ever say anything?'

'Nah, she just sits there being weird. I know it's harsh, but what do you want me to say? She's practically got a sign on her head—"Back off, I'm screwed up".'

'I don't know.'

'Girls with eating disorders, it's such a wank. You're a guy, you don't know. It's like, "Look at me, oh, I'm suffering so much." They're all actresses. They don't give a shit about anyone else.'

She's in line at the tuckshop every Monday, Wednesday and Friday, same as him. He watches her. She's not that skinny. He's seen girls with eating disorders blowing around before. They don't eat sausage rolls and vanilla slices. But maybe that's why she disappears, to do whatever those girls do that keeps them sick. When she passes, she nods at him like a boy and speeds on, as if she's headed someplace important.

At the Glenferrie gym, he watches the older girls in lycra doing lunges and cat stretches, toning their bodies for summer. He pushes the day out of himself and into the machines. There are other Falcons in the gym, like Jovi and Waldo, who bellow through sets of free weights and practise roundhouse kicks on the gym's speedball. He shakes hands with them but sticks to the solitude of his own routine. They may have designer sneakers and full memberships, but they're never there for as long as he is.

. . .

Mud flies into his face as he chases the Magpies' centre half-back to the ball. Overnight rain has turned Victoria Reserve into a stew and after three and a half quarters the players are wearing most of it. It's the second-last game before finals, Hawthorn City versus Glen Iris, with the winner securing second place on the ladder. As the ball nears the interchange bench he can hear Jaffa screaming, 'Get there, Dalton! Get there! Get there! Get there!'

He flexes his upper body, smashes into the half-back's torso, then gathers the ball in one hand and reaches full speed along the wing. A pair of Magpies' players are about to trap him against the boundary line. He stops, drawing them closer, then punches a handpass ten metres to Hoggsy on the edge of the centre square.

The clapping of supporters carries on the wind across the ground. He hears men and women, the parents of his teammates, shouting his name.

The ball tumbles to the opposite flank and his teammates on the Falcons' half-forward line rush to meet it. He drops into the pocket of space they've left behind. It's a risky move—'lairising', Jaffa would say—and it could get him dragged. But when Teddy gathers the ball and boots it across his body he's there to mark it. The Magpies' back-pocket can only lurch into his side and tumble to the dirt. Jason steps over him as if he's fallen rubbish, then squats to hitch up his socks.

'Onya, Dalts!' Hoggsy crosses to him and pats him on the backside. He spins the ball in his hands three times, exhales once and kicks from thirty metres. The ball hangs for a moment above the goal square until the wind drags it between the goalposts. He clenches his fist and runs to the centre of the ground. It's his fifth goal, playing as ruck-rover changing forward-pocket, and the Falcons' twenty-third.

When the final siren sounds, his legs are streaked with mud, grass and blood. His head throbs a little when he turns it. He claps his team-mates as he hobbles from the ground, the niggle in his ankle aflame.

In the change rooms, during review time, Jaffa clutches his shoulder and lowers his head until Jason can smell the Steamrollers on his breath. 'Owned the middle again today.'

'Thanks, Jaffa.' He looks up at the wad of duct tape between Jaffa's glasses.

'Towel off and get changed. There's a bloke outside wants to see you.'

Jason peels off his jumper and showers in his shorts. The hot water comes from heaven. As he lifts his face to the showerhead he thinks about the man outside. He has seen this man before, in his mind. This man has been watching him for seasons now, disappearing each week at the final siren.

He dries off, pulls on his jeans and tee-shirt and zips his gear into his backpack. He passes teammates tilted like statues against the change-room walls and scruffs their hair. Outside, the light is bleak and cool. Parents he knows only by face are milling on the clubhouse's concrete steps and some of them wave at him. Nearby, the Magpies' centreman is holding his little sister on his shoulder and playing with her hands.

'Jason Dalton?' A short, solid man with thinning strawberry hair approaches him. Wearing jeans and a tan-coloured parka he could be just another parent watching the game if it weren't for the black clip-board he's holding against his side. He extends his hand for Jason to shake. 'Gary Shaw.'

'G'day,' Jason says.

'Played a great game today.'

'Thanks.'

'Don't know if Jaffa told you, but I work for the Hawthorn Under-Nineteens. You a Hawks supporter?'

'Yeah. Forever.'

Gary smiles. 'Your dad or mum here?'

'No. Mum's . . . She couldn't make it.'

'Okay. Just so you know.' Gary takes a business card from the clip-board's inside pocket. The card has the brown and gold Hawthorn logo in its top right corner and beneath it his name is written in thin block letters above his title—Recruiting Officer. 'How'd you like to come train with us this summer?'

Jason tries to clear the wobble from his voice. 'Absolutely.'

'Jaffa's vouched for you but I'll need to have a chat with your mum. We've a way of doing these things. Can I get your phone number?'

'Yeah, yeah, hang on, um . . .' He takes a breath. 'Sorry.' He says each digit in his phone number carefully, watching Gary's pen as though the numbers will escape.

'When's a good time to call her?'

'Um, nights. Wednesday, Thursday. But she's a bit, um . . .'

'What?'

'Never mind. Nothing. That's fine. Give her a call.'

'Great.' Gary offers his hand again. 'I have to get to another game. But it was nice to meet you, Jason. We'll be in touch.'

'All right,' he says, pumping Gary's arm. 'Thanks.'

'Keep up the hard work.'

He watches Gary walk out through the gardens in front of the ground to the white Magna parked on the kerb. Soon it pulls onto the road and whispers out of sight. The Hawthorn Under-Nineteens. He covers his face with his hands.

'Hey, Dalts!' Teddy says, swinging his sports bag down the change-room steps. 'What's wrong?'

6. final

Outside the window of the principal's reception area, it looks a lot later than midday. The sky is darkening. Most of the passing cars have turned on their headlights. But the sight of thick rain exploding on the building's front path is cheering. He can see what Daphne meant. It would be fun to walk in, even to stand in, and feel it slowly soaking through his clothes.

The Hawks have called. He says the words to himself. They still don't feel real. But they are: standing inside his bedroom door the previous Tuesday he'd overheard his mum's conversation with Gary Shaw. Next January he'll be stepping into the Hawthorn change rooms at Glenferrie and pulling on a brown and gold guernsey. He relaxes. The rest of Year Eleven and his exams drift before him, weightless.

His mum gets out of her car, umbrella first, from the opposite side of the street. He watches her coming towards the school in her work clothes, her expression hard to make out in the dim light. She doesn't say anything when she sits down beside him, and that's fine.

Burnley Secondary's principal, Mr Lowen, comes out to greet them shortly after. He has a smile like Dean Bennett. But it's hard to picture him in a scarf at the footy. He'd have a seat in the members' stand, not the outer. Lowen shakes his mum's hand with the slightest bow and raises one arm to guide them into his office. His shoes look brand new.

Beside Lowen's computer is a photo of his two daughters, both dressed in private school uniforms. The one on the right's got braces like Hayden.

Jason watches him pinch up the knees of his pants before he sits down. 'Thanks for taking time to come in and see us, Christine. We should talk about the trouble Jason had at the Burnley train station on Monday, I thought.'

His mum looks his way. 'There was a fight, apparently.' It was better when she was ignoring him.

'What have you told her, Jason?'

'I told her I punched a Year Ten kid.' In his mind, replaying what happened, it still feels good. Brett Lieber and his two mates hadn't seen him coming. Daphne had been facing away from them, reading one of her novels as if she couldn't hear what they were saying. But everyone on the platform could hear. Dropping Brett had been justice for himself, too. Catalina and the rest of their year need to know that it's guys like Brett who are the dickheads, not him. 'My friend's had a rough time and he made a joke about her.'

'That was Brett Lieber,' Lowen says. 'He says you threw him into a chair. That's how he injured his back.'

'That's not true, he tripped.'

'So do three other boys who were there. He's had to see a doctor since then.'

'Then I'm sorry,' Jason offers. 'I didn't know about that.' He looks at his mum. The map of lines on her face is growing.

Lowen says, 'The point isn't the injuries. It's the violence in the first place. You know that, Jason.'

He holds Lowen's stare. 'What about Brett?'

'Brett's not the issue.'

'He was bullying one of my friends. What's his punishment?'

His mum's voice is thin as wire. 'I didn't know he needed treatment.'

'Does this sound like Jason to you, Christine?'

'I don't know.'

'How do you mean?'

'I mean, I don't know. I don't know what Jason does a lot of the time.' She looks outside, towards her car. Her mouth is drawn. 'I'm not home very much. It's my fault.'

'I only want to know if there are any family issues . . . ?'

Jason sits up, stung. The prospect of talking about his dad to Mr Lowen sends a wave of disgust through him. 'How's that your business?'

His mum glares at him. 'Jason, don't.'

His chest tightens as it had at the station. 'We're a family, we fight—so what?'

Lowen taps his hand once on the edge of his desk, as if knocking his thoughts into place. 'You're a nurse, Christine. You do shiftwork.'

'Since Jason was born, yes, at St Vincent's. For a long time I worked on the general ward. Now I'm part of the palliative care unit.'

'And Jason's father—he's not in the picture.'

'I'm fitting things together.'

'Brett Lieber's a little shit,' Jason says. He can hear his voice getting louder. 'Get him in here.'

'Jason!' his mum says.

Lowen leans forward and his tone changes—not much, but enough. 'Jason, how I deal with Brett's got nothing to do with you. Are we one hundred percent clear on that?'

Jason looks past Lowen's stare to the streams of rain on the window behind him. 'Yes.'

'Yes what?'

'Yes, Mr Lowen.'

Lowen's stare is easier to handle now that he's angry. 'I want to speak to your mum alone. You can go now. What class are you supposed to be in?'

'English.'

'Reception will write a note for you then. Go on.'

Outside the office, there's still more than half the day to go. He walks unshielded through the rain, past his English classroom and to the boys' toilets on the far side of the quadrangle. Inside, it's silent except for the rhythmic gasp of water flowing into the urinals. As he walks towards the furthest cubicle he watches himself in the long mirror, Burnley Secondary's only VFL Under-Nineteens recruit. He locks himself inside. His initials are still inscribed in the wood behind the toilet roller. He closes his eyes, scowling at Lowen's ignorance of him, and doesn't open them until the next bell.

Things will be different next year, he reminds himself. The Hawks have called. Soon everyone will know what he can do—especially his mum. He recalls with exasperation the guarded questions she had asked Gary Shaw over the phone. 'How much will you be interrupting his studies? What happens when he turns seventeen?' As if Gary is a con-artist and not an expert at the most successful VFL club of the past thirty years. But it doesn't matter. He basks in the radiance of his coming summer. The Hawks have called.

On Thursday morning she wakes him at eight, as she said she would, as part of her plan to stay home with him for the duration of his two-day suspension. It's the longest voluntary break from work he can remember her taking. Even when she's been sick she's always nursed herself out the door with Panadol and cough drops. Maybe Lowen's made her feel guilty. Whatever it is, she won't say.

From nine-thirty onwards, she visits his room every ten minutes to make sure he's working on his overdue assignments. No Walkman, no TV. He slinks between the kitchen and his room like a burglar, unable to find a place beyond her reach.

'I hope you're getting somewhere,' she says at lunch—ham and cheese sandwiches and a Prima, the same as he takes to school.

'Can I at least get a Coke?'

'No.'

'Why not?'

'Because this isn't your day off.'

She cleans the fridge shelving and washes her bedroom walls. She sweeps the stairwell and bleaches their sheets. In the downtime between chores she investigates her cookbooks, picking her teeth and drinking coffee. This is what it would be like if she stopped working so much, he realises.

'I did the windows last week,' he tells her.

'Mmm.' She pulls up the blinds anyway and readies her paper towel and Windex on the ledge.

'Why are you doing them again?'

'Because I am.' The muscles in her back and forearm clench as she wipes nothing from the clean window, her hair limp, in the jeans she's never thrown out.

At a quarter past eight the next morning she's up and vacuuming. He tries to eat his bowl of cornflakes as if she's not there, as if he's alone as usual, but the sound of the vacuum is too much like one of his own sounds.

Outside his window, nothing moves in the day. She's got no idea what happened. Neither does Lowen. It wasn't just what Brett said, it was the way he said it, the way he was standing there, him and all his mates. As if they were the centre of the world. He stabs his pen into the cover of his biology book, harder and harder, until it has penetrated so far it quivers upright when he takes his hand away. Standing up to them had been right. She should understand that. She'd told him to treat girls with respect.

'I'm going to the supermarket,' she calls.

He doesn't reply.

'I'll be checking your work again when I get back.'

When the front door clicks shut he throws his pen onto the desk and sprawls, cracking his shoulders and rubbing his eyes. He rolls his football from beneath his bed and ducks behind their building. No target, but that's not the point. He stabs the ball into the bricks and marks it, counting ten kicks for each foot. His bubbling anger starts to fade. Staying relaxed and focused is important. He pictures himself on the Punt Road Oval before the Falcons' grand final, now less than twenty hours away: Teddy clapping in front of him, the umpire's whistle trilling, the crowd at the edges of his vision. Gary Shaw might be there again, with others.

When she gets back he's sitting in his room. 'How's it coming along?'

'Fine.'

'You didn't go out, did you?'

'Why would I do that?'

'Don't push it.'

Dinner is chicken and rice with mashed potatoes. 'No, you're having it with me,' she tells him, when he tries to take it into his room.

He shrugs and drops his plate beside hers on the kitchen bench. When he's finished his chicken he slices a second helping from the baking dish on the stove. Protein food. He'll get ten hours' sleep and be switched on when he leaves for Richmond station in the morning.

Back in his room he unzips his empty sports bag on his desk. He packs his mouthguard into the front pocket along with his Walkman and house keys. He grabs his footy socks, helmet and shorts from the top two shelves of his wardrobe and searches among his jackets on the coat rail for his guernsey. It's not there. He paces into the bathroom to check the washing machine and laundry basket. It's not there, either. 'Mum! Where's my footy jumper?'

She's still picking at her food. 'How should I know?'

'Where'd you put it?'

'I never touched it.'

'You've lost it again.'

'You're responsible for your own things. That's what you wanted. I don't go near your room anymore.'

'I don't have it. Why don't I have it?'

She rinses her wine glass in the sink. 'Jason, think. You left it at your mate's place. You left it at some ground. Be an adult about it.'

'You've taken it. Where is it?'

She slams her glass into the wash rack.

'You won't even look. It's my goddamn grand final. Have you thought for a second what that means to me? No, you're just going to sit around and be happy I'm not here.'

'This is your solution. Shouting and swearing.'

'How the fuck am I—'

'Get out. I don't care about your stupid game. You're right. Not if it makes you like this. Take your violence somewhere else. I'm not going to let you treat me like this again. I'm not going to be victimised.'

He stomps into the lounge room. 'Brett deserved it. You weren't there. Lowen doesn't know. How can you take his side over mine?'

She grimaces, and looks for somewhere else in the kitchen to go.

'I'd thump him again if I could.'

'Who are you, shouting at me like this?'

He goes back to his room and paces. His boots are in the bottom of his wardrobe, his wallet and Walkman on his desk. In his wallet is enough money for the night. Slinging his bag onto his shoulder, he heads to the front door.

She calls after him, 'You're turning into your father, you know that?' He hears her gasping but doesn't look at her.

The door handle is loose and doesn't turn properly in his hand. He stops and breathes before turning it again. Outside, the wind whines on the communal balcony. It's dark already. He arrows down the staircase. On the driveway he risks a glance back at their flat. She's not at any of the windows. He hits himself on the hip with his fist.

There's a phone booth three doors down from the corner opposite Arthur's milk bar. He shakes a dollar out of his wallet. Arnie's answering machine clicks on after the fourth ring.

'Arnie, it's Jase.' He clears the strain from his voice. 'I need a favour. My footy jumper's gone missing again. Um, if I can come round early tomorrow, if I can borrow one . . . Sorry. I'll be there at eight. Don't try to call me at home. Okay—thanks, mate.'

He hangs up and steps out of the booth to gather himself again. Two cars rip past, drag racing. He watches their taillights until they disappear. In the booth, he takes his school diary from his bag and opens it to the addresses page.

When Daphne answers, she sounds bored. 'Yes?'

'Daph, it's me, Jase.'

'Oh. Hi. What's wrong?'

'Huh? No, I'm right.'

'Something in your voice.'

'It's this phone. I just need a favour. I was hoping I could, um, crash on your couch tonight.' He holds his head, waiting for some more useful words to come. 'I've just had . . . Some stuff at home, a fight.'

'You're coming now?'

'That's what I was hoping. Is your dad around?'

'No. You're not thinking of doing anything stupid, are you?' Her tone is almost irritated. 'To yourself, I mean.'

'No.'

She pauses, as if assessing his answer, and gives him the address. 'See you soon, then.'

'See you.'

Her building is a ten-minute walk towards Glenferrie, across the park next to the tech school. At night-time, the paths look dangerous under the cover of the trees. Daphne's building is at the end of a no-through road on the park's other side. It's the same size as his, four storeys high. Number three is the middle flat on the ground floor. Though the lights are on inside, the blinds are closed, and there's no doorbell.

She opens the door in heavy tracksuit pants and a jumper. 'Hi.'

'Thanks. Sorry.'

Her lounge room has more furniture than his, and some of it looks new. He puts his bag down next to the coffee table. On the far bookcase he spots some photos of her and what must be her dad, a long-faced blond man, but no sign of a younger brother.

She turns the kettle off at the switch and uses it to fill her water bottle. If it weren't for the photo of her dad, the place could be hers. 'You want a smoke?'

'I'm trying to quit,' he says, but takes the cigarette from her anyway.

The hems of her tracksuit pants look as if they're going to trip her up. They're guys' pants, he realises. For a second, he flashes cold on the thought of the boyfriend she must have, some sporto like him.

On the balcony, there's nothing to look at except the grey wooden fence separating her building from the house next door. He watches his cigarette ash flake. 'My mum drives me mad sometimes,' he says finally.

'You had a fight?'

'Yeah.'

'And it's your grand final tomorrow.' She crosses one foot beneath herself, gymnast-like. Her feet are bigger than his, as big as Teddy's. 'I remember you said. You nervous?'

'Pretty.'

'How'd your suspension go?'

'She stayed home with me.'

'Oh.' Her smile is half-mocking. 'There's a Brett at every school I go to. You didn't have to defend me.'

'I'd do it again.'

He waits until she's finished her cigarette. It feels weird, talking here, as if he's meeting her for the first time. She doesn't seem like a student from Burnley Secondary. What about her neighbours? They must see her sitting on the balcony smoking and reading, alone. Then again, there are always people like her in buildings like theirs. 'You should come down tomorrow,' he says. 'We're playing at the Punt Road Oval, twelve o'clock.'

'Sure.'

He watches her toss another mouthful of smoke into the air. It's easy to see her sitting for a whole Saturday afternoon with one of her books. 'So do you mind if I crash? I want to—'

'Sounds fair.'

'I need the sleep,' he says, feeling childish.

She looks at him directly for once, and he remembers what she asked him on the phone. 'You sure you're okay?' she says.

'I'm great,' he hears himself say. 'It's no biggie.'

'You can take my bed. As payback.' She stands up, stretching, yawning. He watches her jumper ride up to the top of her tracksuit pants. The view shows off the curve of her waist but she seems to know nothing about it.

In her room there's a poster above her bed of a band called The Smiths. The two shelves of the bookcase beneath her stereo are full of paperbacks. 'If you want to read something, go ahead,' she says, and raises her eyebrows at the idea. 'Or don't.'

'Thanks.'

She seems to want to duck around him, her weight shifting. Then her face looms in to his and her lips are on the side of his mouth. He doesn't move until he realises what she's done. But she's already closing the door for him. ''Night.'

'Well,' he says to the empty room.

He opens his bag, changes into his footy shorts, and pulls back the sheets of her queen-size bed. Her blankets are heavy. He puts on his Walkman. Metallica thrums through two songs, controlled mayhem, but he fast-forwards to a Bruce Springsteen song from the radio. It's so old it could come from his mum's collection. But it feels right. The keyboards and chorus open into the room's darkness. He sees the umpire in the middle of Punt Road Oval, one arm extended skywards, and Teddy clapping at the beginning of his run-up, and the shouting crowd vast behind them. He checks his watch. Still eight and a half hours till daylight. He folds her pillow around his head, waiting.

. . .

When the police siren blares across Punt Road Oval to signal three-quarter time Jason jogs to the huddle on the clubhouse flank, his spirits low. They lead the East Richmond Tigers by seventeen points, fifty-five to thirty-eight. But ahead, many of his stationary teammates have their hands on their hips and are staring at the grass. The Tigers have kicked the last three goals. Defeat is coming.

Jaffa stands in the centre of the huddle, wearing a white Bonds tee-shirt and black jeans, the remains of his hair flat and sweaty. 'I want you on your man like glue, I want you pushing it forward, I want you choosing the first option. What are you doing, Willo?'

'First option,' Willo says.

'That's how we beat them in the first half. That's where we're losing it now. You blokes on the backline have got to tighten up.'

Jason scans his teammates. Some of them are grappling for water bottles, others look ready to throw punches. Too many have their arms crossed, too few are moving. All of them are as dirty as pigs.

Jaffa holds one finger before them. 'You know how long this season is? Twenty-five minutes. Every lap, every drill, every tackle, every hit you took for your mate, every goal you kicked—it's right here. Twenty-five minutes. Put the heat on these bastards and they'll fall apart.'

The police siren wails again.

'You know what you've got to do,' Jaffa says. 'Get out there and bloody do it.'

The crowd has swelled. Dozens of Geelong and Melbourne support-ers on their way to the semi-final next door at the 'G have stopped to see what's going on. Two small boys hammer the sponsor's logo in front of the old club stand. Parents, girlfriends, brothers and sisters, grand-parents and friends of the players are grouped against the oval's white picket fence and on the grassy slopes behind the goals.

'Step away,' the umpire says. 'Let's keep it clear.'

Siren. In the quarter's opening minutes the ball hardly moves. The game squeezes along the clubhouse wing as players swamp each other. The boundary umpire throws it in three times, then four. No-one can clear a kick.

'C'mon!' Jason screams at his teammates. 'Let's pick it up! Don't wait for it! Let's go!'

The Tigers' ruckman thumps the ball ten metres forward and his wingman gathers it in one hand. Moments later the full-forward snaps another goal. On the edge of the centre square, Jason rips out his mouthguard and curses. Eleven points the difference—two more goals and they'll be in front. He looks at Jaffa for encouragement but Jaffa is facing the clubhouse with both hands drawn behind his head. The Falcons' goal square looks as distant as a mirage.

The quarter deepens. His teammates' mistakes increase. At half-forward, Corbs finds the ball on the edge of the square and handpasses to no-one. Hoggsy tries to tackle the Tigers' half-back but slides off him like a sheet. Jason punches the turf. 'C'mon, Falcons! Man up! Fucken man up!'

The Tigers' forward-pocket mongrel-punts another goal. Five points the difference, ten minutes to go. Jason watches the scoreboard operator on the bank unhook the six beside East Richmond's name and replace it with a seven. He crouches down, concentrating. At the next ball-up he confronts each of his teammates in the centre—Teddy, Hoggsy and Critto—and holds them against him. 'Ten minutes,' he says to each of them. 'Give it fucken everything. We're going to win.'

'We're going to win, mate.' They slap his head.

'We're going to fucken win. Ten minutes, everything you've got.'

The Tigers rush another point. Jason follows Teddy to the forward flank and Critto sends a torpedo punt towards them. It's a perfect strike, the ball tearing upwards and forcing the pack into a handbrake reverse. It lands five metres behind them and spins loose along the roadside boundary. Jason beats the Tigers' centreman to it and sidesteps an oncoming tackler. He takes a bounce, waiting to see which way Rents, the Falcons' full-forward, offers a lead. There he goes—faking left once and charging straight. At full speed Jason stabs a pass to him that seems to quicken across the flank. Rents marks it on his chest, half a metre in the air, thirty metres out.

'Dalts!' Teddy locks arms with him and rubs his ears. 'You champion.'

Rents' goal puts them eleven points up. They can breathe again. On the boundary in front of the clubhouse Jaffa is pacing like an expectant father and slapping one hand with the back of the other. 'That's it! Pressure! Pressure!'

Following the next ball-up Hoggsy boots the ball blindly towards the Falcons' goal. Players from both sides launch themselves upon it. The umpire separates them again. Jason pats each of his teammates on the bum. 'Stuff, Morgs. All yours, Hoggsy.'

One of the Tigers' backmen runs loose behind the umpire. Jason steps away from the other players and trails him at a wary distance. His instinct is right. The Tigers' ruckman drops the ball onto the chest of their ruck-rover, who spins out of a tackle and looks for the backman. Jason streaks forward and steals the ruck-rover's handpass in front of the backman's eyes. Every player seems to stop, stunned, as

Jason closes on the goals. It's a tight angle, the space between the goal-posts half what he'd normally be aiming for. Then he sees Kirby, one of the Falcons' forward-pockets, back off his opponent. He checks his kick, stabbing the ball to the other side of the goal face. Kirby marks it and falls backward, somersaulting after he lands, ten metres out. His shot for goal is clean and straight. Around him, Rents and the other Falcons forwards erupt.

Jaffa has moved along the boundary towards them. A spike of sweat has bled down his tee-shirt. His voice is like a shovel on cement. 'Five minutes! Man up! Five minutes!'

The score is unchanged when the siren sounds. Jason closes his eyes and falls forward. The din inside and outside of him is the same. Feet whir across the turf. He rolls onto his back and looks up at the white swab of sky. They're forming a circle on the flank, all of his teammates. Jaffa is coming from the boundary like a dog set free. Jason finds his feet, sprints towards them; when he gets there he leaps over Morgs, toppling into the centre of the group. They crowd in until he can't stand up and then someone—Critto—drags him out. They run in again. Hands, faces, mud, shoulders. Twenty voices at full pitch. Someone pushes Critto into the centre of them and the big man takes the weight of three players at once. Somehow, beneath the bodies piling on top of him, Critto finds room to raise his arms.

Jason stops shouting and looks towards the centre, remembering what Arnie had told him in the morning. The Tigers ruckman is there, and the ruck-rover, and most of their forward line. They look the same way the Hawks looked on TV after they'd lost the '84 grand final. He jogs towards them. Corbs comes from behind to join him, then Critto, Daffy and Teddy. Jason takes out his mouthguard and holds out his hand to the Tigers' ruck-rover. 'Well done, mate.'

• • •

Around the circumference of his premiership medallion the words 'U/17 PREMIERS EASTERN SUBURBS LEAGUE 1989' are engraved in gold. As he turns into the driveway of his building and floats up the stairs to the flat, Jason runs his fingertips over each etched letter and weighs the medallion in his palm. The cloudy suburban afternoon around him is difficult to adjust to. It's as if the game and its presentation ceremony happened in another, better reality.

His mum is sitting on the couch, her hands on her knees, when he opens the front door. The weather in her face is bad. Her hair is matted on one side. How long has she been there?

'Hi,' he says, but doesn't wait for a reply.

He places the medallion carefully on the top pillow of his bed, undresses and wraps himself in a towel. In the shower he washes his bruises and scratches, recalling the Falcons' final celebration on field. Something had been forged then. He can still hear their voices. He goes back to his room. His reflection in his wardrobe mirror impresses him. He sees a dangerous resolve when he squints his eyes. He pulls on his jeans, hoodie and black sneakers, then lowers the medallion over his head and stands in front of the mirror again. The after-party at the club starts at four-thirty—they'll be taking photos for the rest of the club to see.

The new answering machine by the phone is blinking. He checks it: a message for his mum from Lori, one of the younger-sounding nurses, offering another shift. In the kitchen he pours himself a glass of water from the tap.

Her eyes are on him. 'I got a call from that boy's mum. The one you hit. She wanted to talk to me about the chiropractor's fees.'

'Did you?'

'We need to figure out how we're going to deal with this.'

'I've got a thing at the club.' He refills his glass.

'I'm not going to start arguing.' She holds her sides and looks at the floor. 'It's hundreds of dollars, Jason. The club thing can wait. This is a bigger responsibility.'

'I'm late already.'

'You're not going.' In her shapeless tracksuit it's difficult to tell where her upper body ends and her legs begin. Her scalp shows through the accidental part in her hair. 'You hit this boy and there are consequences. If it means you miss whatever your club thing is, so be it. You don't get to walk away.'

He goes back to his room and takes his Walkman and cigarettes from his bag. The stain on his ceiling has spread overnight. At his bedroom door he stops, listening for her, but she hasn't moved.

Before he reaches the front door she says, 'What thing?'

'Huh?' He pushes the doorknob into place.

'What thing have you got that's so important?'

He drops his hand. 'We won.'

'What? What did you win?' He can see the look on her face as if through the back of his head—the way her mouth turns down, the way her eyes drift. 'Oh, your football.'

He closes his eyes for a second, but when he turns around and opens them it's no different. She's still sitting there, in her crumpled outfit, where she's probably been since the start of the match. 'That's right. My football. We just won the flag.'

'I don't care what you won. You hurt that boy and now you're going to pay for it. This is the real world, Jason. It doesn't go away. Are you listening? Four hundred and fifty dollars. They could take you to court.'

'Fuck the money.' Looking at her, he can't control his tone. 'Just take it from what you've saved up for the house. You're loaded.'

'No, I'm not paying for your violence.'

'What are you working for then? Where's the money going?'

'I work to look after you.'

'You never looked after me.' Anger hurts his throat. '*I* looked after me. You didn't want to be around. Now you're taking their side. Some arsehole bullies one of my friends, and I'm the criminal.'

'I didn't choose this.' She stands up. 'You think I wanted to work this hard for the last seventeen years? When you were born, I had nothing. I was renting a bloody bedsit in North Melbourne. Twenty years old. St Vinnie's were putting your food on the table. I had to call them for a bloody pram.'

'You're right. It's my fault, and I get it. Thank you.' He hits the nearest stool. It travels further than he intended and thuds into the far wall. A chip falls off the plaster. When he closes his eyes and backs away the pain travels up his arm.

'That's your answer, is it?' The quiver in her voice is shocking. 'Don't stop there. Go on. Throw your fists around.'

'I don't need this.'

'You and your thug mates. You don't care for anyone but yourselves.'

'Right. I'm a thug footballer. You and everyone else reckon so. I'm a meathead with a ball. I'm dead weight.' She's so close he could throw out his hand and hit her. His chest feels ready to pop. 'You slept with some guy and got pregnant and it's my fault. Picture's clear to me now, Mum. You've got it off your chest. Thanks.'

Her face is ashen. 'That's not what happened.'

'Some shit happened to you in Echuca and it's my fault. No. You made your choices. Whatever's shit about your life is yours, Mum. I just won the goddamn flag. Are you listening? I trained five nights a week for that. You weren't here.'

'I didn't—'

'Now you're taking sides against me. You think I'm a thug. Anything I do, you tear it down. No matter what I say, you back a stranger over me.' He steels himself with another breath.

She starts to shake. Like a trapdoor closing she locks her body against her knees and stays there, submerged in her clothes, just her fingertips visible above the cuffs of her sleeves as she covers her ears.

Her sobs pierce him. He turns away. 'It's down the fucken road, two minutes away. But I don't give a shit you don't come. I don't give a shit.'

'He raped me, Jason.' Her voice is brittle. 'He and three of his mates from the club. They held me down and he raped me.'

It's a long way to the door. He reaches blindly and the doorknob falls into his fingers. 'Fuck!' He kicks the door once and grapples with the knob until it clicks in and he thrusts it into a turn.

The staircase railing vibrates under his hand. Soon the driveway concrete is rushing beneath him. Down the street, two boys are sitting against the wall of Arthur's milk bar and drinking Coke. He steps into the gutter and a sedan cannons past him, honking in shock. He crouches and presses his head between his arms.

A queue has already formed outside the pub down the road from Victoria Reserve. He keeps his head low as he steps around them. The streetlights outside the ground are on, and the sounds of the families on the clubhouse steps seem too loud. He turns around.

The park next to the tech school is falling into darkness. A group of young guys is huddled by the toilet block, the tips of their cigarettes flaring. He pulls up his hoodie and draws in his shoulders. Daphne's no-through road is tight with parked cars that hadn't been there the night before. Public Enemy booms through the open front door of a weatherboard he passes. At the top of her building's driveway he can see her on the balcony, reading, in jeans and a tee-shirt. It's not cold but his left hand refuses to stop trembling. He puts the hand in his pocket and holds in a breath, trying to relax. She doesn't seem to hear his footsteps. He stands in front of the balcony until she looks up. Her bare feet hit the ground. 'Where did you come from?'

'Hey.'

'Hey yourself.'

Standing at her front door, he takes another breath. When she opens the door he doesn't look at her face straightaway. Instead, he looks at her hips, where he'd noticed the curve the night before. She's put on weight. For a hot second he sees himself making out with her right there, her jeans at her ankles.

'I saw you win,' she says.

'Did you?'

She steps aside. Passing her he puts a hand on her bare arm. The touch of her skin makes it hard to think.

'You look pale,' she says.

He steps into her lounge room and realises he's not going to sit down. The room looks murky with just the couch-side lamps on. He flinches at the snap of the latch when she closes the door.

'Coffee?'

'No.'

'Sit down.'

'That's okay.'

After stirring herself a cup of instant she carries it to the couch and puts her big feet up on the coffee table between her copy of *NME* and some unlabelled videos. There's a certainty to her movements that isn't there at school. He looks again at the seat beside her and she nods at it. 'Sit down.'

He waits until he's sure his voice will be steady. 'You stuck with us the whole game?'

'Until you all did your boy thing at the end, yeah.'

He and three of his mates from the club . . . He dawdles towards her white singlet—the one she slept in—on the kitchen table, where she must have taken it off in the morning.

'You can sit down when you want.'

'I'm still a bit . . .' He takes his hands out of his pockets, then puts them back. 'I don't know.'

'Is it your mum?'

He looks for something in the room to hold his attention that's not Daphne. Nausea spirals in his stomach. 'My mum?' he says. He looks at her until he can't anymore. 'Just another fight.'

'What this time?'

'Everything.'

'That's all?'

He tries a small laugh but too much feeling explodes in him—the match-day energy with a rabid edge. He backs away from it and into the kitchen.

'You can stay.'

He opens the fridge, closes it, and pours himself a glass of water from the tap, then another.

'If you want to talk about it . . . Or I can just stay here.'

He leans against the sink, not looking at her and wondering what he's still doing there, the trip across the park from the reserve blurring as if behind a wet screen. 'Can you . . . ?'

'Hey.' She stands up, her voice softening. She stops at the edge of the kitchen, one knee bending towards him, waiting. Everything she does could mean five different things. Her fingers graze the tops of her thighs.

It's only three steps to her. His voice doesn't come. Before he can think again he closes the space between them and squeezes her, pushing his forehead into the darkness at her throat. Her arms draw tight. Holding her, he hears his mum's voice again and it slices through him, quivering.

'You're okay.' Her whisper is warm on his neck.

In a rush he closes his mouth on hers, his breath shaking. The push will come, another Catalina moment, and he grips her harder to deny her room. She doesn't resist. Her breath comes hard on his mouth and her hands on his back pull him closer until their hips meet.

He lifts her tee-shirt above her breasts and pulls her bra up her chest.

There's not enough of her. The threads of her tee-shirt's neckline break against his hand.

'Wait,' she says.

He kisses her to her knees. He kisses her until her jeans are at her ankles and her hand is working against his buckle. They find the floor. She fills the room above him. Someone walks past outside the front door of her flat, male steps. He envelops himself in the warmth of her body until there's only her and the rough fabric at the couch's base and the prickling carpet on his back.

Her mouth moves above his ear. 'My room.'

She leads him there with one hand, naked except for her green underwear. A purple bruise on the back of her thigh, stretch marks on her lower back. Her step is sure, as if she knows what she's doing.

Afterwards he clutches her damp shoulders, inhaling her. She takes his hand and drops it over her face. No words, just the empty space beyond her, and then a buzzing on his fingers. 'Jason?'

He doesn't move.

'In February, we're moving again. To Sydney.'

He doesn't reply.

'I don't want to go, either.'

He presses against her. There are no noises in the flat. No pipes, not even a ticking clock in another room. Her sweat runs down his thigh. He kisses her until there's nothing left between them and he can't feel himself trembling.

part two
away 1991–1995

7. the recruit

Home, he thinks, though it doesn't yet feel like it. After stepping off the coach and grabbing his bag, he stands in front of the Spencer Street station terminus and absorbs the gothic, tarry cityscape. Trams lunge down the hill towards Swanston Street, the first he's seen in thirteen months. Despite the clear March sky above him the air feels cold. He crosses his forearms, comparing them. His tan is better than he thought. In his bright northern colours, he looks just like the Gold Coast tourists around him.

He finds a phone box outside the station and fifty cents among the remaining change in his wallet. Striking his hip with his fist, he listens to his mum's new number ring. Her answering machine clicks on, as he'd hoped, and he relaxes. 'Hey, Mum, it's uh, me. I, um, need a place to stay a few days. I got your letter. So—yeah. Right, bye.'

He follows the station tunnel to the metro platforms and collects a timetable from the ticket booth. She's in zone three, twenty-one stations away. It costs twice as much to get there as it did to get to their old place in Hawthorn, even with his healthcare card. The Belgrave platform is mostly his. He sits on his bag, feeling an echo of the angry nights he'd spent at train stations when he was younger, seeking an escape he hadn't found.

It's an hour-and-a-half train ride to Belgrave. Watching the top of Hawthorn pass by the window is unnerving. For a long time there's nothing to do but remember. He sees himself waking on Darren's couch in a fug of pot-stink. He sees himself gasping through Under-Nineteens drills at Glenferrie Oval in the January heat, a reminder of his dad in each of his teammates' faces. Students board the train, Year Elevens and Twelves wagging, and seeing them he feels older than he should. Past Ferntree Gully the view out his window turns green and forested and hills rise on both sides. By the time they slow into the Belgrave terminus he can see cloud shadows streaming across the Dandenong Ranges and there are only five other passengers getting off with him.

Her address is on the back of the envelope that still holds her letter. At a newsagent in the shopping strip that curls above the station he finds her street in the directory. It's ten minutes away. Walking there, it feels like the kind of neighbourhood she wanted. The mountain air is thick on his face. Most of the houses down the hill are on half-acre blocks. Some of them are as wide as the old block of flats in Hawthorn.

Her house number is on a tin letterbox at the front of the downward sloping driveway. He knocks six times on her front door but no-one answers. The spare key is under one of the three pot plants at the end of her porch, and he lets himself inside.

The fresh carpet along her hallway parts softly beneath his sneakers. The second room past her newly furnished living room has his bed and desk in it, and a pile of boxes of what must be his old stuff. He closes the door without putting his bag down.

The kitchen looks like something from a magazine. He slides open the screen door beside the kitchen sink and stands in her backyard, smoking. Everything around him is so green. A lyrebird's falling whistle comes from somewhere close. He backs away from it.

He isn't ready, he realises. He should have stayed on the Gold Coast for another month. At least up there, looking out at the high rises and palm trees, he could see no trace of himself. He'd forgotten what the suburbs in Melbourne feel like: the flatness of their days, the memories they contain.

At five-thirty a key turns in the front door. He stands up from his kitchen stool, waiting. She stops just inside the entrance and puts down her handbag. 'Jason,' she says. Her hair's shorter and she's wearing eye make-up. She looks younger, a lot younger than he can remember her being. 'When'd you get here?'

'Hi, Mum.' He stays where he is.

'What happened?'

'I should've called.'

'Are you okay? When'd you get here?'

'Couple of hours ago.' He takes the front door key from his pocket. 'Found this. Sorry.'

'Well, what?' She looks down the hallway and back at him as if tracing his steps. 'If I'd known you were coming, I could've—'

It's difficult to look at her.

'Well, give me a hug, then.'

The top of her head only reaches his chin. She seems heavier, filled out somehow, and softer around her shoulder blades. He breaks her embrace with his elbows and avoids her gaze. 'I won't be here long.'

'What happened?'

'No, nothing.'

'I mean, I assumed—' She doesn't finish. 'You never called me.'

'I got in this morning. If you check your machine.'

'I was at work.'

Cornered, he steps around her and halts in the centre of the kitchen. 'How are you?'

'I'm good. Good. How are you?'

'Good.' He clears his throat. 'Listen, I've been eighteen hours on the bus.'

'Sure. Right.'

He escapes to the room with his bed in it and lies down with his shoes on. He looks at the boxes, thinking again of his stuff stacked inside them, and her letter in his bag. *You can always come back.* He listens to her moving through the house while watching television. He rolls off the bed to remove his shoes and sits in his socks, staring at the boxes and his closed new cupboards and his desk with the old slashes in it. Somewhere among them is Daphne's first postcard from Darlinghurst with her phone number on it. After reading it, he'd smoked half his stash at Darren's, and gone to training with the Under-Nineteens the next day. Thinking back on the choices he'd made empties him.

After rising the following day at one in the afternoon, he leaves the house as quickly as he can and roams the shopping strip again. No-one knows where he is. No-one can contact him. It's a pleasing feeling. The shops have simple names and there are no franchise restaurants yet. It's slower than Hawthorn, and it's hard to imagine the slowness working for her. But what she was like in Hawthorn is part of the life she had wanted to escape.

Further along the road is a small cinema that hasn't been redecorated since the 1970s and a pub with ten-dollar counter meals. In the pub he buys a beer. There's a copy of the previous day's newspaper on one of the empty tables. He flicks past Iraq to the job listings. They're as barren as up north: no need for bartenders or bus boys, lots of 'experience required' and 'must have own licence and transport'. He watches the blonde bartender glide across the bistro and mount a stool to turn on the television. Her voice. It's enough to work the rest of the afternoon around.

None of his teammates who made the cut for the Under-Nineteens have been elevated yet. The same senior Hawks are in the liftout, playing the same positions. He spares himself from reading on but nevertheless feels the judgement they offer: if he'd been ten percent better he might have made it, ten percent he'd cost himself on those write-off summer nights at Darren's and in the park near Daphne's place. He circles his glass between his thighs.

At six-thirty his growling stomach and empty wallet force him back to the house. She's locked the front door and he uses the spare key from the pot plant to get in again. She's wide awake in the kitchen, in neat casual clothes, flicking through a cookbook as the dishwasher grunts behind her.

'Where have you been?' she asks.

'Just out, you know. Around.'

'You didn't surface last night.'

'I was tired.' He finds the remains of some fried rice in the fridge and searches behind the new cookware in her cupboards for an old pot.

'Here.' She presses some buttons on the microwave beside the sink and springs its door open. 'One minute on high. You can do just about everything in it. Have a look, so you know. You don't even have to take the food out of the containers. They're microwavable.'

He watches the food rotate inside the machine. How much did it cost? How much, in total, had she been sitting on all this time? He thinks of the old cloth couch, his fold-out desk, the pipes in the walls of their flat and the hours he spent cleaning the place, alone.

'So.' She slaps the cookbook shut. 'What do you think?'

'What?'

'Belgrave.'

'It's nice.' He finds a fork, eventually, and after taking the fried rice from the microwave realises she's still waiting for him to say something. 'It's nice,' he says again.

'You still haven't told me anything about, well, anything.'

'Sorry.'

'Don't apologise. I just want to know.'

He swallows another spoonful of rice and another, and finally empties the last clumps of it into the sink with the container. 'It sort of
happened all at once. This friend wrote to me, and it felt as if I didn't
know what I was doing up there anymore. So I came home. This is
home.'

'Right.'

'I really should've called. I know, it's not—' He backs towards the
hallway. 'No, really. This place is great.'

'Okay.' She watches him, surprised. 'Where are you going now?'

'There's a pub up next to the cinema I want to check out.'

'Really? Well, okay, see you soon.'

'Yeah. Bye.'

The pub on the shopping strip is now crowded with people his age.
Someone's having a party, it seems. The guys standing in an open circle
in the corner remind him of the old crew in Richmond: relaxed and
baseball-capped, their jokes getting louder and louder. The Marg had
always been a good hangout, he remembers. Before they'd turned eighteen, the crew had made it their own. It would be good to hear their
stories again, no matter how successful Darren is.

• • •

The following Thursday night he leaves Belgrave at seven to get to the
Marg by nine. Darren's band, Mule, is on the chalkboard out front.
They're filling the slot after Hummer and before Skrieg. Inside, most of
the old crew are sitting at one of the tables beside the stage—Sev, Blain,
Fish and Darcy. Shaking hands with the guys, he can feel their surprise
at seeing him. It would be great if Robyn was still on the scene, not off
in Byron or wherever she's gone. She'd be cool about it.

'When'd you get back, mate?' Darcy says. 'You look like a bloody Abo.'

'A couple of days ago,' he lies, not wanting to have to explain his delay in seeing them. 'It's freezing down here.'

Blain says, 'Reckon I'll give Queensland a crack myself next year.'

'Yeah? Hope you like the dole. I was on it for five months.'

'Cheers to that,' Fish says.

Blain buys the next two jugs. They're all out of school now. He thought they'd be older, somehow, that they'd be working full-time and would have moved out of home, like he had. But after half an hour of hearing about Crow's TAFE course, Abigail Taylor's fiancé, and Darren cutting Sev's lunch, he is in the same place he was the previous February, when they were still in school and he wasn't. With each beer he can feel himself receding from them, his part in their stories now assumed by others.

After buying another beer, he takes it to the front of the stage where Darren is unpacking his drum kit. It's the same one he bought at the end of Year Eleven, but there are political stickers on it now: a Greens logo, a silhouette of Mandela, the stripes of the American flag bleeding. 'You still at the restaurant?'

'Yeah, yeah. Still busting my balls.' Darren's hair looks as if it's been chopped with a knife. 'Get you a shift, if you want.'

'Nah—too far, you know?'

'Yeah.' Darren seems to reach for something else to say. 'You still playing footy?'

The word pangs. For a moment he's back in the Under-Nineteens' locker room among the other ten members of the squad about to find their names cut. 'No, not right now.'

'It's good to see you, J.D.'

'Yeah, we should catch up.'

'Totally. Look, give us your phone number.'

Jason hesitates. 'I don't know what it is.'

'Okay.' Darren raises his eyebrows and puts on a smile as he does when he's talking to a girl. 'Call us when you do. We'll go to the footy sometime, all right?'

In the men's he freshens up. Being drunk again is like slipping into an old coat. The men around him look the same as they did when he was sixteen. Except he's one of them now, he tells himself, as his dad must have been.

Onstage, Darren hammers his snare. Fish layers dirty electric guitar over the top of it until their lead singer—some bald guy from Darren's design course—puts down his beer and steps up to the microphone. They go loud, then quiet, then loud again, like one of the Seattle bands. No-one else from school shows up before the end of their set. Between songs Blain tells the joke about three condoms sitting at a bar and Darcy shows off his party trick, filling his fist with gas from his lighter and sparking it into a flaming ball. The next band, Skrieg, are a four-chord thrash act with a Goth on vocals, and Sev makes wanking motions with one hand.

At midnight the house lights come on and the manager asks them four times to leave.

Outside on Victoria Street, two punks in leather jackets and nose rings step around them, eating souvlakis, and Fish whistles at them through his teeth. Jason stops a cab in the middle of the road and climbs in before the others have finished smoking.

'Don't be a pussy, Dalts,' Darcy says.

'We're going to Chasers, right?'

'Don't puss out, you weak bastard.'

'See you there.' He closes the door. 'Camberwell station, mate.'

His cab pulls into the bay above the station just as the last train to Belgrave is rumbling under the bridge. He stumbles down the ramp-way. No inspector is at the gates. The rear doors of the middle carriage close on his shoulders. Three guys, underage and drunk, applaud him as he takes a seat by the window opposite them and drops his head on his knees.

The train passes Burnley station and the laneway leading to his old school. Being the one in the crew who'd dropped out had been cool for a while, and so had the idea of escaping to the Gold Coast. To them, he'd made it sound like a gamble. But had they believed him? Not Darren, he knows. The pot and the need for couch space every other night had left him with nothing to hide behind.

For days after seeing the crew, he drifts. Things come back to him in the stillness of his mum's house, their meanings tangled, their links unclear. His football cards, his posters, the training timetables he used to make, the chalkboard targets he drew on the rear of their block of flats. The self-assurance he gained from each routine, as if it were medicine. His mum's ageing face wavers before him, her expression contorted.

It would be so easy to call Darren and get in touch with their old dealer. And he wouldn't use as much this time, only for help to sleep. Then he remembers the fog, the uncomfortable loss of time it brought on, especially in the later months up north when whole weeks had unravelled into the air and disappeared. Worse, Darren would know he still needs it.

Hayden's mum picks up the phone with a sigh in her voice.

'Hi, Mrs Bennett? It's Jason Dalton. Hayden's friend. From school.'

'Jason! I didn't recognise your voice. How long has it been?'

'A while, yeah.'

'Hayden's in Sydney with his father at the moment, Jason. On business. I'm sure he'd love to hear from you. When will they be back? Let me think . . . Dean's got him learning Japanese, would you believe it. *Konichiwa! Arigato!* I don't think poor Hayden knows what he's got himself into. It's a lot different to what he got away with at school. A dose of the real world, I think.'

'Exactly.'

'How are things with you and Mum?'

He pauses, thinking of Hayden, now a businessman, out making money in the world. The handshake he'd have, and the smile of a man on the move. Hayden would quickly see the path he'd taken, too. 'I'm heading overseas, actually,' he lies. 'Thought I'd give Hayden a bell before I went.'

'Wonderful. Where to?'

'World trip,' he hears himself say.

'Well, let me get your number.'

'I'm staying at my girlfriend's place. Better I just call him back when he's around.'

After hanging up he unpacks his cassette player from the boxes piled in the corner of his room and plugs it in beside his bed. Turning the dial to triple j, he lies spreadeagled on his mattress. Gangsta rap, then the Beastie Boys, then a song by the Red Hot Chili Peppers takes him back to his sharehouse up north. With his eyes closed he tries to hear the music as he did when he was stoned, the way the riff uncoiled and came alive.

There are new, unfamiliar voices leaving messages on his mother's answering machine. A woman named Leanne with a hard country accent, a younger woman named Tina who calls at random in need of cooking instructions. The following night, there's a message for him. 'Jason, are you there? It's me. Listen, I won't be home tonight, I'm going to the movies with some friends from work. Bye.'

• • •

In the first week of May he gets up before midday to check out a two-bedroom sharehouse in Collingwood. It's twenty minutes north by train from the city, an hour and a half from Belgrave. The streets around the house feel like his old street, including the video store with bars on its windows. Many of the local houses have been split into units and the kerbs are choked with second-hand cars. The sky feels much more distant than he's used to, its light swallowed by the brick and concrete.

From the outside, the house doesn't inspire. It's three steps from the tiny front gate to the door, and the brass turnkey doorbell doesn't work. The ad said two hundred and ten a month, plus bills, which is five bucks less a week than he'd been paying up north—except up there he could walk from home to the beach in one cigarette.

The man who opens the door is as tall as the doorway. His face looks as if it's been knocked into shape with a hammer and his nose has a depression in it like a rivet. 'You Jason?'

'Yeah. Hi.'

'I'm Barnaby.' His handshake is painful.

A tour of the house takes less than three minutes. There's a bathroom with some mould on the walls, one bedroom cramped with clothes and sports equipment, a lounge room with a covered fireplace and a narrow rear kitchen where Barnaby's two-minute noodles are steaming on the wrought-iron stove. In the backyard, a black labrador is lying in the bare veggie patch, his nose between his paws. 'That's Dundee,' Barnaby says. 'Don't pet him—he doesn't like strangers.'

The TV in the lounge room is the same kind Daphne had, though its stand is a milk crate with a sheet thrown over it. 'Where you from, Barnaby?'

'Toowoomba.'

'Long way to come.'

'Beats the dole.' Barnaby's smile is lopsided. 'You get enough of that.'

In the silence that follows Jason can hear the dog's paws scraping outside.

'So tell us a bit about yourself, mate,' Barnaby says.

'Right. I'm working in the Safeway at Glenferrie—stock and that.

I'm saving a bit there, what I don't blow on the weekends, anyway. Me and my mates are always in the neighbourhood.' It comes out more easily than the truth. Thinking his story over beforehand, it wouldn't come together—dropping out, the couch-surfing, heading up north— without having to go into everything else.

'Second bedroom's a bit smaller but that's why she's cheap,' Barnaby says, showing him the empty room one more time on the way to the door. 'I got a mate who said he'd come over and meet you, too. But it looks as if he won't get home from the pub till later.'

'He a barman, is he?'

'He'd like to be.' Barnaby plucks a biro from his back pocket and touches the nib to his broad forearm. 'You'd be moving in the first week of June, so you know. Call me on Monday. I'll know where I'm at by then.'

They shake hands again at the door.

Out on the street, Jason unfolds his black beanie from his jacket pocket and pulls it over his ears. A group of younger Vietnamese girls passes in a cloud of sniggers and maybe they're laughing at him, the lone guy with the glum face and his hands jammed in his jeans pockets. They could be. He sits against the fence inside the train station, smoking, disappearing into his bomber jacket and earphones. When the Metallica chorus ignites in his head he grunts the lyrics to himself.

Eighteen years. In the quiet of his room at his mum's he looks back at their life in Hawthorn and longs to vanish again as he had on so many afternoons up north, his bong a shelter from his thoughts. He sees his mum's face in her hands as she sits trembling on the couch. Who would he be now if she'd never told him about his dad? And what had he cost himself? In the dark, sober, there's no way to avoid the questions.

When a shower breaks the bleak sky and layers his mum's windows in rivers of water he stays in the house, in his tracksuit pants, using the TV to block out the quiet. The footage from Iraq is fascinating and he finds himself surfing channels for more of it. The night vision, the desert fatigues, the rubble. A new world is happening up there, to guys even younger than he is.

Ads for the navy and air force make service seem like being in the cast of an action movie. What would the reality be? Sleeping in a bunk, scrubbing floors, following orders all day, hard drinking on weekends. But the travel would be free, and the ads are right: by the end of it, you'd have been part of something bigger than yourself.

On June tenth he leaves everything in his mum's spare room except the atlas and his sleeping bag. He makes the bed and vacuums the carpet before she gets home. His clothes take only ten minutes before dinner to pack.

'I understand you need your independence,' she tells him. 'But staying here an extra month, you could save. There's your bed here, food in the fridge. You wouldn't need to pay any board.'

'I'm sorry.'

'Don't be sorry. I just thought—'

He doesn't respond.

'It must be hard for you up here.' She takes their cleared dinner plates and slots them into the dishwasher. 'Away from your friends, Danny and—no, it's not Danny, is it? I always call him Danny. Darren.'

He watches her wipe the kitchen benches with a dishtowel. She doesn't seem lonely, as he thought she'd be. She doesn't talk like a lonely person. Her back is still fragile but she hasn't been groaning or sighing. Is she happy? Is this what she's like when she's happy? 'You've got new flowers in the lounge-room window.'

'Carnations. There's a little florist downstairs at the hospital.'

When he kisses her on the cheek at the front door she hugs him unexpectedly. It occurs to him that he might be the first guest she's had up here. 'I'll call you,' she says. 'To check in.'

'Okay.'

Walking up her driveway and the dark quiet hill to Belgrave station, a dull anger throbs in his chest. The way she'd talked to him about money, as if he was fifteen again. By the time he reaches the deserted, glowing station, words are coming easily. Yeah, there are things I want to talk to you about. How about the letter you wrote me? How about the things you told me about my dad? But when he screams at her in his head her face soon crumples and he's back in Hawthorn, reaching for the door.

On the station platform he pitches stones onto the tracks. The train pulls in a few minutes later and he walks along to his old seat against the rear wall of the last carriage. He closes his eyes for the length of three stations; when he opens them he takes out of his bag the school atlas he'd found in the same box as his stereo. Eastern Europe is out of date and the CIS is still the USSR. But the names of the major cities are the same, and the distances. With the right job, he could have money for a plane fare by August.

The stray newspaper on his tram to Collingwood says that the state's unemployment has hit twenty-one percent among people his age. At least he's not queuing at soup kitchens. He thinks of Daphne in Darlinghurst among her university crew: is she still okay? He should call her. But hearing her voice would open up a hole in him again that he only knows one way to seal.

• • •

The sharehouse, he discovers, has no protection against winter except the column heater in the lounge room and the kitchen stove. When he lies in bed in his new room, the June air comes in around the door and up the disused air vent opposite his mattress. He plugs the gap with a towel and covers the vent with his wardrobe, but each morning he can write his name on the inside of his window with his finger. In the window's lower corner, half a rainbow from a child's sticker book remains frozen to the glass. What must it have been like to grow up here?

Barnaby arrives home from the brewery at the same time each afternoon and lurches onto the lounge-room couch. He complains about the inflammation in his neck and shoulders, his left knee. Between dinner and the late news he doesn't move except to answer the phone. The cheery voices of his friends on the answering machine suggest he must be a different person around them: hard-drinking, sarcastic, good with women—a great bloke to know.

'I'm thinking about joining the navy,' Jason tells him one night.

'You're kidding me.'

'I called them about it the other day. All you need is Year Ten.'

'There's a war on, mate.' Barnaby's eyes don't move from the screen.

'Beats sitting around here being broke.'

'You don't want to be in any kind of army.'

'What do you know that I don't?'

'My old man's a sergeant,' Barnaby says. 'And you don't ever want to meet that bloke, let alone work for him.'

On the inside of his bedroom door Barnaby has taped a blown-up photo of himself, aged sixteen or so, standing beside Wally Lewis in the Maroons' change rooms after a State of Origin match. With one hand resting on his hip, just like the King beside him, he already looks big enough to hold down a place in a senior team.

In the backyard, Dundee snarls and nips at Jason's fingers when he gets too close. Clumps of his black coat stand up stickily in the air and parts of his hind legs show pink. 'Easy, mate. Easy.' Moving quietly around him, Jason picks up his bowl and takes it inside to wash out the ants and fill it with water. How much is a dog his size supposed to eat each day? One of the vets on Johnston Street must know.

'He's not mine,' Barnaby tells him that night. 'I'm minding him till his owner gets back from Europe.'

'Some owner.'

Barnaby makes a sound that could almost pass for a laugh. 'She had me wrapped around her finger. Never again.'

A week later, watching Dundee finish his morning can of wet food, Jason leans forward and touches him on the back. The dog doesn't stop eating. The hair around his neck is oily, and along his back it looks, in places, like the bristles of a brush. 'Easy, mate. I won't hurt you.' There's something willing and predictable about him under his damaged coat and encrusted face. He must have been a different dog at some point if he can recognise kindness like this, if he can trust it as he does.

• • •

None of the local Collingwood or Fitzroy pubs are advertising for work. He applies to them anyway, aware of his unemployment like a bad smell. How many guys his age have asked the same string of questions to the same bartenders? The queue backed up to the electric doors of the CES on Johnston Street has the answer.

Using the first thirty dollars of his next dole payment, he buys the strongest lead he can find. Dundee snorts when he attaches it, then whines from a place deep in his chest.

'We're right, mate. We're walking through the house, okay? Let's walk through the house.'

Once he's out on the street Dundee surges forward like a speedboat, setting his own pace. Passing the children's playground, he rears and yips at the open grass and what must be the smell of other dogs who have been there before, his lead stretching cable-taut.

'Come on, mate. Enough of that.' Jason lets him circle the metal poles of the swings in search of a place to shit. Dogs his size need to be walked every day for at least half an hour, according to the vet's leaflet. He should eat at the same time every night, half a can of wet food, not the random serves of dry food and biscuits Barnaby keeps him on. No wonder he's vicious. If a person was tied down in a yard all day he'd be vicious, too.

When they arrive home, mail is waiting for him in the letterbox: an A4-size envelope with the Defence Forces logo on it. He takes the envelope to his room. Inside are two brochures, one with an application form and the other describing the naval base in Westernport. He could be a mechanic, a combat systems operator, a clearance diver. Lying on his back, he can see the bunk rooms at the naval base numbered like the dorms in one of the hostels up north.

His mum's voice on the answering machine is stilted. 'Hello? Jason? Are you there? No? . . . I'm just calling to see how you are. Give me a call, okay? Take care. Bye.'

• • •

Football in July is impossible to avoid. Hawthorn is back near the top of the ladder, he learns. They have a star import from Adelaide, Darren Jarman, who seems to slow time when he has the ball and is so skilful he looks lazy. In the news footage of Hawthorn's round-fourteen win against North Melbourne, Jarman dummies his opponents around goal as if he's still in the schoolyard. Watching him, Jason sees himself standing behind the interchange bench at the MCG, holding a shovel and dreaming of the crowd.

Arnie must love Jarman.

The following Sunday Jason puts Dundee on a leash and catches the train with him to Hawthorn station. In the back of their carriage Dundee whimpers and trembles, heavy against his legs.

'I'm here, mate. You're okay.' The other passengers give Dundee a wide berth, but he has to learn to be with people.

Arnie's house looks the same from the outside, but his street feels smaller than it used to. Walking up the driveway to the front door, Jason remembers how good he felt, kneeling below the front fence, turning and clearing the dirt. He presses the doorbell and skims his shoes a few times on the faded welcome mat. It's just Arnie, he tells himself, though his hands continue to sweat. Dundee sniffs out the door apprehensively. Jason crouches and holds Dundee to him—'Your first train trip, mate'—reminding himself to be the calm one.

The latch clicks open and Arnie appears behind the flyscreen door. 'G'day, stranger—come in.'

Inside, his house still smells of cut wood and paint, except there are now tapestries of Japanese women on the walls and the lounge-room couches have been covered with new, matching throw rugs. Jason lets Dundee roam the backyard while Arnie fetches a bowl of water.

'Was good to hear from you, Dalts.' Arnie leads him to the lounge room and settles into the seat next to him. He hasn't put on any beer-drinker's weight and his face, though thicker, is still clear of lines. 'What's it been—two years?'

'It makes me remember stuff, being here.'

'I would've still been working on the pool room when you were here last, eh? I'll give you the tour in a tick.' Arnie looks towards the back room and smiles in remembrance. 'Yeah, dragged my arse a bit, but it got done. So what's been happening with you, mate? When was the last time?'

'Before the premiership.'

'The premiership, that's right. Then you disappeared on us.' The look on Arnie's face puts him back inside the Falcons' change rooms. 'Bit of a Houdini act. Couldn't figure you.'

Putting reasons to the choices he'd made in the summer following the Falcons' 1989 premiership is like looking through dirty glass. So many of his memories are shards. Lone mornings at Darren's and brutal afternoons among the thirty-strong Under-Nineteens squad are clear, but what he can't pin down is who he was among them. Someone that Arnie doesn't know. He watches his hands.

'Timing, was it?'

'Something like that.'

'Need a beer?'

'Here.' Jason unzips his backpack. 'I brought some for us.'

'This way.'

He follows Arnie to the back of the house. The carpet stops just before the final room and becomes pine floorboards. Inside are a three-quarter-size pool table and two thin windows looking out onto the backyard, where Dundee is still inspecting the bushes. The walls are covered with photos: Arnie and his mates on fishing boats, in front of mountains, around fireplaces and restaurant tables. While Arnie fetches a bottle opener from beside the minibar, Jason studies the more recent photos. The same woman is there, again and again. She's slight, with black hair and big eyes. In most of the photos she's making a funny face: not again, you dag.

'Who's she?'

'That's Tamara.'

'Where'd you find her?'

'Don't laugh. A pub in Thailand.'

'You're married?'

'Nah, we're having too much fun for that.' Arnie takes two pool cues from the stand by the little TV. 'On the phone, you were asking me something about footy.'

'I've read some of the local clubs will pay pretty well if you're a decent player.'

Arnie smoothes his cheeks with one sandpaper hand. 'There's a lot of thugs playing district.'

'I know.'

'Not to turn you off—I'm only telling you like it is.'

'How much do they earn?'

'Hundred, two hundred a game. More, if you're ex-AFL.'

The opposite wall shows pictures from Arnie's football career, including his time coaching the Falcons. Some of the photos go back to when he was in his Preston guernsey. He had more hair back then but the same grin, the same mates.

'That's a fair bit. I could use that.'

'Could you?'

'I could.'

'What's your job these days?'

'I don't have one.'

'Okay. I know a few blokes up at Brunswick in the EDFL. You probably won't get a run this season, but you can check them out.'

'Thanks.'

Arnie chalks his cue and nods at him to rack up again. 'What happened, mate—can you talk about it?'

'I don't know.'

'It's not drugs or booze, is it?'

'I had to get away.'

'But you came back.'

'I'll be off again. When I get the money. London, maybe the States. You told me once, you can learn everything you need to know backpacking. I remembered that.'

'Me and my big mouth. Go the six. But don't whack it, hit through it. I get the family stuff, mate. Kids I've coached, even some of the blokes you've played with—you know, you'd be surprised. Your story's probably not as bad as you think.'

'Right.'

'I'm just saying, when you're ready to talk, you can give us a call. You know that.'

'How are your Under-Sixteens?'

'Still thinking it's schoolyard footy. Never mind. They'll come good.'

They play until the sun disappears behind the back roof and Arnie has to turn on the down lights. Jarman is the club's best recruit since Platten, they agree. With him in form, the Hawks might have another flag in them. But pretty soon no-one will be able to touch the Adelaide Crows, Arnie observes. It's already happening in Perth. Listening to Arnie's talk is relaxing. Jason peppers him with questions about the Hawks' season, savouring the gruff humour of his answers.

At dusk he puts Dundee on his leash again and precedes Arnie out the front door and into the driveway. The rosebushes are getting messy again. For a second he considers offering to trim them. But no, going back would be wrong—worse than wrong. 'Thanks again. For everything.'

They shake hands. 'Door's always open, mate,' Arnie says. 'Take care.'
'I will.'

On the train home he curls over Dundee, whispering to him and shielding him from loud noises. The press of Dundee's head against his hand offers reassurance from his own feelings. The thought of pulling on a jumper for the Brunswick Redbacks fills him with trepidation. He won't have the skills anymore. He won't have the fire to compete. His focus will be shot, just as it was in the Under-Nineteens. What would Daphne say? Make your own life. But she'll be graduating in two years, same as Darren. They'll go to their offices in the city. Isn't that where people as smart as them end up? What about people like him?

At home, after Barnaby has shut himself in his room, he lets Dundee inside to sleep on his bed.

• • •

The East Brunswick Redbacks' home ground is two tram rides west of Collingwood, on the northern edge of the city, a murky oval unprotected by trees and bordered on its far side by a wobbly line of house

fences. Walking through the ground's front gate the following Wednesday night, he finds himself almost overcome by the desire to turn
around and walk out again. For a few minutes he watches the team
training beneath the ground's scant lights—twenty-five players in tee-
shirts and club guernseys. They aren't playing for the same reason he is.
They'll know it as soon as he laces up.

The inside of their clubhouse looks much like the Falcons' had:
mobile furniture, a television attached to the ceiling, and a covered
pool table pushed into the corner. A middle-aged man is drinking a can
of VB at the window overlooking the ground. 'You right, son?'

'Arnie Singer told me to come down.'

'So you're Jason Dalton.' He eases himself down from his stool and
holds out one hand. 'Les Abernathy. I'm the club prez. Maddox's the one
who knows Arnie.' He nods through the glass at the tracksuited, pink-
faced coach hollering on field. 'Thanks for coming down.' Les frowns as
the team hustles past the window. 'Heard you trained with Hawthorn.'

'Mostly I played on the ball with Hawthorn City Falcons. With
Arnie. Then I trained with the Hawthorn Under-Nineteens for a while.'

'What position?'

'Ruck-rover.'

Les appraises him, stockman-like. 'You've got that build.' The older
man shows signs in his arms and shoulders of being a former player,
though it seems unlikely he could raise more than a jog now. 'Let's get
you out there then. Introduce you to the place.'

They meet Maddox at the boundary fence, where he's gathering
footballs into a net. His handshake is so much like Les's they could be
father and son. Maddox is skinnier than Arnie, and taller, with a fuzzy
haircut years out of fashion. 'Thanks for coming down, Jase. Arnie gave
you a rap—said you played some Under-Nineteens for the Hawks.'

'Trained with them for a summer.'

'So long as you're keen.' Maddox motions to the squad to begin their warm-down by the fence. Under his gaze his players seem apprehensive. He must be that kind of coach. 'We could use you next season, mate. We're a bit slow through the middle this year.'

'Think you're interested?' Les says.

'Sure.'

'Let's get you signed up then. Plenty of time to chat later.'

Inside the clubhouse, Les disappears into the locked office in the corner. Jason watches the Redbacks clap themselves into the change rooms. They're a straggly-seeming mob. He could have beaten any of them when he was at his best.

Les soon comes back from the office with three A4 sheets stapled together and gives him the pen from his pocket. Ambulance cover provided on match days. In fresh pen Les has written '$150' into the contract's per-game salary clause. It's compulsory to appear at all training sessions and club functions, the contract says. 'We like to see the boys putting some money back into the bar on weekends.'

'Says here about my sign-up fee.'

'That's some incentive. Come down to the game this Saturday, we'll give it to you then. Now, you want to say g'day to the boys?'

Jason follows Maddox and Les outside and through the door into the change rooms. Inside, the laundry and old liniment smell brings back his teenage years. They're in the cold stone floor and low benches and row of coat hooks, the blackboard on the rear wall and the match summaries pinned to the cork board beside it, the fluorescent lights in the ceiling, and the murmur of players winding down, their sports bags scraping the floor. Once, he had pinned so many of his hopes to this: a concrete room full of strangers, a woollen jumper with his number on it. He starts nervously hitting himself on the hip with his fist. It seems every player is either sizing him up or ignoring him.

'Fellas,' Les says. 'This is one of our new recruits—Jason Dalton. Make sure he feels at home.'

8. redbacks

At lunchtime on the last Friday in September he meets Arnie on the steps of Parliament House for the grand-final parade. Arnie's grin, as deep as a carving, reassures him that getting out of bed to meet him was the right thing to do. In his jeans and polo shirt, Arnie looks like a lot of the other supporters still coming up out of the subway who've draped Hawks scarves over their work clothes. 'Not too many Eagles about, eh?' Arnie offers.

Down Bourke Street, the footpaths are as crowded with supporters as standing room on match day. In the mall, the Hawthorn cheer squad has set up in front of the David Jones windows and two teenage boys have climbed a lamp post to get a better view. Jason watches them, their passion stinging him with its reminder of what he used to be like. He shadows Arnie to the front of the crowd. 'When was your first?' he asks.

Arnie doesn't hesitate. 'Sixty-three, it would've been. Me and my mum.'

'We lost that one. Geelong.'

'You've done your homework.'

'You went to the game?'

'No. I was gutted to miss it.'

In front of the Myer windows two buskers, on saxophone and trombone, strike up the Hawthorn anthem. Here they come, the 1991 grand-final team, along the tram tracks in a swarm of confetti and tickertape. Michael Tuck, still their captain, is in the first car: a Batmobile on loan from what must be a theme park somewhere up north. 'Where's your cape, Tucky?' Arnie shouts. The other Hawks follow in brand-new convertibles. So many are the same faces from the eighties: Langford, Ayres, Jencke, Collins, Platten, Hall, Brereton, Dunstall. Some now have kids. In their suits and ties they look comfortable with the attention, laughing and taking photos of the fans. He used to idolise those men.

'Stick it right up 'em, Rat!' Arnie shouts.

Jason claps for Arnie's sake and then stops. Half a block away, on the post office steps, Daphne is standing with her back to him. Looking at her, he feels his ears turning red, then his neck, then his cheeks. But it's not her, she's in Sydney. It's just a girl who looks like her. He looks the other way to clear his mind.

Afterwards, in the Royal Arcade, Arnie buys them each a pie. 'So, how'd the Redbacks treat you?'

'Pre-season starts in November.'

'They paying you decent?'

'Enough. I've still gotta find a job.'

'I'd take you on myself, if I had the work.' Arnie makes a face at the world. 'You going to the grand final tomorrow?'

'No.'

'Come round, if you want.'

They shake hands on the Flinders Street station steps. Arnie grips him on the shoulder for a moment, his face widening into the same grin Jason'd welcomed him with. 'Whatever time you can make it, mate.'

The following afternoon he and Dundee arrive at Arnie's house for the last fifteen minutes of the match. Arnie is already doing victory laps around his TV set. The Hawks are on fire. 'Brereton started the quarter with two from the goal square,' Arnie almost shouts at him. 'And Dunstall's going for his fourth in a row.' The final margin, fifty-three points, gives them their fourth premiership in six years—a stretch longer than Jason'd been in high school.

Arnie's bag of footballs for Falcons training is in the back of his Kingswood. His driveway is long enough for a kick. Dundee runs between them and sharks the ball when it spills into the rosebushes.

'Ready for the Redbacks?' Arnie calls to him, the ball singing from his feet. 'They'll test you out, the seniors. Keep your eyes open.'

Arnie's respect is disarming. Packing his bag in the kitchen afterwards, Jason wonders what would happen if he started talking to him about his dad. Even if he got the words out, he decides, a look would come over Arnie's face: you're a troubled kid, the look would say. We're different. From then on, they wouldn't be at ease with each other.

Arnie shakes hands with him. 'Let me know how the Redbacks works out.'

'I owe you one, Arnie.'

. . .

Starting the first week of November, pre-season training with the Redbacks is on Tuesday nights. Two of his teammates once played for the Collingwood Under-Nineteens. Another four had played reserves with Preston. You should see the deals they get in the country leagues, he hears. A mate playing in Warrnambool's so deep in chicks every Saturday night, he can't stand up. Arnie's right—they won't have him if he's a pretender.

The spring sun has hardened the ground and their boots clap on the dried boundary mud. Maddox instructs them to do dumbbell flies using the renovator's bricks stacked beside the change rooms, to wind-sprint around the cordoned-off cricket pitch, to hold squats until their thighs are hard as bone. In the change rooms they hang gasping from the chin-up bars beneath the windows. After the initial shock Jason's muscle memory returns and his body expands to its former size. Within a month, he's among the fittest on the team.

The challenge of leaving the Gold Coast behind shapes his days. His tee-shirts are soon tight on his shoulders and loose at his waist. When he tires, he imagines his dad with a skinny country build. He works out until his arms shake.

'Group psychology,' Maddox tells them. 'You're as strong as your weakest link.'

Through the club, membership at the Brunswick Baths is two dollars a visit. Jason packs a towel and a change of clothes into his backpack before he heads over each day. It's easier, and cleaner, to use the showers there than shower at home after Barnaby's left for work.

In the afternoons he sits in the backyard with Dundee, playing fetch and tug-of-war. He's such a smart dog. If only he wouldn't try to eat Barnaby's ashtrays or chew on the lounge-room cushions when he comes inside. But the fur on his hind legs is growing back now and he jumps to his feet at the sound of the back door opening. Training would be good for him, the company of other dogs. But after his inoculation fees, worm tablets, flea cream, shampoo, a basket to sleep in and a new blanket and brush from the pet store, there's hardly enough money left for rent.

'Jason, it's me,' his mum says into the answering machine. 'How are you settling in down there? I hope you can still make it for Christmas. Give me a call.'

• • •

On Christmas Day, the Belgrave train from Richmond station is almost deserted. The other passengers are single people like him, their faces blank. He takes his new Nirvana album out of his ears to listen to the sounds the carriage makes on the tracks. The temperature drops and soon thick rain from the mountains is streaking the windows. When the train arrives at Belgrave, he scans the empty rows of seats for a newspaper to use as an umbrella.

The sky above the Dandenong Ranges is touching the tops of the trees. On his mum's street, the gutters have become rivers and the newspaper soon comes apart on his head. Daphne would have loved being out in this.

His mum appears in her front doorway wearing a summer dress he hasn't seen before and a red hair band like a girl in a sixties movie. He lets her kiss him on the cheek. 'You forgot your umbrella, you duffer.'

'It's not raining in town.'

'I would have picked you up from the station.'

Smells of rosemary and mint are in the hall. For a second, it feels like their old flat again. After standing in front of the blinking tree with her for their Christmas photo, he unwraps his present: two new work shirts and a tie. This must be how she imagines him in the city, he thinks.

'You've lost weight. How are you eating?'

'I've been in the gym.'

'Take home what's left over from dinner.'

'No, I don't want to. Mum—'

'How am I supposed to eat all of this by myself?'

Waiting on the kitchen bench are carrots, beans, roast potatoes and dinner rolls. She has more in the fridge—olives, ham, cheese, and a chocolate Christmas cake. 'I got a recipe book from Cleo at work. I guess I got started and just decided to keep going. Never mind. You'll have food till the new year, anyway.'

Outside, he listens to the rain as it sheets across her porch roof. She still hasn't fixed the creeper on her fence, but her grass looks newly mown. A rosebush has appeared in the corner. He tries to imagine her on hands and knees, digging into the dirt as he used to at Arnie's, but the version of her in his head never had the energy.

She stands watching him from the doorway. 'That's right. You had that gardening job with one of your teachers, didn't you? How am I looking?'

'You really need a man to come in about that creeper.'

'Just leave me some instructions.'

He sets the table with her good cutlery, then opens the bottle of champagne while she serves their food. Sitting down feels awkwardly formal. But this is the Christmas she used to talk about, he tells himself. Be happy for her.

'Your hair's grown terribly long. I liked it better when it was short.'

'I don't.'

'It's the fashion, is it?' She frowns over the words as if they're bad news. 'I don't like it, the cardigans and tracksuit pants. There's no colour.'

'You're not supposed to like it.' He refills his champagne glass and swallows half of it, hoping it will hit him quickly. 'You working today?'

'I don't work Christmases anymore. Where did you say you were off to tonight?'

'Darren's.'

'If you had your licence.'

'I don't have a car, do I?'

'You'll get there.'

'Last time I checked, they weren't handing out cars at the CES.'

'Have you thought about going back to school?'

'Not today.'

What would she do if she found out about the Redbacks? he wonders. The answer comes quickly: she'd blame herself. Neil Diamond's voice is floating around them. He looks at the CDs stacked beside the player, unable to make out the titles but certain of what they are. He watches her bring her fork to her mouth. Even the way she sits in her chair is different. It's as if she's grown a history, except of course it had been there all along. He'd just been too—what?—to see it. Young? Self-absorbed? Obviously it had been his fault, again.

At four o'clock they walk together along her street towards the station. The rain has stopped and the sun has come out, illuminating crystals on the tree leaves and roofs of parked cars. A basketball bounces and crashes into a backboard behind one of the local houses. At the top of the hill leading to the main road, two boys are propped on shiny bikes and are glaring at the descent. He watches her suck her lower lip until the pair reach the bottom unharmed.

At the main road she kisses him on the cheek goodbye.

'See you,' he says.

'See you.'

The next train to Richmond doesn't arrive for twenty minutes. He sits under the station's maroon awning. The envelope with her letter in it is still in the side pocket of his bag. He takes it out, wanting to compare the person she is in her house now to the words she'd written twelve months before. It's a full A4 page long, typed. When he reaches the first line of the second paragraph he turns the page down, the same shock and nausea coursing through him now as on his first read.

He unfolds it and keeps reading:

No-one in the town would talk about it, even acknowledge what had happened. He was a local legend, a promising footballer. No-one wanted to ruin his career. His name was Mick Casey. Afterwards I spent the day in hospital, and then three weeks later found I was pregnant with you. I left then, Jase, I couldn't stand to have them look at you and know how you came about.

He reads on until the final paragraph, where she has included her address a third time. The sentences don't sound like her. The words are too formal. But her sign-off is the same five words she always uses: *I love you very much.*

She was his age when he was born. The thought casts a shadow over him. She'd moved to the city and gone to work. What had his father done? Run away and shielded himself among his mates. Imagining what it must have felt like for her—to be a girl, held down—he flinches, unable to cope with the connection between what happened and himself.

Back in Collingwood the house is empty, but Barnaby hasn't left a note. Dundee is at the back door and paws at his thighs as soon as he opens it. 'Merry Christmas, mate. I've got us some Christmas dinner.' On the back step, he shares with Dundee the hamper of turkey his mum prepared for him, Dundee's rough tongue and cold nose tickling his hand.

• • •

Five days into the new year, he gets a call-back. The Brunswick Arms Hotel, one of the Redbacks' four sponsors, needs a part-time bartender.

On the afternoon of his interview, he wears jeans and one of his new collared shirts: the same uniform as the bartender he'd first handed his CV to. Before leaving home he feeds another two biscuits to Dundee, who rolls onto his back for his belly to be rubbed. 'Wish me luck.'

The hotel is just off Nicholson Street, two blocks from the Redbacks' home ground. Counter-meal specials are listed on a fold-out chalkboard beside its front door, and the bar inside looks as worn as the pensioners leaning on it. Beneath the TV in the upper corner is the 1991 Redbacks' team photo, signed by half a dozen of the players, and a framed Redbacks' guernsey is hanging beside the spirit shelves. After sitting down at the bar he unfolds his résumé from his bag. But the publican and manager, Ross, seems uninterested in his story—except his life in football.

'So, what chance d'you give the Redbacks this year, Jase?' he asks. 'If you can bring a flag home for that mob, they'll name the ground after you.'

Eleven dollars an hour, cash in hand, three nights a week. His first shift is the following night. His hands are still limber enough from his work in the bar up north to carry four towers of glasses at once, but most of the evening he spends stocktaking in the storage room, the beery smell seeping into his skin and hair. In the bistro he sets the tables and clears plates under the fuzzy gaze of the corner television; he keeps his watch in his pocket to stop himself glancing at it. It's work, he reminds himself, good work, and the half-price dinners are better than anything he could put together at home. One day a girl will come in. He pictures her as he shovels six-packs into the fridges beneath the taps: a blonde his age needing a drink and some time out, maybe a local office worker, or a student taking a break from study. He'll collect her empty drink, share her cigarette, and she'll leave her phone number underneath her glass like girls used to for the bartenders up north.

Knock-off is eleven-thirty. Walking home from the tram stop, he can feel his feet throb. From the front porch he can hear the washing machine rattling at the back of the house. Inside, Barnaby's leftover dishes are still floating in the kitchen sink. Dundee's nose is against the base of the back door. He's found a way to escape his lead, and his front paws are covered in dirt from where he's been digging against the fence again. 'You poor bugger, you've been waiting for hours, haven't you? Come here.'

. . .

Five members of the Redbacks squad have shaved their heads for the new season. The Velcros, Maddox calls them, impressed. There's something about their look from a distance. He's right: their haircuts make a point about being part of a team.

Three weeks into March, the Redbacks play their first home game against the North Coburg Bombers. Upwards of sixty locals have milled at the fence in front of the clubhouse to cheer them on. Many have brought their kids and dogs along. The supporters know his teammates' names and numbers as if they've been following them for years. As the team walks through the picket gate onto the field, two men in duffel coats come out of the crowd to slap his teammates on the back. 'Heads up, lads.' They look proud to be there.

From the opening bounce Jason patrols the backline, sweeping around his teammates to collect handpasses and intercept his opponents' kicks. The Bombers hit hard, as Maddox said they would. Fifteen minutes in, his opponent lines him up with a hip-and-shoulder and sends him wheezing across the boundary line chalk. The hit makes him hesitate, and the more he thinks, the more the ball stays out of reach.

At half-time, as Jason's teammates head for benches inside the change room, Maddox stops him at the door. 'Dalton.' Maddox has no eyes beneath the peak of his baseball cap, only a small gritty mouth. 'Where are you today, mate? You were running around as if you wanted it bloody gift-wrapped.'

'I didn't put in enough.'

'I could see that. You're about the best runner on the team. I ought to be playing you on the ball, but I'm not. You know why?' Maddox pokes him in the chest with his pen, four times. 'That's why. Ticker. Show it to us.'

During the third quarter he throws himself into every pack he can. His body surprises him. The gym and the pre-season have made him as strong as the tradies and renovators on the team. He's remade himself.

With ten minutes to go, he crumples the Bombers' rover in a tackle and snaps a goal from the forward flank that has car horns trumpeting around the park.

'Onya, Dalton.' One of the supporters in front of the clubhouse has found his name in the *Record*.

In the showers after the game he leans against the tiles and encloses himself in the falling spray. It fills his ears and distorts his teammates' voices until their taunts blend in the steam.

'Hey, Matty, is that your dick or your little finger?'

'Quit checking out my piece, faggot.'

'Who dropped the soap?'

Benny strides in, whistling, and takes off his towel. Hose, the rest of the team call him. 'You coming to Storm tonight, Dalts?'

'Yeah.' Something about the way they talk makes refusing them feel like whingeing.

Jason stays listening to them until the water goes lukewarm. When they're naked around one another, their arrogance is unnerving. In the change rooms he towels off slowly, the post-game daggers in his shoulders and hips already sharp. But it's his first win in a long time. The feeling of the ball gliding off his boot as he gathered pace inside the Redbacks' fifty-metre arc is still effervescent inside him. He'd seen the goal and made it happen, same as he used to.

He goes back to his Falcons routine of cleaning his boots at home on Tuesday and Thursday nights after training. Dundee lies next to him, occasionally sitting up to eat the dried turf that springs from his stops. The boots carry his feelings in them of breaking free, of kicking goals, of being good at something. As long as he keeps them in condition, the feelings will stay. A kid's superstition, he knows, but sharing a ritual with Dundee gives shape to the empty nights.

• • •

When he gets home from work on the Monday night following the Redbacks' third win—away, against the Reservoir Stingrays—Barnaby is waiting for him in the kitchen, the same dishes from three days ago still crowding the sink behind him. It's as if Barnaby can't see them. In his bathrobe, bent over a bowl of noodles, he looks like a patient in a hospital. He doesn't bother saying hello. 'We've got fleas. Why do you reckon that is?'

'Dundee must have left them on his way through.'

'You're paying for it.' Barnaby nods casually at the back door, where the edges of the flyscreen have been torn out and Dundee's teeth have left marks in the wood. 'The door, the fleas, the lot.'

Outside, Dundee waits at the fence to see who it is before limping towards him and lying on the concrete with his chin between his paws. He doesn't move his tail, just his eyes, and snuffles a sigh. Two puddles of piss are in front of him, and a thread of blood is trickling from the side of his mouth where Barnaby must have kicked him earlier.

'Jesus Christ.' Jason watches the back door until he's certain Barnaby has shut himself in his room. Inside, he unearths one of his jumpers from his bedroom laundry hamper and strips the sheets from his bed. After folding the jumper and sheets into Dundee's basket he lies beside him, in the dirt, and rests his hand gently against Dundee's neck, scratching him beneath the collar. 'I've got your back, mate. I'm home now.'

The cut on Dundee's lip will heal. He still cowers under the washing line when he hears Barnaby inside the house. But he's a different dog to what he was last June. Having a routine has calmed him. His eyes are bright. He has energy again. But he needs a place to live where he can run around like dogs his size are supposed to.

The next morning, after breakfast, Jason makes an appointment with the vet for the following Friday and sets to work on a flyer. In the afternoon he attaches it to each of the community noticeboards at the

CES, the YMCA and the Collingwood library. 'Room wanted—21yo male bartender and his dog, adult male labrador, well trained. Am willing to pay up to $100 p/w. Call Jason.'

According to the street directory at the service station there's a good stretch of beach between Mordialloc and Chelsea. It takes them an hour to reach it by train. At the beachhead he takes off the lead. Dundee's paws leave craters in the sand as he bolts to the shoreline.

'Hold on, mate. I'm coming.' The ocean's horizon is silver. There's so much more light here, like there used to be in the mornings up north. Jason sets down his towel and sports bag, takes off his thongs and tracks Dundee's pawprints to the water as Dundee nips at the incoming waves. 'Where's the ball, mate? Where's the ball?' Knee-deep, he skims the tennis ball across the open stretch of water. Dundee collapses into a paddle, his ears arrowing back. This is what he must have been like when he was a puppy. 'Back here, dummy. That's it. Good boy.'

After lunch, they lie together in the shade of the grass parkland behind the beachhead. The salt-matted fur on Dundee's belly and back is clumped with sand, but at least he's finished throwing up seawater. Jason strokes his ear, keeping an eye on the four girls settling and undressing beneath the tree alongside them. Dundee sighs. He'll never be a people dog, not like Maddox's kelpie, Tagger, who can't wait to get on the ground with them after training and chase the ball. But it's not his fault he got lumped with the life he did.

. . .

By the midpoint of the season the Redbacks have won six of their eleven games. It's not much of a return after the pre-season they've put in. Their problems are clear: they need more talls on the backline, a forward who can kick straight, some speed in the middle. And they need a coach like Arnie, Jason reckons quietly. Arnie had a way of making every player feel gifted, even the ones who weren't. He made it a class-room as well as a sport.

Before their training session the following Tuesday Maddox demands they grade their performances from the previous Saturday on the blackboard in the club change rooms: their hard yards, their one percenters, their teamwork. Afterwards, he scratches his own grades beside each of their names in blue chalk. 'Commitment,' he summarises. In his rain jacket and ancient sneakers, he's easy to dislike. 'It's not complicated, all right? You get in there, you chase, you back up your mates. Right? So you'd better get out on the bloody track and show it to us.'

When the session's over, Jason sits on the sheltered concrete step outside the clubhouse and cuts the mud from his boots. Unscrewing and rescrewing the stops, he can smell his old flat in Hawthorn and remembers again the pipes clanging in the ceiling and the sounds of his mum getting ready for work. What would the teenager he'd been think of him now? he wonders. What could he say to his teenage self that would be comforting and not a lie?

Walking Dundee home from his follow-up appointment with the vet the next morning, Jason checks his account balance at the ATM. After the consultation fee, his balance is one-third what it was. They pass the Collingwood library and he ties Dundee to one of the bike rails out front. 'Two seconds, mate.' Inside, he checks the community noticeboard. No more stubs have been torn from his flyer, but next to it, hidden beneath promotions for meditation classes and rotary clubs, is a 'for lease' ad: room for rent in a two-bedroom flat in North Carlton, $260 per month, contact Erin Daniels.

He calls her as soon as he gets home and arranges an interview for the afternoon.

At four o'clock he gets off the tram outside the Carlton cemetery, not far from where Dean Bennett's secret parking space used to be.

For a moment he can see himself and Hayden scrapping for the ball alongside the cemetery fence. He crosses Lygon Street to a bluestone laneway that should lead to the address Erin gave him. Behind him, the knuckled city horizon looks more open than it does in Collingwood.

Erin's flat is on the third and highest storey of a tea-coloured building that dwarfs the brick and slate houses on either side of it. From its communal balcony he can see the dividing lines of the neighbours' fruit and vegetable gardens and their sagging sheds.

The deadlock on her front door unlatches. 'Hello!' She's a pale girl his age with short brown hair and a smile that makes her a lot prettier. Her slippers are as big as gumboots. 'It's freezing out there—quick, quick.'

'Thanks for letting me come so soon.'

'I was supposed to be at uni.'

'Yeah? I'm supposed to be at work.'

'Wednesdays, right? There should be a law against them.'

The room for rent is bigger than he'd expected, and there's a working power point in the corner. Apart from that, he doesn't know what else to look for. The only heating she has is the reflective electric panel in her lounge room, and her long tiger-striped tabby is absorbing most of it. She scoops the cat from the carpet and droops it over her shoulder. 'So what're you like to live with?'

'Pretty cool,' he says, trying to keep his hands out of his jacket pockets. 'I'm a bartender. That's not my career. But it pays the bills and that.'

'Cool,' she says, and then, 'I don't know how to do this. This interviewing thing. I mean, if you like the room, great. But you don't have to make up your mind now. Have a think about it, I'll think about it, I'll give you a call.'

'Sure.'

She looks worried. 'Did I just fuck that up?'

'No. Why?'

'I feel like I just fucked that up. Like I'm listening to myself and I'm thinking, "Christ, way to sound like a bitch, Erin." It's just in my head, though, isn't it?'

'No, you were fine. What's your cat's name?'

'Napoleon,' she says grandly.

He scratches Napoleon's neck, feeling the tiny motor in his throat. 'Napoleon's a funny name.'

'I thought it would be good to give him a name to live up to.' She cradles Napoleon in the crook of her arm. 'And you did, didn't you? Yes, you did.' Napoleon purrs indolently beneath her tickling fingers.

'It's a good room, I reckon.'

'Oh yeah. That's a question I should've asked you. What else do I need to ask that I've forgotten?'

'I have a dog.' He realises that his hands are in his pockets and takes them out. 'He's a labrador. Dundee. Well, technically he's not my dog, but I look after him.'

'Ah.' Erin casts a guilty glance at Napoleon. 'We're not supposed to have any pets. The landlord doesn't even know about this guy.'

Jason nods, crestfallen. She's right, it's a small flat, and there's not much of a yard out front. Dundee would have to spend all day tied up again. The thought doesn't sit well with him. 'That's okay, I can probably figure something else out. As I say, he's not really my dog.'

Erin's apologetic look somehow makes it worse.

'So what do you do?' he offers.

'I work at the Twin in the city.'

'The little cinema?'

'Yeah, the black tee-shirt crowd.'

'Metallica?'

Her grin is real. 'No, the other one—Jim Jarmusch.' She opens the door for him. 'Degenerate art fags.'

'I think I'm more of an *Alien 3* man.'

'You should hear my bloody cinema studies lecturer going on about Sigourney.'

'She looks like some of the blokes I play footy with, actually. She'd fit right in.'

She laughs. 'See you, Jason.'

'Cheers, Erin. It was nice meeting you too, Napoleon.'

At the front of the driveway he looks up at the white railing of Erin's empty balcony and its backdrop of dank sky. It hadn't been the usual charade. He dwells forlornly on Dundee. What chance is there that anyone will want to share a place with a stray man and his dog? Instead of going home the way he came he follows her street in the direction of the city. Terrace housefronts gape at him above tiny yards. Most of the porches have couches on them and one has prayer flags strung above it. A student district: this is where Daphne would be living now if she'd stayed.

Two messages are blinking on the answering machine when he gets home. He presses play. 'Jason, it's me,' his mum says. 'You wouldn't believe it, but the tap in the shower's—' He skips ahead. The second message is from Erin. 'Hey, Jason. I know you only came by this arvo, but I figured, you know, you seem like a good guy. So if you want the room, you've got it. Give me a call and let me know.'

Dundee yaps in the yard at the sound of him in the kitchen. After assaulting him with licks on the back step, the dog stands obediently for his leash to be attached. Jason hugs him, heavy-hearted. He's a regular dog now. He could live with other people. He just needs someone to trust him.

. . .

The following Saturday night is Storm nightclub's fifth-birthday party: two-dollar shots till midnight, a live performance by Ratcat, girls drink for free. Two of his teammates, Sheff and Mirrors, have turned twenty-one. Knocking back another of their invites would be an insult.

By one in the morning the club's two extended dance floors are full. Some of his teammates have already pulled and have slunk off with their partners to the walls. Tequila rings in his head as lasers scissor the crowd. The girls on the dance floors are wearing more clothes than they do up north, but their sweat says the drugs are the same.

'Dalts!'

'Huh?'

It's Hose. 'You're up.'

Behind the dry ice he finds the remaining Redbacks at the bar. A bottle-blonde on autopilot measures shots of tequila into the seven glasses before them. Jason taps his shot with McKee, whose swollen cheek from the day's game is starting to colour. The tequila goes down hard. He reaches for his wallet but one of them has already paid.

'You and that bloke on the flank,' Mirrors says. 'The wing-nut.'

'Shown you the bruises?' Jason lifts up his shirt.

'Just a couple of love bites, mate. You should've had a crack.'

'Sheff was a step ahead of me.'

'That's right, the mad bastard. Where is he?'

He follows Mirrors through the throb and flicker back onto the dance floor. The room rolls temporarily but he blinks away the worst of it. Better take it easy. Girls in iridescent bras appear through the dry ice falling on either side of him, too young to be there.

Sheff is standing by the podium. 'Fire up, Dalts.'

'Where's your woman tonight, mate?'

'Blush, I reckon,' laughs Sheff.

'Hey?'

Sheff's arm reaches around him like a tail. 'Mate, you should've spoken up. We would've got you there earlier.'

'I'm up for whatever.'

'Let's get Mirrors then. Mirrors! Dalts is up.'

Jason follows Sheff to the exit and past the ponytailed bouncer on the door. Outside, the city air scrapes his face. 'Where's the rest of us?' he says to the traffic.

'Get in the taxi, wombat.'

He tumbles into the back of a silvertop, Sheff behind him.

Mirrors rights himself in the front seat. 'Rose Street, Fitzroy, mate. What's your name? Oh, it says here. Rahid. Hey, boys, this is Rahid.'

'Rahid!'

The city's northern bank rises around them, first the Victoria Market sheds and then the university alongside the parade. Jason spots a booze bus parked next to the Carlton cemetery, not far from Erin's place, and winds down the window to get some fresh air. 'I'm not having a spew. Don't worry.'

'You and that redhead, Sheff,' Mirrors says. 'You know the one.'

'Mate, I'm coming in off a run-up.'

Soon they're on a dim footpath somewhere off Brunswick Street. The taxi can't get away fast enough. No streetlamps, just lights on in the upper storeys of warehouses. Sheff and Mirrors are already vaulting the steps of a terrace house with tinted windows.

A woman, middle-aged and Russian-sounding, shows them inside. The hallway has the same kind of staircase on one side as some of the sharehouses he'd inspected. But the bedrooms have numbers on them. Another guest, a young Indian man in a neat shirt and pants, is waiting on a seat by the wall. A girl in a white slip and suspenders wisps past. Too late, Jason realises the Russian woman who showed them in is saying something. '. . . she take you upstairs.'

He feels for his wallet.

'No, after. She will tell you.'

Compared to Storm, the house is as quiet as a doctor's clinic. He leans against the wall alongside the reception desk at the end of the hallway. The ringing in his ears gets louder.

'Dalts,' Sheff says. 'Can you get it up, mate? Hang in there, old fella.'

Soon a curvy girl in a black slip appears from behind a closed door. Her face is so well made-up it seems to float. She holds out her hand to him, her smile warm and heavy. 'I'm Kendra. How are you?'

'I'm Darren,' he says.

'You look like you've been having fun.'

'At a club, yeah.'

'Dancing?'

'That's it.'

'Would you like me to dance for you upstairs?'

He almost trips on the final three steps but Kendra helps him keep his balance. The second-floor hallway is darker than the first and smells of incense. She leads him to the furthest numbered room, a bedroom with a shower and spa bath in one corner. She passes him a towel from the bed. 'I can help you undress.'

'No.'

She lets herself out. After showering, he waits for her on the bed, the towel around his waist. When she comes back she climbs onto the mattress and straddles him easily. 'What do you like?'

'I don't know.'

She kisses him on the neck. There's no tension in her. He can smell scent in dabs along her arms and breasts. With one hand she unhooks his towel. She holds her other palm against his face and tugs down her underwear. Her breasts fall free of her slip and he kisses them, unable to close his eyes.

'I like your shoulders.' Her voice is soft in his ear.

Then he's inside her, this stranger, Kendra, her breath quickening but her hand still light on his cheek, her hips heaving forwards and her scent enveloping the smoke-and-beer tang still on his body.

A door slams outside. At the sudden noise he shudders and comes. For a second, with his eyes closed, she could be Daphne. Her elbows collapse and she smothers him. He holds his hands together in the middle of her back, using her body as a blanket. The smell of her hair pushes the loneliness from him.

'I can keep going. Do you want me to?'

He shakes his head, watching the ceiling, and for some time can't place himself. It feels like a memory already. But no, it's real—the brothel ceiling, the girl, the strange room. He's nineteen years old, it's almost August, and in December he'll be twenty. 'Kendra?'

'Yes?'

'How old are you?'

She seems to calculate. 'Twenty-one.'

He looks over her shoulder and down her body. 'This is the first time I've been in a place like this.' Her skin is so soft, like Daphne's had been. When he finds his voice again it comes out staggered. 'Can I say something?'

'Okay.'

'My mum was raped.'

She looks at him, nodding—she's younger than twenty-one. 'Okay.'

'It's how she got pregnant with me.'

'Okay.'

He tucks his head into her neck. She draws him closer, her body so calm and loose. He folds his hands into the slip now bunched around her waist, their legs entwined and one of her hands still on his cheek. It feels good to have said the words out loud, to have survived them, though his pulse is still thrumming at their fading presence in the room. Soon their time will be up.

. . .

Barnaby's temper is getting worse. In their rubbish bin at home are his empty packets of Panadeine Forte. No wonder he's a black hole on the couch every night. But so many girls leave messages for him on the answering machine. It's like there are two of him—one out there, at work and at the casino with his mates, and one here.

The morning after Kendra, Jason wakes to Dundee's whine in the hallway and jumps from his bed. Too late. Barnaby is already dragging Dundee by the neck through the kitchen.

'Barnaby!'

Dundee rears and trips against the strength of Barnaby's hand. He must have bolted inside in anticipation of his walk. Barnaby loses one slipper kicking him back into the yard. 'He's pissed on the kitchen floor, idiot.'

'You don't know a damn thing about looking after dogs, Barnaby.'

'He was doing fine before you showed up.'

'Right, when your solution was an old rope and some tin stuck together.'

'Fix it.' Barnaby drops a sponge on the puddle at his feet.

Through the kitchen window Jason watches Dundee moping around the backyard. The prospect of leaving him in Barnaby's hands puts a stone in his throat. Things will only go back to the way they were.

Shifting his belongings into Erin's flat on the fifth of August takes half a morning. His clothes fit into a single garbage bag, his mattress on the back of Sheff's ute. The wardrobe he leaves for Barnaby's next housemate, along with the ash on the couch and the month's stubbies around the bin.

The beach at Edithvale is empty when he and Dundee arrive, and the ocean is ink past the buoys. No girls today, just an elderly lady walking an alsatian along the beachhead. He holds Dundee by the collar until she and her dog have climbed the shrubby trail behind the lifesaving club and disappeared, then lets him go. In his backpack are

Dundee's things: his tennis ball, his biscuits, his vaccination papers. The kennel's re-homing program had sounded good. Their criteria had been reassuring. Maybe a uni student will want him, or someone who has a bigger house and a proper backyard. He leaves his shoes on the cold sand and tracks Dundee to the water. 'Come on, mate. Race you.' Dundee looks up from the cuttlefish he's found and streaks through the water between them, his face bright above the splash of his paws. He barks happily at the waves. One chance is all he'll need.

9. full-forward

The Redbacks finish the 1992 season in eighth place on the EDFL ladder, three wins from a spot in the finals. It's an improvement on their previous season, but Jason is surprised at the relief he feels coming home from their last match. He can look to the end of spring and the long stretch of summer, the nights he can fill with work and the days he can spend hanging out with Erin.

Each morning of spring he strolls the two blossoming kilometres from his and Erin's apartment to the Carlton Gardens on the northern lip of the city or to the commission flats at the top end of Brunswick Street. More shops seem to be open than in winter, and the local coffee drinkers have spread onto the footpaths. There are so many places to roam. It's a greener neighbourhood than Collingwood, and friendlier. By the time he gets home and Erin is through her morning coffee, the day feels well spent.

He thinks she's too smart to wind up a teacher like she says she will. There are metres of fat serious-sounding books on her shelves—*The Manufacture of Consent*, *The Apartheid Reader*. It would take him five years of reading every day just to finish them all. But then, he figures, maybe if he'd had a teacher with her personality, high school would have been more interesting.

On her bedroom wall is a map of the world colour-coded with pins—red for the places she's been, white for the places she wants to go. Between Australia, New Zealand and South-East Asia are six red pins. Most of the white pins are organised around northern Europe: Oslo, Helsinki, Copenhagen, Warsaw. After looking them up in his atlas he can see them in his mind, each a city in a snow globe.

'We should be Norwegian,' she tells him over coffee one morning. 'They tax fifty percent and everything's free. School, uni, dental, transport—everything, mate. That's what Australia would be like if we were a proper socialist democracy like Whitlam was aiming for, instead of this economic-rationalism crap. Which I don't care what they say, it doesn't bloody work.'

Her balcony ashtray is a leftover takeaway noodle box. There must be two hundred butts in it already. Her boots tap restlessly against the edge of the railing while she talks. My caffeine beat, she calls it, though she does the same thing when she's smoking.

'So where you headed first, mate?' she asks, as if her world map and pins are the usual thing to have in your room. 'Tell us your list.'

'I haven't got a list,' he says.

'Rubbish. Where do you want to go?'

'Too many places. I can't decide.' He tries to think of something he's done that's more interesting than getting drunk and stoned on the Gold Coast. 'Maybe I should.'

She cooks with ingredients from strange sections of the supermarket: chickpeas and lentils, coconut milk, pita and pesto. In fifteen minutes she can turn three vegetables and spice into a meal that will feed her for three days. Together they munch bowls of it in front of the ABC news, talking back at the commentators and anchormen. Watching news grabs of the upcoming US presidential elections, he feels as if he should have something to say. But it's always easier to wait for her to go first and figure out what line to follow from there.

'Where'd you grow up?' she asks him.

'Hawthorn.'

'South side.' She raises her eyebrows. 'Lah-di-dah.'

She keeps her car, a rusting VW, wedged along one side of a local lane without parking signs. The back seat is as hopelessly scattered with stuff as her bedroom floor. The dashboard has no glovebox and he has to mind her cigarettes and water bottle between his knees. Ophelia, she calls the car, though to him it seems more like an old man than a rich-sounding girl.

Her favourite hangout is a live music café—the Cosmopolitan—only five minutes' drive from their flat, between a continental grocer and a locked-up supply store on Brunswick Street. She always changes into buckled shoes and vintage dresses before she goes, as if one of the local student photographers might suddenly ask to take her picture.

As they weave through the crowd inside he finds it hard not to feel self-conscious about what his jeans and surfwear tee-shirts are saying about him. The other men all seem to know the waitresses or have girlfriends just like them. If Erin wasn't there, he'd probably stick with pizza and Coke at the souvlaki shop across the street.

It's funny how easily words come with her, as if their conversations are never finished but only paused for a few minutes or hours, and then rejoined. 'I once lived with a bloke who was music-mad, when I was on the Gold Coast,' he tells her. 'This bloke Joonie, he spent half the year trying to convince me The Pixies were the greatest thing to happen since The Beatles.'

'Guys and bands.'

'It was like a religion for him, like I was about Metallica for a while.'

'I feel sorry for your deprived childhood. Let me guess—you had pictures of naked girls on your wall.'

'Like you didn't have guys on your wall.'

'Yeah, but I didn't masturbate about them. I know about you boys—I have a younger brother. They should put all of you on an island and leave you there.'

Boredom suits her, somehow. The way her voice gets when she's talking about her sleeping patterns and the condition of her fingernails, the way she can flick through a street press at the same time as listen to him. He can't imagine her ever chasing a ball around as a kid. It sounds as if she spent all her time in front of her VCR and the newspaper, waiting to be a grown-up.

'When's your birthday?' she asks him.

'December sixth. You're not going to star-sign me, are you?'

'I'm just trying to get a handle. You don't talk much about where you're from.' She can do a look, sometimes, as if she's waiting for him to catch up on a joke he's missed. 'How'd you do at school?'

'Next question.'

'Don't be a clam. It's boring.'

'What can I say? I dropped out and smoked pot.'

'Okay, but why?'

'Why does anyone do anything?'

'You're impossible. So what am I getting you for your birthday?'

'I don't know. Nothing.'

'You're turning twenty, for Christ's sake.'

'Okay. Driving lessons.'

'Great. I'm off my P-plates January fourth. And show me some photos sometime. I want to see what you looked like before me.'

. . .

On the night of his birthday he sits down with her in their lounge room with the bottle of good vodka she's bought him and her three shoeboxes of photos. When she said they could spend the night going through them, she was right: there must be more than three hundred altogether, from her soup-making class in primary school to travel photos with her two best friends, Polly and Luce. She had blonde hair when she was a kid. Between eight and thirteen the shade of her hair darkens and she expands. Then sometime in later high school—Year Ten, it looks like— streaks appear in her hair and she becomes the girl he knows.

'Hi, Jason,' his mum says into their machine. 'Are you there? No? Okay. Happy birthday! I got your message—I hope the place in Carlton is going well. One thing, um, I was hoping to speak to you in person. I've got some trouble with my taps up here and I remember, one time, you knew how to fix them. I have some screwdrivers here and I thought . . . well, if you want to give me a call. Bye.'

By three o'clock the following Tuesday the December sun is high in Belgrave and the tradies' utes have vacated his mum's street for the day. Leaves and sticks have blown from the neighbourhood yards onto the footpath. His footsteps crackle. Anyone could hear him from a block away. But her car's not in her driveway, as he expected. The carnations in her window have been changed for fresh ones and she's bought a stand for her plants on the porch.

He has bike oil and a shifting spanner from the hardware shop above the station. After grabbing the spare key from under the pot plant he lets himself in and inspects each of the taps in the kitchen, bathroom and laundry. What was it Arnie had said? It comes to him quickly. Funny how he can remember a five-minute phone conversation from three years ago about plumbing as if it was something he had studied.

Each of the taps takes only twenty minutes to fix. Being there seems strange; he feels like an intruder, reminded of the hostility he'd felt in their Hawthorn flat in the months after the Falcons' grand final. He battles through it. Afterwards, he oils the hinges on her screen door. The rosebush in her backyard looks a lot better, but the creeper has taken over the porch roof. He stands in front of it with his jumper around his waist, planning it out. A three-hour job, at least, and then he'd have to bag it all. There's not enough time.

After putting his things back in his bag he gets a juice from the fridge. One of his high school photos is under a flower magnet stuck to the lower door. In it he's a skinny, put-upon kid with a messy part in his hair. His smile is half-concealed, his ears more normal than he had thought. Year Nine—Darren's parties, working in Arnie's garden, exercising in his room, graffiti. Not long before his raging started.

He recalls his promise to Erin to show her his family photo album and goes to his mum's room. She has enough space now for her things to fit—her knitting boxes, her collection of magazines, her old LPs and the broken record player she refuses to give away. Their photo album isn't under her bed where she used to keep it. He finds it, finally, in the neatened bottom drawer of her bureau, beside an A4 exercise book and a new manila folder labelled BILLS 1992.

Sitting cross-legged, he leafs through the opening pages of the album. The photos' repetition is jarring—Christmas, school and birthday, again and again, with few signs of their lives in between. His stomach aches as each photo triggers memories of the forlorn and lonely kid of those years. He had a way of standing, he realises, that was just like her.

The exercise book beside the album in the drawer looks as old as one of his primary school books. Maybe she held onto one of them and he hadn't known. Its first few blank pages smell of their old flat. Twenty or so pages in, she has pasted two cut-out listings from a newspaper. The dates penned above each one are different, except for the year: 1975, when he was three years old.

JOHNSON-TATE: The marriage of Allan Johnson
and Susan Tate will be celebrated at Blacktown on
Saturday, 16 April at 3 pm.

McDONALD (Wilson): Lauren and Ben have much pleasure in announcing the birth of Renee Louise, at Echuca District Hospital on 23 June.

Three more listings have been attached to the pages that follow. Each cut-out has yellowed. He reads them slowly. The first is the birth of a boy, Jonathan Fraser, on August ninth at the same hospital. The second is a memoriam notice for Arthur Harwood—died 15-2-75—from Penny, Chris and family. The third is an engagement notice from a Mr and Mrs Buxton, Echuca, on behalf of their daughter, Carmel. Different dates again, but the same year. He would have been in day care at the time.

Every few pages another notice appears—for Simone and Luke Adams; for Bridie and Clark Hanlon; in memory of Esther O'Connor; for the birth of Duncan Graham—and in the book's final pages are two folded newspaper photographs. He unfolds them carefully. One carries a photo of a twenty-year-old girl, Joyce Devine, returning home from a Rotary-sponsored exchange to Italy. The second is even simpler: 'Down Come the Decorations', reads the caption beneath a photo of three nurses, also his age, taking down a hospital Christmas tree—January fourth, 1977.

Where could she have got them from? He stares at them, waiting to understand. She'd never been back—he was certain of it.

After returning the exercise book to its place, he carries the photo album downstairs and puts it in his bag, the image of each notice and their neat placement in the book scratching at his mind.

By quarter to four, local schoolkids are swarming over the two plat-forms of the train station. Watching them from across the street, he feels old enough to be one of their teachers. The payphone on the cor-ner takes change and he slides a dollar into the slot. 'Mum, it's me,' he says when her answering machine clicks on. 'I had some time spare to fix those taps. But I couldn't stick around—I had something on. Listen, you really need to get a guy in about that creeper, otherwise it's gonna wreck your roof.'

She'd never mentioned her friends in Echuca by name. His dad had driven her from all of them. That's how much he'd hurt her. Had she called them? When had she stopped? Maybe she'd started feeling the same way as he'd felt last time around Darren and the crew, that she'd become an outsider to them.

At home, to escape the oven heat of the apartment, he plugs Erin's good earphones into his Walkman and wears them to bed. The dirty crashing sounds of his American albums replace his thoughts and carry him to sleep. Nirvana, Soundgarden, The Pixies, The Smashing Pumpkins—Erin calls it fuck-you music but he can't explain to her the peace it gives him, or the strength. Without them he'd only toss and turn.

Between sessions in the gym and his work behind the bar he scrubs their bathtub and the bathroom floor. He vacuums the lounge room, wipes down the skirting boards and takes out the garbage. He cooks and freezes his meals for the beginning of the new week: pasta bake, spaghetti sauce, vegetable soup, red curry.

'You're unbelievable,' Erin tells him, marvelling at the apartment's condition. 'I want to put you in a bottle and sell you to my friends.'

He shrugs. 'Keeps me busy.'

'Jase, I'm telling you. There's chicks who'd crawl for miles to find a man who does all this.'

Two nights before Christmas, he lies awake in his bed listening to his Walkman while she sits in the kitchen and wraps presents for her family. In the morning she'll drive down the Calder Freeway to stay with them. She's as guarded about them as she is about her relationships with guys. What would she do if she found out about his night with Kendra? She would probably stop speaking to him, he decides. There are too many things that wouldn't come out right: his mum, the letter in his bag, the thing with Daphne. She'd think he was a mess, or a woman-hater, or something worse.

He arranges to drive with her to pre-season training on Tuesday and Thursday nights. Getting the VW out of the laneway and circling the broad nature strips in the streets around the cemetery is easy. But on the main roads out of the city, it feels as if any of the passing four-wheel drives could flatten them. 'The engine tells you when to change gears,' she instructs. 'Don't go any higher than third unless I tell you.'

'Sounds right.'

'How are your nerves?'

'What nerves?'

'Clever.'

From their flat to the ground is a ten-minute drive. By the time he pulls into the car park, releases the clutch and has turned off the engine, his legs are stuck to the seat and he has to wipe down the steering wheel with his training towel. Parked beside his teammates' sedans and utes, the VW looks lost. 'I'll have to drive you down to Hawthorn,' he tells her. 'Show you where I grew up.'

'One day.' She can wink like a TV starlet. 'We'll have to get you into fourth for that.'

In the change rooms he sits on the cool, smooth concrete floor and listens to his music. His teammates arrive in ones and twos, some in suits and the rest in shorts and tee-shirts. Most have a private pre-session ritual that's easy to spot: Freo's singing, Cole's hand washing, Tank's hunched stare, Mirrors' stretches. Jason remains alone where he is until his tape finishes and then he stands, ready to join them outside.

Each session of pre-season starts at six pm and finishes before dusk. They lap the cordoned-off cricket pitch and use witches hats for goal-posts. The sun is still bright enough for the Velcros to have to rub sunscreen into their scalps. Some new faces have appeared on the team but the core is the same: Mirrors, Freo, Cole, Sasha, Hatto, D.C.,

Shwatta, Tank and the Velcros. Storm would be going broke without them. Local die-hards gather around the boundary line with their eskies and camp chairs to watch the squad play while the sun sets over their heads. One has a dog, a ropey dalmatian with ears that flop over its eyes. Its barks and yips are Dundee's, only cleaner. Hearing it, Jason replays Dundee's expression as he stampeded across the backyard to him each night. When he gets home, the apartment feels quieter than it usually is.

On Thursday nights they eat for half-price at Bertolucci's, a club sponsor at the terminus end of Nicholson Street. Enough of his teammates drive to get everyone there. All of the tables are plastic and there are fake vines hanging along the walls, but the owner's waitressing daughters are both gorgeous. For two hours, their pot glasses are never empty.

'Who's your woman?' McKee asks him.

'Forget it. That's my housemate.'

'You telling me or are you telling you?'

'We're mates.'

'Bring her up for a beer then. I want to meet her.'

'It's not her kind of place.'

After the Cosmopolitan's moody lamplight and sunken couches, Bertolucci's is as bright as a fast-food store. The tablecloths are vinyl and the owner plays birthday music on request. Erin wouldn't rate it— no way. She'd have a word for it that he hadn't heard before. But it would be fun to see her with them, trading insults with McKee and Cole over a stubby.

Rolling home afterwards, it occurs to him that her little put-downs could mean something more. She's so quick to put the boot in about Metallica, the *Terminator* movies, his travel plans. That challenge in her voice, the same as Daphne's: you've got me, but you'll have to work for it.

...

The 1993 season is going to be about playing football the Redbacks way, Maddox has told them. After the pre-season's last training session he points out the premierships in the clubhouse trophy cabinet and team photos alongside them. Jason studies the faces in the 1972 team, their shaggy heads and buckled teeth. Is that what his dad had looked like? The players in the most recent photo, 1978, would be Arnie's age by now. You're part of something bigger here, Maddox tells them. Think about who you represent.

At the end of their first game, against the Moreland Tigers at home, they form a huddle on the clubhouse wing and raise their voices one more time. It could have gone against them, especially after McKee went down, but in the final quarter they'd found something more. They slap each other's chests, they rub each other's heads. To their left, the old black and white scoreboard shows the result: 87 to 72 in their favour. A memorable win, though they wouldn't have expected it at half-time.

A dozen of their supporters have clustered at the players' gate to clap them off the ground: mums and dads, some with cameras, hollering their sons' names. The team walks in single file onto the concrete and through to the change rooms. Maddox's expression is a reminder that there are still seventeen games to go.

McKee is getting his corked thigh dressed in the change rooms with an ice pack almost as thick as his thigh. Only Megan, the volunteer physio, is taking an interest in him. When she's done, McKee stares at the ceiling, alone. Jason hoists himself onto the heavy bench beside him. Sometimes it seems the only team spirit among his teammates is in the bar upstairs, he reckons. 'How you getting home, mate?'

'The Mazda.'

'Don't be stupid. Let me get myself right, I'll drive you.'

With his arm around McKee's waist he helps him to the door. McKee's car is behind the roadside goals, a new blue Mazda sedan.

Jason opens the passenger door and clears the paper trash from the back seat so McKee has room to lie down.

'Since when did you have your licence?' McKee asks him.

'You've seen me behind the wheel.'

'Yeah—in that bloody rustbucket. This is a real car.'

'It's good practice. Where's home?'

'Oh, bloody hell. Elling Street, Princes Hill. Number fifty-eight.'

'Just off Carlton cemetery.'

'That's where I'll put you if you scratch it.'

The Mazda's gear stick slides easily under his hand. Driving is more relaxing without his L-plates on the windows. Down Nicholson Street he stays in third, but there's no jolt between gears as there is in Erin's car. 'I have to get one of these.'

'It wouldn't suit you,' McKee says. 'Too much under the hood.'

'So what do you see me driving?'

'A tram.'

'Clever.'

Fifty-eight Elling Street is a block from Princes Park. Jason boots the shell of a soccer ball from the path inside the front gate to keep McKee from tripping over it. Before he can get the key in the door McKee's dad opens it, a ginger-haired man with no eyebrows. 'Cripes, what's this?'

'Special delivery,' Jason says.

The bike-cluttered hallway ends with a stained-glass door and there are Bob Dylan LP covers lining one wall. Together, they step McKee into his bedroom.

'Thanks, Jason,' McKee's dad says in the hallway. 'The one bloody game I miss.'

'The ambos had a look at him at the ground. He seems pretty clear.'

'You a nurse, are you?'

'Bartender.'

'I'm Ryan, by the way.' They shake hands. 'So how did you boys go today? Give us the rundown.'

The pair of them seem less like father and son and more like brothers. They have the same way of smiling when they're not talking, of saying 'me' instead of 'my', like one of the older men at the Arms. 'Want some grub?' Ryan says. 'I was about to put on some sausages.'

'Thanks, but I'm cooking with my housemate tonight. We've got a tradition.'

'Let me give you a lift.' Ryan disappears into his son's room and comes out with the car keys. So they share the Mazda. Following Ryan to the door, Jason imagines them working together on meals, doing the laundry, watching the replay on TV. Envy stirs in him.

Ryan's place to the flat is a three-minute drive. Sitting in the passenger seat he wishes he still had the car under his hands. 'What do you do?' he asks Ryan.

'I manage a backpackers in the city, on Lonsdale Street. Which pub are you at?'

'You know the Brunswick Arms?'

Ryan laughs. 'The Army. Bit of an old man pub.'

'I'm back there tomorrow night,' Jason says. 'Whoopee.'

'Well, we've got a couple of jobs going at reception. You ought to send us your résumé. It's a good little place, as long as you can handle the Poms. Central Backpackers. Just make sure you print it up nice and stick it in a folder. Some of these jokers we get applications from, it makes you wonder how they finished school.'

Jason hoists his bag onto his lap as Ryan brings the car to a gentle halt in front of his apartment building. Outside, he returns Ryan's salute through the passenger window and watches the Mazda glide away. They're good people.

At the letterbox he stops. A thin fancy envelope is poking from their slot. He must have missed it earlier. A fine hand has looped his name below the single stamp. Inside he finds a perfumed card dripping flower petals. Arnold Singer and Tamara Shultz are to be married in September and Jason Dalton is cordially invited. 'Arnie,' he grins. 'Bugger me.'

At the Brunswick Arms that night Erin roams among the Redbacks memorabilia mounted on the walls, clicking her tongue. In her scarf and boots she has a liveliness that doesn't match the rest of the pub. The Nick Cave songs she plays on the jukebox are nothing like the Beatles and Kinks mix tapes she has stacked in columns around her vanity mirror: death row growls and murder lust, a soundtrack for the neighbourhood's sinking cottages. But this is pub Erin, not home Erin. Joking about it would ruin her performance.

He's seen Army punters try it on with her before, older guys who look at her as if she's the brightest thing in the room. Usually she handles them fine and they go away. But they're good at it, some of them, better than he is, and in the time it takes to smoke half a cigarette they can make her blush.

'I hate clubs,' she tells him on his dinner break. 'Nightclubs, sports clubs, lawn bowls, all of it. It's just an excuse for those buggers to go home drunk to their families.'

'They need a place to go,' he says.

'What—their families aren't good enough?'

'You don't know that.'

'I know,' she says.

Later, when she's left to meet her friends on Smith Street, he wonders what else she might have told him if he'd asked. Her parents' voices have never appeared on the answering machine, and she's spoken of them even less than he's spoken of his mum. Maybe she wanted him to ask.

He shakes hands with the remaining Army punters at the end of his shift, older guys with gnarly tattoos on their forearms who've lived in the area since before he was born. What secrets are they hiding? He imagines his dad in Echuca among the regulars for last drinks, a club hero, sharing his glory days.

. . .

The Central Backpackers hostel is only two streets from the Twin, its three brown storeys nothing like the palm-treed hostels he'd stayed in up north. Before his interview he tours the dorms. The third-floor balcony at the back of the building overlooks a city he doesn't know: tenement staircases and mysterious lofts, large fans turning on the tops of buildings.

'I've been working in pubs since I finished school,' he tells his interviewers. 'I'd call myself a people person. And I'm really interested in other cultures—I've got a map of the world on my bedroom wall at home where I've stuck pins on all the places I want to go. Copenhagen's next.'

He starts the following Monday at seven am, catching a quiet tram down Lygon Street in the pre-dawn cold. Fourteen bucks fifty an hour, full-time, with three weekends off a month. Guys his age come tramping through the door wearing arctic jackets from the New Zealand ski slopes and bum bags full of foreign money. They all want to see the things he never thinks of as Victoria, like the penguins at Phillip Island and the Great Ocean Road. So many Swedes, so many Poms, unshowered, grinning, carrying their lives on their backs. It's easy, they say. You want to go somewhere, you buy a ticket. If you plan any other way, you're kidding yourself.

Lunch breaks are half an hour, though nowhere on rumbling Lonsdale Street is a good place to relax. He takes his smoke breaks on the third-floor balcony, imagining his way across the city. What would it be like to pick up and go someplace else forever? It's strange to think how easily it could happen: one plane ticket, one bus, a job to get you started and there it would be, a new life waiting, your old life wiped away. Then he thinks of his mum staying in a hostel like his, a lone pregnant nineteen-year-old, in 1972, the strange city howling outside.

There's time at the end of his shifts to pop in and get a free ice cream from Erin at the Twin. At three o'clock the cinema is always deserted, and she has time for her Dead White Guys, as she calls them, in her university readers. When he reads their introductions, every paragraph is like a wall of cold air.

'I wish I was a bimbo,' she tells him. 'They're happier than I am. They don't have to think—they just do. They walk around, being hot, and the world falls over for them.'

There are girls who come through the hostel from the tropics and northern Europe who could be another species. They live in a world of complimentary drinks and taxi rides, and they clearly know their smiles and laughs are magic wands on guys like him. Erin has an edge on them, though, something punchy and funny and complicated.

'I'm a bimbo,' he replies. 'I haven't been to uni, I play football, I watch action movies. Compared to you and your friends.'

'You're lucky. Everyone at uni's cut off at the neck.' She assumes a perch on her chair, her knees to her chest, a position that reminds him of the winter girls in scarves and stockings he's seen in their local cafés. 'What good's smart, anyway? The more you learn, the angrier you get.'

'No, I should go back to school,' he says. 'I can only bullshit my way through interviews for so long.'

'I admire what you've done.'

'Why?'

'The way you keep getting up,' she says. 'This job, your last one, the stuff you do at home. I wish I had what you had. You just can't see yourself from the outside, that's all.'

'Neither can you.'

'Thank God.'

She could be better looking if she wanted. She could dress like she dresses at the Cosmopolitan all the time, instead of retreating into her bulky jumpers and slipper boots. She'd fit right in with the funked-up waitresses who every guy in the place wants to put his hands on, including him.

. . .

Arnie and Tamara's wedding is on the beach at Port Melbourne the day after the Redbacks' seventh win of the season. It marks the anniversary of when they first met in Phuket, according to the invitation. Arnold Singer and Tamara Shultz: Arnie and Tam.

After mixing with the other guests at the reception's buffet table he drifts onto the hotel's beachfront balcony. Across the parade, bike riders and rollerbladers are cruising the wall in front of the beach, Gold Coast style, and the calm bay water shows the places where the sunlight has broken through the clouds. Life feels bigger here.

'What did you think of the wedding?'

He turns to look at the woman who spoke to him. She's close to his age, but older, and is wearing a satin dress with a split to the thigh. An indie girl in disguise. 'This is my first.'

'You're a friend of Arnie's?'

'He used to be my coach.'

'Really?' Her interest seems genuine, not merely polite. 'The Hawthorn team.'

'Hawthorn City.'

'He'd be a good coach to have—especially for young guys. Inspiring.' Large eyes, freckles along her shoulders, a nice curve in the way she holds her arms across her chest. Where had she come from?

'Jason.' He frees his right hand from the cuff of his hired suit.

'Zoe.'

'You know Arnie?'

'I know Tam.' She leans closer, conspiratorially. 'She's just like Arnie.'

'Ah. Beer-drinking, pool-playing . . .'

'Table-dancing, Monty Python–loving . . .'

He laughs. 'You heard how they met?'

'That pub in Phuket. Romantic, isn't it?' There's something in the way she grins that makes him step closer. 'They were hungover for a week.'

'You've got the inside story.'

'I get all the dirt.'

He empties his beer, enjoying the girliness of her laugh, waiting for her boyfriend to show up. It's what always happens.

'So what else do you do, Jason, besides play football?'

'You first. I haven't got anything on you yet.'

'Media buyer.' She taps him on the shoulder with one finger, as if making sure of something. 'You still haven't answered my question.'

He shrugs. 'I haven't said g'day to Arnie yet. Do you want to—'

'You want to chaperone me?'

'That sounds like the right way to put it.'

In the function room, he finds her a glass of champagne. She seems used to guys getting drinks for her. Already she's talking to three other people. She's short, compared to Daphne, and laughs in a way that says she likes people. Chaperone. A word Daphne would have used, rolling her eyes.

Arnie and Tamara are seated by the window like mannequins in a store display. When Arnie sees him his face opens up and he stands. Boyishly, he overworks their handshake. 'Jase. You made it. How are you, big fella?'

'I had to be here, Arnie. Congratulations.'

Arnie's face is ruddy with excitement, his cheeks flushed and his neck thick in the collar of his tuxedo. 'Hey, Tam. Tam? You've got to meet this one. This is the kid I was telling you about.'

Tamara's smile is as wide as a hammock. 'He's not a kid anymore, bub.' Beside Arnie, she looks fairy-sized, and could be one, if it weren't for the glass of beer in her hand. She pokes Zoe's hip. 'Where'd you find him, Zo? I want one.'

Arnie makes a show of ignoring her. 'How's life, mate?'

'Good. Better. Got a place in Carlton, got the footy.'

'You've filled out.'

'Have I?'

'Dead set—you're an axe. We've got to play pool again, mate. Catch up.' He winks at Zoe like an embarrassing parent. 'And bring this one along. I've got some weeding for her to do, the windows, the gutters, the drains. You can talk her through it.'

Zoe kicks him in the foot, not softly.

'Ease up,' Tamara grins. 'My boy's got a big night ahead of him.'

Soon the guests begin pulling the tables and chairs back and forming a loose circle in the centre of the room. Jason follows Zoe to the edge of it. 'I love this part,' she says.

They stand aside for Arnie and Tamara, cheering. Some of the guests start to chant their names. Looking at each other's feet, Arnie and Tamara embrace as the music begins. It's an Elvis song, slow and partly spoken. Arnie and Tamara turn in soft rocking circles, their heads together. Soon older couples enter the circle, more sure-footed than the bride and groom.

Zoe leans back and Jason accidentally looks straight down her dress. 'You're sticking around, aren't you? I'll need someone to dance with.'

'Can I get another beer first?' he asks.

'No.'

'Okay.'

When he takes them her hands are damp. Then they're in the circle, moving, and he's holding her bare shoulder. Plenty of the other guests

are watching. Elvis finishes and more Elvis begins, still crooning. Arnie
and Tamara are not far away. He watches their steps for guidance.

. . .

'People who work in advertising are sharks,' Erin says to him over their
balcony coffee the next morning. 'How South Yarra is she?'

'Is that a fair question?'

'I'm just saying.'

'Because I play football and I don't have a degree—what? I should
stick with my own?'

'I'm not against you, Jase.'

'I'm into her, she's into me. Good for us.'

'Yes. Good for you.'

Zoe Ford. She could have chosen any guy in the room. That night,
lying in bed, he can still feel the weight of her body as she danced
against him. Dinner, she'd said, like he was an older guy. A woman he
normally would have been scared to look at in case she saw how much
he liked her. The strap of her dress falling off her shoulder as she danced
away from him. Having her hands on his shoulders had felt the same as
being in Kendra's arms at Blush, when the world, for a while, had been
safely outside.

On Wednesday night he catches a taxi past the MCG to South
Yarra. The bottle shop around the corner from Zoe's street clearly
caters for customers who ride in Mercedes, not trams. The only thing
he's sure about red wine is to avoid the stuff they used to serve at the
Arms. Her apartment building looks nothing like what he's used to:
white stone, bird baths, flowers and trees among the picture windows.
'Lah-di-dah', he says to himself, in Erin's voice.

'Hey, hey.' When she answers the door, she's still in her work clothes.
Water is boiling somewhere and the aroma of pasta sauce meets him two

steps inside. The apartment is small without feeling crowded: a couch, a chair, rugs and a television, a small square dinner table with a vase on it. House music is thrumming from the hi-fi system on her bookshelf and for one glorious second he can see her on a dance floor, in a tight singlet, the beats pulsing around her. This is what being twenty is supposed to be like.

'Sit down, I'll make you a drink.' She closes the door behind him.

10. full-back

'Hello, empty flat, it's me.' Erin's voice on the answering machine battles the buzz around her. 'Is Jason there, too? No? I'm at the Cosmopolitan, so . . . I'm just gonna leave a message on top of the two from his mum. Jase, come down, I'm in the window, give me someone to bug. You'd like it—they're playing Mudhoney. What else? Oh yeah, I was gonna catch up with you for your driving lesson last night, but no, you must've told me it wasn't on. I do that, don't I? Don't ever tell me anything in the morning. Christ, those first years look about fourteen. Anyway, I'm just hanging out here. You're still alive, aren't you? You should let me know.'

Each night in Zoe's apartment, when she's asleep, Jason listens to her snore, a deep drone that would make her blush if she was awake. He studies the pinprick moles behind her armpit, the freckles on her shoulders worn in from summers gone. To bed she wears the same slip she did on his first night in her apartment, when she wriggled out of its straps and rode him to the lounge-room floor. Strange, how the weeks since then have bled together around her. Even the Redbacks' season, now, is a mash of drills and lazy dinners with his teammates at Bertolucci's, of rainy matches and team meetings in the change rooms. Every memory he has of the past month seems to be of her. The door to her balcony rattles in its frame. He holds her to him, sheltering in her calmness.

Afternoons before going to her place stretch out like an elastic band refusing to snap. As soon as he arrives, they help each other out of their work clothes. 'You're impossible,' she says, while she still has breath to talk. Afterwards they eat naked, deep in the softness of her bed, until the traffic hushes and her balcony feels like a castle window looking down on the night. 'I pay through the arse for this place,' she tells him. 'But I can't handle other people's grot. I'd jump off the roof.'

Her wardrobes are her grandmother's, the bed a present from her father. A lace quilt, so many pillows, so many perfumes on her bureau. In the photos taped next to her media arts degree, her dad looks flattered to be standing beside her.

'Arnie was my first-ever boss,' he tells her. 'Every Sunday afternoon, I'd have a job at his place. Half his backyard's my work. Kept me in beer money and out of trouble.' Hearing himself ramble about high school, it doesn't come out as it actually was, which is good. It sounds full of adventure.

'I was a juvenile delinquent,' she says dramatically.

'Liar.'

'I got booted out of St Mary's. I know! Daddy's little princess.'

'I thought you were a state schooler like me.'

'I was, in the end. God, it was so much better.' She was a private school girl, all right: it's in the rhythm of her voice, the way she holds her glass. 'Now my St Mary's girlfriends are having engagement parties, and I get to corrupt them all over again.'

Weekend mornings he spends with her on Toorak Road and Chapel Street, following their reflection across the glass storefronts, Jason and Zoe, the couple. Flashy sports cars and four-wheel drives lounge at the kerbs. The skating rink has gone, he discovers. It's in the past. But so are Darren and Fish, and so are his Metallica tee-shirts, and so is Hawthorn.

'I want to get you something that shows off your shoulders,' she tells him. 'For when I let you out of my bed, I mean.'

'But then I'll look as if you dressed me.'

'I'm better than that.' With her hand inside his bomber jacket, she scratches his tee-shirt. 'Your wardrobe's hiding you away.'

The sales assistants in the men's boutiques seem to enjoy dressing him. He models jeans and a shirt for her. In a black coat he could be one of her co-workers. 'A-ha,' she says, holding up a tight pair of boxer shorts. 'I'll pay for these.'

'We should go out to dinner down here one night,' he tells her. 'With Arnie and Tam.'

'They're all *married* now.' She says the word as though she could fall asleep in the middle of it. 'Married couples are scary.'

'Arnie would be cool.'

'Maybe.' She reaches for his hand. 'But I like it better just cruising with you.'

At the tables outside her favourite restaurants she drinks nothing but German beer. It's charming, her blokey taste in drinks. When her friends pass she jumps up and hugs them like dolls. 'This is my friend Jason,' she tells them, but it's obvious from the way they smile and shake his hand that they know exactly who he is.

When he's home he checks the answering machine for her messages and pieces together meals from what's left in the fridge. Crumbs have hardened on the kitchen table, dirty footprints mark the shower floor. He finds Erin's notes at the base of his door: the milk to get, his share of the electricity bill to be paid. When had they started communicating by pieces of paper? It doesn't feel as if he's been away that much.

The Redbacks are tenth on the ladder and will slide further, he senses, before the end of the season. They're not playing with any discipline.

Something granite in the Pascoe Vale Swans and Tullamarine Jets has smashed them twice. They have to get tough again, Maddox tells them, tough like they were back in January and February, hitting the ball as if they'd die for it. At training he sets up their brick pyramids again, their witches hats, their crash bags. It's easy to beat the other guys, especially now that they spend more time in Storm together than they do at the gym. They've become a tribe. 'You're missing all the fun,' Sheff tells him privately. 'Some of these high school chicks, mate, you wouldn't believe it. They queue up for us older blokes.'

In the change rooms at the end of sessions they point out his new underwear and necklace, his clean shirt and the aftershave he dabs around his neck. 'Look out,' they say. 'Dalts is dolled up for his chick.' Their wolfwhistles bounce off the walls and surround him as he leaves.

'My ex wanted an itemised list of who I'd gone out with before him,' Zoe tells him the night following the Redbacks' last match of the season. 'I keep waiting for you to interrogate me. You're the first guy I've dated who hasn't freaked out at the thought that I've slept with other people.'

He reaches up and finds her hand, watching her face. 'Why are you going out with me?'

'Oh, boy.'

'Well, you've got this place, and your Chapel Street friends. I sometimes wonder.'

'You're not good enough for me?'

'Or something.'

'You're sexy and fun and I like you, okay? Shut up.'

On the night of her birthday, with her windows open to the warm rain outside and the slushing traffic two floors below, Zoe reaches into her bedside drawer and slips a blindfold over her eyes. 'You're next,' she says, laughing. He can have her however he likes. She won't see his fumbling, or the tremor in his hands, or the stupid grin he knows he puts on when he can't unhook her bra. He relaxes, freed of the mirror she becomes, the expression in her eyes that says she's used to being with more experienced men.

. . .

The Lygon Street Foodstore, along with the Cosmopolitan, is one of Erin's favourite places to have coffee. On the first Wednesday of October he walks there with her to queue among the other young people in dark clothes peering into the display cases of bocconcini and prosciutto. Her big sunglasses hide what she's thinking. At their table on the footpath, she jiggles her knee while she nurses her cappuccino.

'I don't know what I'm doing,' he tells her.

'You said you had a girlfriend once. Daphne.'

'That was different. That was school. Zoe's got this fundraiser at Flemington today. I keep thinking about all the dickheads in suits who'll be hanging around her. I'm a jealous bastard, I know.'

'Where's your invite?'

'It's a company thing.'

'Bitch.'

'Huh?'

'One of us had to say it. I mean, turn the tables. She's a guy. No way I'd cop that. What are you, a fifties housewife?'

'She's not a bloke.'

'What's the difference?'

'Everything.'

Erin goes through her routine with her lip balm and her rollies, both from the discount Smoke Mart on Sydney Road. So much of what she does is making do, filling gaps, as though she doesn't understand how far she could go. 'All I'm saying is, if you were my boyfriend I wouldn't treat you like that.'

'Treat me like what?'

'Like a doormat. Like a little puppy to play with when it suits me.'

'Well, I'm not your boyfriend, am I?'

She falters. When she speaks her tone is sharp. 'You said she's not a bloke. What difference does that make?'

'You said I was a fifties housewife.'

'It was a metaphor, Jason.'

'I know what it was. I know what you were saying.' He looks at the whirlpool he's created in his coffee and waits for her to skewer him. She can be so hard to read. And if he tries, he knows the look she'll give him: you're not clever enough to know what I'm thinking, you poor thing. 'And I'm not a puppy,' he says, loud enough to be heard over the traffic.

'Not if I can help it.' When he looks up at her, she's smiling again. This is how she's used to spending her mornings—teasing him. He's glad when she stands, dropping her share of the bill on the table.

As they pass the restaurant next door a woman his mum's age eating pasta at a wooden table clutches Erin's arm. 'You almost got away.' Her laugh is as startling as her outfit.

'Leanne. I didn't see you.' Erin steps away from her hand.

'Noel and Karen said you were living around here now.'

'Yeah. Lucky you caught me.'

'Have you eaten?' The singsong in the woman's voice perfectly matches her practised expression. 'I've just started. Sit down. How are you?'

'We're on our way somewhere, actually. Good to see you.'

The woman's smile gets wider. 'Gerry and I have some friends in Flemington. We're having a flutter or two. I've sent him to put a bet on for us, pay for my lunch.'

'That's the way to do it.'

'Who's your gentleman friend?'

'No, Jason's my housemate.'

Jason waves, staying mute in case something he says puts Erin in a worse position—whatever her position is with this woman, Leanne, who's still smiling as if seeing Erin with him has made her day.

Leanne wags her finger playfully at Erin. 'I saw you walking along and I thought, "Does Noel know about him?"'

'No. Still on my own, I'm afraid.'

'Good for you.'

'Listen, we're off to a barbeque, Leanne. So give my regards to Gerry.'

'Well, I'll be sure to report back that you were looking lovely.'

Halfway up the hill to North Carlton, Jason says, 'Well, are you going to tell me who she is?'

'A small-minded fucker, Jason. I went to school with her daughter. Living in a small town, that makes me her business. Fucken snobs. And it's not even a community—it's just who's still there.'

Back at the flat she reaches for her doona and her journal, drawing down her shutters. He recognises one of his own moods in her and packs his sports bag. No way would she ever end up like that lipsticked woman, if that's what she's worried about. It goes against what he knows of her: the car she's saved for, the job she's kept, the books she buys more often than food. Sometimes she's so blind to who she is.

• • •

November twenty-eighth is his mum's birthday. He arrives at her house just before noon, as he said he would. She opens the door to him in bare feet and jeans and an apron, her longer hair smoothed into a ponytail. 'Look at your clothes,' she says, turning him around in front of her after they hug. 'You look so grown-up.'

He passes her the present Zoe had helped him choose and wrap. 'Open it before we do the photo.'

'Let me get out of this daggy apron first.'

The awkward photo of him is still on her fridge. It's good that she'll have a better, adult version of him to compare it to now.

'You've still got all those boxes in your room,' she says. 'I haven't been through them. But if you could throw out the things you don't want . . .'

'After lunch.'

'You're lucky I believe in hoarding. Some of the junk in my wardrobe must be as old as you.'

He opens the champagne, moving around the table so she can put down their plates and her new gravy jug. Having the food in front of them, finally, is relaxing. He glances at her between forkfuls. For a moment he can see her if he wasn't there, a lone forty-two-year-old sitting over her dinner with the evening dark outside. Those names in the exercise book, probably her friends, how often does she still go over them? The discomfort he'd felt reading those cuttings spills through him again.

'I'm going out tonight.' She watches him for a sign of approval. 'My friend David's coming to pick me up at five-thirty.'

He stops chewing, his appetite gone. 'David?'

'Can you stick around to meet him? I've told him about you.'

'You and he are . . . ?'

'No, nothing like that. There's a whole group of us going to one of the restaurants in the mountains.'

'Oh.' He finds himself again. 'Okay.'

'You'll like David, I think. He's hard not to like.'

When the dishes are finished he heads along to the room she calls his and closes the door behind him. David. The name leaves him puddled in a dull resentment he doesn't understand. He lies on the bed, waiting it out, recognising his protectiveness of her. She's forty-two, he reminds himself. She can look after herself. She put up with you.

He dozes, sleepy from the champagne, until her voice comes through the door. 'David's here. Want to say hello?'

When he opens the door he finds her wearing a long sleeveless red dress, a pair of new black heels and holding a matching bag. She smiles at him as if he's a mirror. He follows her down the hallway.

The man at her front door is thin and gangly, with a receding hairline and a doughy nose. His chocolate-brown suit and white shirt look fresh from the drycleaners. 'G'day, mate,' he says, holding out his hand. 'Good to put a face to the name, finally.'

Jason moves slightly to let David inside the door. 'Where are you taking Mum tonight?'

'A little pasta place I know off the tourist trail. Smells as if you've had a real feast here.' David winks at him. 'Best meal in town, isn't it, mate?'

'It's nothing,' his mum says, eluding the compliment.

'Have a great night, Mum.'

'Walk us to the car?'

'Okay.'

David's white Saab is parked in the driveway. There's something outdated about the car, as if he inherited it from his parents. When David opens the driver's side door the inside lights show leather seats. His mum climbs carefully into the passenger side. Seated, she taps the windshield and waves, as if he might have lost her behind the glass. David reverses up the driveway.

Jason wanders to the front gate and looks up the hill towards the shopping strip and the whispering Sunday night traffic. Back on the porch, he lets himself inside. The house is his again, the photos in her room, her exercise book of names. But he leaves those things alone, wary of the questions they ask. In the room where he'd been dozing he opens the boxes of his high school things and stuffs the freestanding junk into garbage bags.

The resentment David's presence had provoked remains with him at work across the next week. He tries to remember to double-check his takings, he leaves messages on Zoe's office phone. But David's face becomes his dad's in Echuca, its detail shadowed. What would Mick have now, twenty years on from his mum? A wife, kids, family traditions. Hard not to like, his friends might say.

In the Brunswick gym he works even harder than before—dumbbell squats, barbell lunges, calf raises, farmer's walks. The muscle he packs onto his arms and thighs tells him who he is: a modern athlete, an outdoors person, a hot girl's boyfriend. David and Mick don't have what he has. Schoolboys in weight belts approach him at the scales for advice on their routines and to check if what they're reading in the magazines is right. Like Arnie said, he's an axe.

He helps the other Redbacks at the bench presses. Their end-of-season trip sounds as if it had been a riot: the Swedes staying in the hotel with them, the porno Ned and Woosh had made, the casino, the golf-cart races on the local course.

'How's your missus?' McKee asks him.

'She's a star.'

'If that's the way you feel about her, maybe it was a good thing you didn't come, mate.'

Some of his teammates haven't got much else, he realises. After school, they'd gone straight to work at building sites and for road crews. They've been set alight, they've had concrete poured on them, they've been nail-gunned to support beams. Imagine waking up to that every day. He's been lucky.

Zoe Ford. She doesn't like the word girlfriend, but that's what she is. She makes him sharper, more adult. He can feel it in his stride alongside her and hear it in the way he talks with her friends. His teammates can see it. She's changed him. The parts of himself that flare at the thought of Mick and his mum don't belong with her.

• • •

When he gets home from the hostel on the last Wednesday of January a message from his mum is on the answering machine. 'Jason, it's me.' Her voice is a lot flatter than usual. 'I need you to call me. I have an appointment with a specialist on Friday and want you to come with me. I can explain if you call. Thanks.'

She answers on the fourth ring.

'Mum.'

'Oh, thanks. I don't know if you get my messages, sometimes.'

'What's going on?'

'There's an appointment I have up here. It's at work, at Belgrave Private.' The flatness in her voice is gone but something brittle has replaced it. 'Can you come?'

'Can't you drive?'

'I can, I just . . . It's my nerves at the moment.'

'What's wrong?'

'It's a women's doctor. It could be breast cancer, they're not sure.'

Coldness overcomes him. 'When do you need me there?'

'Before eleven, if you can.'

'See you then.'

He arrives at her house at quarter past ten on Friday morning. When she answers the door she's in a starched work blouse and acrylic pants. 'Have you had breakfast?' she says.

'You're going to work after this?'

'I feel better wearing this, that's all, more normal.'

When he lowers himself into the passenger side of her Corolla his head almost hits the ceiling. Cancer. He looks for something reassuring to say. She starts the engine and puts it in gear, one step at a time, gripping the steering wheel tightly. She drives so slowly he can read the numbers on each of her neighbours' letterboxes.

'It's a biopsy,' she says. 'It's one of the things they do when they can't say what it is. What the lump is.'

'Okay.'

'I have a family history. I should've got it looked at earlier.'

The car park at Belgrave Private is on the opposite side of the street to the main building. He follows her through the sliding doors, close enough to hold her hand if she wants to. She nods hello to the receptionist. They catch the elevator to the second floor alongside a nurse and a very old man in a wheelchair. So this is what she does every day. They suffer badly, she'd told him many times, especially at the end, when their cancer is so advanced that morphine is all you can do for them.

She confirms her appointment with the secretary inside and sits beside Jason. There's nothing to look at except the stand of information flyers and the box of toys in the corner.

'Christine Dalton.'

His mum finds her feet. Then she's gone.

Family history, he thinks—he doesn't know any of it. He sits, elbows on knees, hands supporting his forehead, waiting.

When she appears again she doesn't smile at him as she normally would. She pays with her health insurance card and chequebook, and he opens the door for her again on the way out.

'Do you want me to drive?'

'Yes, thanks.'

The Belgrave roads are wider than the ones in the city. He travels at the same speed she did, avoiding any sudden braking. No clouds in sight. He tries out a few questions in his head but decides to keep them there.

He parks at the front of her driveway and when they step out he can hear the rustle of gum leaves around the telephone wires. Inside her house, the stillness is unsettling.

'I'm going to lie down,' she says.

He watches her walk into her bedroom. Her colour's back but there's still no sign of what's going on inside her head. Maybe nothing is. The only food in her fridge is the end of a loaf of bread. No milk, no cereal in the cupboards, no fruit in her fruit bowl. He stands still in the kitchen, tight with dread. How long has she known something was wrong? Would she call him if the news was bad? Maybe that's why she won't talk about it.

He gets back from the supermarket in the midafternoon. After unloading the groceries into the fridge and pantry he calls Zoe. On her answering machine, she sounds like a secretary. 'Babe, it's me,' he says. 'I can't make it round tonight. I wish I could. My mum's not well, so I'm up in Belgrave. I'll fill you in tomorrow night, okay?'

At twilight she comes out of her room. Below the sound of the TV he can hear her in the kitchen heating the chicken and mashed potatoes he'd left her. After a while she comes down the hall and into the lounge room to join him, carrying her food. She's still wearing the clothes she wore to the appointment and doesn't look like she's slept.

'I have to be on the last train to Melbourne,' he finally tells her. 'I have to play tomorrow for my club, East Brunswick. If I don't play, I don't get paid.'

'I didn't know you could get paid.'

'It keeps things steady.'

'I see.'

At the front door he hugs her.

'Please get a haircut,' she says. 'I can hardly see your face.'

Between phone calls at work over the next week he sits in the staff toilet with his hands against the door, unable to play along with the backpackers checking in and out who want to know how to get to Bells Beach. In six months, three months—how long do these things take?—she could be dead. And after she's dead, what? He puts himself back in Hawthorn, blaming her, another self-obsessed teenager.

'Sure she'd be scared,' Zoe says in bed one night. 'Being a nurse, especially. You haven't spoken about it with her?'

'We don't really . . . communicate well.'

'It could just be a cyst. That's what happened to one of my girl-friends' mums.'

'So what are the chances of cancer?'

'I honestly don't know.'

At two am he gets out of bed and sits in her kitchen with the light on. How long would it take? Chemotherapy, radiotherapy, surgery, morphine. Images of her funeral play in his mind, then the time after, the months and years. All the hours he'd spent yelling clever things at her in his head: how would they sound then? He'd done nothing to change things.

No new messages are waiting for him on the answering machine when he gets home from work on the following Wednesday afternoon. Maybe the results aren't through yet. He puts down his bag, collects the phone and stares at it for a while before he dials. She answers quickly.

'It's me,' he says.

'Jason, I'm sorry.' Her voice is heavy. 'They called this morning. It's benign, it's no problem.'

'Wait. What's benign?'

'It's just a cyst. I'll go in for surgery in a fortnight and they'll take it out.'

'You don't have any cancer.'

'No. I'm fine. You don't have to worry. But if you could drive me home from the hospital, I'd appreciate it. There are some things I want to talk to you about.'

On the morning of her surgery he calls in sick at six and is at Flinders Street station in time for the seven forty-five train to Belgrave. The train dips into the loop and howls.

The sky above the Dandenong Ranges is still early-morning blue when his train pulls in to the station. To steady himself, he buys a coffee from the café next to the newsagent. The journey from the shopping strip to the hospital by bus is twenty minutes. In the bus's back seat he takes refuge inside his Walkman, but his thoughts find a way through Soundgarden's barrage.

Belgrave Private has its own bus stop. He follows the blue line on the tiles inside to the post-surgery ward. Her room is the corner suite. Inside, she's already packed her belongings into her overnight bag and stripped the bed sheets for the nurse to collect. He hugs her carefully. She smells of antiseptic and cheap soap. It scares him.

'Looks like you got the special room.'

'I hated it.'

'Are you in pain?'

'No. Yes, some.' She picks up her bag gingerly, ignoring his offer to take it for her. 'I had to do my bandage again. My post-op nurse must have been a man.'

In the car park across the road she climbs into the Corolla's passenger side before he can open the door for her. The bandages around her chest peek through the top of her shirt when she puts on her seatbelt. Her expression is set hard like his teammates' faces when they're hiding an injury from Maddox.

'You look really healthy, Mum. Do you feel well enough to go to the lookout?'

'Do you know the way?'

'You'll have to show me.'

'Okay.'

The tourist trail is ten minutes down the highway. He drops the Corolla into second gear on the incline, its steering wheel and gear stick shaking under his hands. He grips the wheel harder.

She rolls down the window to take in the fresh air and scenery. 'How was your game on the weekend? You said you played.'

'The season starts at the end of March.'

'You still go to the gym, though.'

'I have to. If I didn't, the other players would knock me over too easily.' The road straightens again. He feels for something else to say. 'In most team sports, you have to build your core strength so that you can stay on your feet. Your core's your hips and your pelvic floor, up to your abdominals. That's what we spend a lot of time working on.'

'It's good you keep fit,' she offers. 'You won't get osteoporosis when you're older.'

The car park at the top of the trail is smaller than he remembers. He guides the Corolla up to the fence and stalls. 'Sorry. I relaxed.'

'Who's been giving you lessons?'

'My housemate, Erin. But she drives a VW.'

They climb out and lean against the Corolla's bonnet. Clouds have formed to the west. Below them, cars bank up at the traffic lights in Croydon, another suburban morning drifting by.

'Hey, Mum.' He presses on, wanting things to be different. 'Sorry for those times I yelled at you. When I was playing football, back in Hawthorn.'

'No.' She shakes her head.

'You didn't deserve that.' He looks at the gravel. 'I took a lot out on you, I reckon. I'm sorry. I didn't know what I was doing. You were there, so you copped it.'

She shrugs, more at herself than him. 'I've got more good memories than bad.'

'Really?'

'It's funny.' She looks at the city. 'Stuff you wouldn't even remember, like you coming home after school. Splashing me when you were little. That kind of thing. Small things. They're the brightest.' She waits. 'Now you're older, and I feel as if I don't know you. Not like I should.'

'When you wrote to me when I was up north, why'd you do that?'

'I could never have said what was in the letter to your face. Out loud. I'm sorry.'

He lets her apology go. He walks to the fence and back. 'I'm seeing this girl at the moment. Zoe. I met her at this wedding. We've been going out for five months now.'

'What's she do?'

'She's a media buyer. It's pretty—what's the word—corporate. She lives in South Yarra. We go out there a lot. She's a couple of years older than me, but that doesn't make a difference.'

She nods, thinking over what he's told her, and turns his way appreciatively. 'That man you met, David, I'm not going out with him.'

He looks at her.

'I'm so used to being on my own. It's hard.'

'Zoe says I'm an ice-man. I tend to keep it all . . .' He pushes his hands together like a vice.

'You learned that from me.'

After he drops his mum at her house, he trudges back to the train station. No-one else is there. He slumps into a chair, as drained as if he's been crying, but can't get a grip on his feelings—relief or confusion, tiredness or edginess. He doesn't know whether to go to bed or hammer out at the gym what the day, the month, has put him through. He pictures Zoe in her blue slip, in one of his work shirts, in her bra and underpants, waiting for him by her bed. He tastes the saltiness of her skin on the tip of his tongue and hears the small sighs she makes when she's under him and pressed so tight he can feel her heartbeat against his.

He searches his back pockets for telephone money. A woman waiting on the other side of the platform gives him ten cents, but when he tries the booth at the bottom of the rampway there's no dial tone. He leans his head against the receiver, willing it to work.

On the train he watches the backs of the houses flash past the window and lets his thoughts return to Zoe.

The following evening he sits with her on the bank of the river as the last of the day's sun fades behind the city. The grass is a cool cushion under his hands. Behind them, evening joggers pace along the Yarra bend, their feet rough on the track. It sounds too much like Redbacks training.

'What are you thinking about?' she asks.

'I keep telling myself I'm gonna go somewhere.' He runs his hand down her dress to her thigh. Having hold of her when he's saying something always feels better. 'I have this atlas at home that I used to flip through every day, imagining places. And Erin's got this map of the world in her room with pins in the places she's been.'

She nods. Her silences are trustworthy now. 'You should do that. Travel, I mean.' She looks at the darkening sky above them. With the funky line of her fringe and her tinted sunglasses pushed back on her head, she could be in one of the commercials her agency makes.

'You're quiet.'

She drifts again. 'Do you know what you're going to do, eventually?'

'I hate that question.'

'I guess that's the answer, then.' She hunches, and something about the way she holds her ankles makes her seem younger. 'I think we need to cool off.'

'Why?'

'I think you've become dependent on me. In a bad way.'

'I'm not dependent on you.'

'I think you are.' She blinks, almost scared. 'You've been at my place how many nights in a row now? And every night you're not, you call.'

'Not every night.'

'And I've never seen your place. You've never, ever asked me over. Not once. It's been five months.'

'We can get a drink and you can stay over tonight, okay? I'm sorry.'

'You're not hearing me.'

'I'm hearing you don't want me around.' He begins pulling the grass. 'This is the part where you try and make it easier on me, isn't it?'

'Jason—'

'Cool off. Whatever the fuck that means.'

She holds her ankles, squinting at him sadly. 'You're always hiding something from me. You are.'

He watches a man and his son stroll, one behind the other, along the riverbank, the son bent slightly beneath his backpack, following his father's footsteps. A girls' rowing team glides towards the Punt Road Bridge and beneath it.

He stands up. 'I'm going home now.'

'Jason.'

'I'm going home.'

• • •

In his room, too many parts of her remain: his clothes in the closet, the aftershave, the condoms in his bag, the bottle of wine in his cupboard. He stuffs them all in a garbage bag and throws it beneath his bed. The only clothes he has left are his old ones, as shapeless as curtains.

When the tram coming down Lygon Street to take him to work is her tram, he lets it pass and takes the next one.

At night she appears next to him in bed, just behind his eyes. The words come easily now, turning to acid in his throat: You think you can just drop me and move on like I never happened? You and your slut friends, you think you're better than me? He thumps her side of the mattress again and again.

If only he'd acted less keen, as his teammates had advised, or if he'd dropped her after their first night. He should have kept her as something on the side, like McKee or Sheff would have done. There would have been plenty more just like her to sleep with if he'd only kept his head.

'It's me,' he says to her answering machine. 'Call me. You owe me that, right? We haven't even talked. So call me, I'll be here.'

Training at six o'clock that night is the Redbacks' final preparation for the Tullamarine Jets and the 1994 season. After two wind sprints up and down the ground he has to bend over, hands on his knees. Pain rattles through his ribs and shoulders each time his teammates tackle him. The newest players in the squad seem armour-plated. He makes a show of hamstring tightness to avoid the last three drills and jogs laps instead, alone.

'You need to come back out on the town with us, big fella,' Sheff says to him. 'Only way to get past it. Between you and me, mate, I wasn't gonna say anything, but I reckon you could do better. Seriously. You don't want to get too worked up over a bird. It's not worth it.'

After stumbling home from Bertolucci's, he finds Erin waiting for him at the kitchen table. Since the start of the year she's lost weight and tonight she's wearing tights instead of tracksuit pants, a turtleneck skivvy instead of a jumper. 'You made it. I thought you might not be coming home.' It feels as if she's new, somehow—the weight loss, the polite questions.

'Training ran late.' There's no food in the fridge. He pours a glass of water down his throat.

She holds the edge of the table for a moment. 'I think I want to move out.' She looks at him plaintively. 'It's not you. My honours fin- ishes in October. I don't know what I'll be doing after that. I might not even be in the country. But I didn't want to leave you hanging.'

'Well, you kind of are.'

'Jason.'

The four pots he drank at Bertolucci's have filled his skull and he can taste them on his breath. Work at the hostel tomorrow is going to be hell. 'You could have picked a better time, that's all.'

'Is it Zoe?'

'Yes, it's Zoe. She bloody . . . No, it was my fault. You never liked her anyway. You were right.'

'I never met her.'

'Well, you're not going to.'

'You broke up with her? If you'd told me earlier—'

'Look, I've got all this shit in my head right now, okay? I don't need this, I really don't.'

'I'm not psychic, Jason. If you'd told me about this before instead of—'

He raises his voice over hers. 'Erin, my mum had a cancer scare at the start of February. It's probably made me a real arsehole and you've had to put up with me. And since I met Zoe, I haven't been the greatest housemate. I know that. I'm sorry. How many times do I have to say it? I'm sorry.'

'This isn't about you.'

'Bullshit it isn't.'

'Sit down.'

'I don't want to bloody sit down. I just want to get some sleep and go to my bloody job.'

'Fine, have your tantrum. Goodnight.'

She deserved it, he tells himself later, lying on his bed in the giddy dark. She could have approached him differently—asked first, seen how he was feeling. And she was the one with the bad news to deliver, not him.

He slides his hand inside his pillowcase. The warmth there is like that of Zoe's body. The traffic under his window sounds like it did from her bedroom. Where to next? he thinks. Echuca is four hours away. He could get some answers. Mick would be in the phone book, or someone at the football club would know him. He thinks back on the Gold Coast and its beaches three minutes from his apartment, the sand sucking his feet at the water's edge. It wouldn't take much to get up there again. This time, he could do it properly: travel around, stay off the dope, keep his mind clear. A day or two on the bus and he'd be there.

He checks the phone, but there are no new messages. He picks up the receiver and dials her number one more time.

. . .

By three-thirty the following Sunday morning, Storm's dance floors are full. From a table in one corner he watches the girls on the podiums. Most of them are underage and wearing the kinds of clothes Zoe used to wear: sparkly dresses and tight singlets that show off their breasts. A rap song erupts, another teenybopper anthem. How many victories had they rung in to this kind of stuff now?

'Big fella,' Sheff mouths at him from the back of the drinks queue. His high-five falls into a sloppy hug. 'Let's get back on it.'

Three bourbon and Cokes costs twenty bucks. Sheff polishes his off as they weave towards the remaining Redbacks by the wall: Leon, Ned and Woosh. The blonde girl between Woosh and Leon is glazed with sweat. Her head lolls in search of her drink. The bracelet on her wrist is from the uni party that left two hours ago. She closes her eyes and doesn't open them until Leon nudges her. But she can still stand up.

'Should've seen how toey McKee was.' Woosh laughs. 'He was begging change off me so he could get to Blush.'

'Tragic,' Leon says.

'But we've got a winner here,' Ned says. 'Right, love?'

She opens her eyes again and smiles in Ned's direction. Somehow, she manages to swing her glass to her mouth.

'What did you say your name was?' Woosh asks.

'Alex,' Ned says for her.

'Sexy Lexy. I love it.'

She tries another smile until her head docks on Leon's shoulder. Where had they found her? She doesn't look like the type who'd stay at a club without her friends. Blinking quickly, she makes a face as if she's going to walk off and falls into Leon's arms again.

'Grab her drink off her,' Jason says.

'She's right.' Leon squeezes her against him. 'I'll get her a glass of water in a sec. She'll sober up.'

'Where'd her mates go?'

'Ease up, Dalts. We're looking after her.'

Jason puts down his second empty glass as another Zoe-lookalike floats past them. Walking to the men's is like moving across a skating rink. 'This rap crap,' he says to the dance floor. At the urinals he uses one hand to steady himself over the trough. His hair sticks to his cheeks. The bourbon and Coke is carpet on his tongue. One more, and he'll be wrecked.

Outside, the dance floor flickers. He lunges around it to where the boys were standing by the wall, but they're gone. They're not at the bar, either. He eases down the carpeted entrance stairs and past the bouncers. There are still clubbers queuing to get in. On the street, the 7-Eleven two doors down is so bright it hurts his eyes. He holds himself against a bus sign. Seventy bucks left in his wallet. It would be good to walk off some of the journey first, rather than get sick in a taxi.

He starts towards the next main city block, the local court buildings looming above the streetlights. For a change he turns right and up one of the city lanes. A truck beeps past, violent among the dumpsters and shadow.

Laughter floats from somewhere nearby, a laugh he knows. He stops and looks down the alleyway on the opposite side of the street. It was Leon, he's sure of it. They must be taking a piss. The grate at the front of the lane clanks under his foot. The laugh comes again, no mistaking it—an asthmatic hacking he's heard in the Redbacks change rooms a hundred times. Closing in, he can hear murmurs and someone coughing. He follows the wall towards the end of the lane.

It's them—belts open, flies undone.

'Hey, dickheads,' he says.

Leon grins at him, his cock standing up, and raises one finger to his lips.

Ned has her on the bitumen, her upper body squashed between the lane's right wall and the blue dumpster in front of it, his arse flexing against hers. All her hair has fallen forward. She's still awake, though her body's limp. Below Ned's gasping they can hear her sobs occasionally broken by the wheeze of her breath into the wall.

'I want in,' Woosh says.

'No, fuck off,' Ned says.

Her ears and the back of her neck are crimson. She's slack now, a bundled thing, like something they found on the street on the way out. One of her hands comes up from her chest to stop her face scraping the wall.

'Shove over,' Woosh says.

'I said, fuck off.'

'Let's check out her tits,' Leon says.

'How do you feel about that, sweetheart? What have you got under there?'

Her knee jerks. She works herself closer to the corner between the bin and the wall, kicking backwards to free herself. Leon laughs again as she falls on her side, coughing. He taps Ned to make room. Woosh has her dress scrunched up to her shoulder blades.

Jason unbolts his feet from the ground and finds the wall opposite them. Crowding in, they don't see him coming. After slinging a punch into Leon's side he tackles Ned into the wall.

'—the fuck?' Ned says.

Someone's hands are on his shoulders and are pulling him backwards.

Leon. The wall behind them breaks them apart. Leon's second jab takes him on the ear. Jason straightens enough to knee Leon in the ribs and clear him out of the way.

'Fucken idiot, Dalton.' Woosh hitches up his pants.

The girl's gasps turn into shrieks when he kneels beside her. Behind him, Leon laughs again. The side of her face that scraped the wall is bleeding. Jason fends off her fists, her fingernails lashing his neck and arms. 'Wait.'

Ned and Woosh join Leon in laughing as the girl staggers away from them dripping tears. The back of her dress is caught in what's left of her underwear. Heaving, she follows the wall to the side street with her hands.

'Arseholes.' Jason staggers into the street after her. His feet can't find a straight line. He drools and retches on the spinning gravel but nothing comes up.

'Fuck off, Dalts. You're spastic, mate.' Woosh finds and lights a cigarette while Ned and Leon retreat into the alley shadows to make themselves decent again.

A block down the side street he vomits into a sewer grate. When he comes to, slumped between the grate and the wall, vomit is on his sleeves and jeans. His body is aching from the chest down. He hears above him the voices of two men, tipsy. Behind their legs, a glowing cab has its door open. They lift him to his feet. 'You're right, mate. Can you stand? This way, we've got you.'

. . .

Six hours later he climbs out of bed, sleepless and reeking. Erin's morning newspaper is open on the kitchen table. She must have left for work already. Through the kitchen window there's no sky, just Melbourne grey, the nearest clouds drifting like factory smoke. At the sink he pours himself a glass of water, gripping the bench to keep it down, and throws the glass at the wall. He picks another glass off the wash rack and throws it at the same place. It shatters onto the bench and around his feet, leaving a dent in the wall as big as his thumb.

The girl had thought he was one of them. Outside, he sits at the base of the stairs, holding his head. If her friends had stuck around as they should have, it wouldn't have happened. Wind comes up the stairwell and into his clothes. He sees his mum's face in her hands as she shakes on the couch in their Hawthorn flat.

Woosh, Ned and Leon will be there on Tuesday, laughing in the change rooms with the rest of the team. They'll know what he saw, but it won't matter. They were drunk. It never happened. He walks out onto the driveway and down the middle of the road past the churchgoers on the sidewalks and then the church. His stride is wooden. He makes fists and digs his fingernails into his palms at the thought of the girl crumpled in the alley, her scratches on his neck stinging now. Five blocks down he crosses into a laneway between two miner's cottages. At the end of the laneway he finds a vacant lot with a hole in its wire fence large enough to crawl through. No, she'll never tell anyone. Who could she tell? If she told, there'd be people who'd think she deserved what she got, walking into an alley with three guys in that part of the city. She was a dumb slut who got burned, they'd think. They wouldn't say so, but that would be the message.

Amid the debris inside the vacant lot are broken fence palings, moulding chipboard, lengths of frayed rope and half a cricket bat. He picks up the bat by its gaffer-taped handle and goes back to the fence. When he strikes the edge of the crawl space, the whole fence vibrates and pain wires up his elbow. The bat soon cracks through its centre. He doesn't stop.

At home later he picks up the phone and dials Zoe's number. It rings until her answering machine clicks on. He hits the wall with the receiver and the knots in his chest tighten.

He pulls off his jumper and throws it on his bed, then his shoes and jeans. Showering, he grimaces as the water strikes the burning red welts she'd left on his arms. Afterwards he sits against his mattress, watching his knees. He pictures Mick at home on the morning after, showering and moving on with his day, his life. Only his teammates had known. That would have reassured him.

The clean clothes remaining in his cupboard are his tracksuit pants, jeans, black Bonds tee-shirt and hooded jumper. He folds them carefully into his sports bag, followed by his Walkman and wallet. After sweeping up the broken glass and leaving a message with the hostel, he writes a note for Erin and leaves it standing folded on the table.

Had to go away for a while. Family stuff. Home soon though.
Can we talk when I get back? J

The tram stop on Lygon Street is open to the wind. He paces from one end of it to the other. He has change in his wallet and Friday's fortnightly pay in his account. The tram soon arrives. Aboard, he moves to the back corner and sits, his heart thrumming.

At the Spencer Street bus terminal the ticket seller behind the wire-grille counter looks as though he's been sleeping. 'Where to, brother?'

'I need to get to Echuca from here. Can I do that?'

The ticket seller feels for the clipper below his desk. 'Next bus is at one-thirty. Just over here, at the orange sign.'

Nausea churns in his stomach, and rage—an old feeling, frightening but overpowering in the confidence it gives him, the sense of purpose. He thinks again of the girl in the alley. Her name was Alex.

11. heartland

The antique sign at the top of the main street says Echuca. He'd thought the town would be smaller than this, just a scattering of shops on the Murray, but there's a community hall and a tourist information centre and cafés along the main strip. Like in Belgrave, the lettering on most of the retail stores is tourism-quaint. It must have a population of ten thousand, even more.

When his coach reaches the town depot at five pm, he climbs off and walks towards the pubs near the river, uncertainty slowing his feet. The Murray Hotel is a block from the river and looks as good a place to stay as any. Only one person is working the front bar, an elfish girl with dyed red hair wearing the hotel shirt and black jeans. The customers look like locals—a man in sheepskin with his teenage daughter, and two older men in flannel shirts like his own. He waits for the girl to finish her conversation with them.

'After a drink?'

'I was looking for a room.'

'Just a basic?'

'That sounds right.'

239

'We've got a footy team coming through tonight, but I reckon I can find something for you.'

For twenty-five dollars he rents the cheapest room upstairs: a double bed, a sink in the corner, a view over the main street. After dumping his backpack he finds a quiet window seat in the bar. The biggest meal they serve is a twelve-dollar steak. He orders it, suddenly famished, and a jug of beer. The trots on the two screens above the hotel's TAB room offer a comforting drone.

As dusk encroaches he can feel the coldness of the street on the window. How do you find people? Erin would know. If only he had someone brainy with him. The steak soon arrives, as big as his plate. It feels like weeks since his last good feed.

The pub begins to fill with customers. Some of the women are his mum's age, but plumper, with flatter accents. What would they say if he introduced himself? Would they make a connection? She'd said, sometime, that everyone here knew each other's business. Then again, that had been twenty-two years ago. Echuca probably didn't have a McDonald's outside of town then. It would have changed a lot since she was here.

He programs Nirvana on the pub's jukebox. It's good to hear some of his feelings out loud. Two hours later, he rises slowly from his chair by the window, spilling some of his remaining jug on his shoes before leaving it on the bar. He stands at the base of the hotel stairs, hunting his pockets for his key. No-one knows who he is or what he's doing. A guy like him must pass through here every couple of nights. The thought is shelter.

His room at the end of the hallway on the second floor is noisy with the customers and the music downstairs. It doesn't matter. He kicks off his shoes and crawls beneath the blankets. With the light off he listens to the trucks passing on the main street outside, the two-and-a-half-hour trip on the bus blurry in his mind. His anger had abated on the journey, the drone of the bus lulling the shock and the violence out of him and leaving just an ache in the pit of his stomach. He sees the girl again, Alex. It had only been the night before. He wraps his pillow around his head to keep her out.

• • •

The following day, he rises at lunchtime and for twenty minutes stands under the dimly-lit shower at the end of the hallway. Afterwards, he wipes the steam from the bathroom mirror and looks at himself. This is the face Mick could see. Find a name, find an address, knock on a door, and there he'll be: some strange man staring at him. Is this how it's going to happen? He goes back to his room and sits on his bed, waiting for a better idea to come.

Downstairs, he heads into the main street and the nearest café. The day's newspapers are in the rack by the door but he doesn't pick one out. He orders a toasted sandwich from the heavy-set woman behind the counter and sits with it on the blue vinyl seat by the drinks fridge.

'You been in before?' she says.

'No, I'm from Melbourne.'

'You don't look like it.' She smirks. 'You've got a country face.'

'I've got relatives from here.'

More people come into the café, tourists in city coats. It's so easy to pick them. He looks through the window at the Murray Hotel on the opposite side of the street. After finishing his sandwich he brings his plate back to the counter. 'Excuse me, could you tell me where the local footy club is?'

'Depends which one you're after.'

'How many are there?'

'Echuca Central's round the corner, off the river. Echuca-Moama's nearer to the bridge.'

'Which one's older?'

'Central's been there since I was in primary school. Can't speak for the Goannas. You a rep, or something?'

'Just a tourist. How do I get there?'

'Here.' She pulls a napkin from the dispenser beside the cash register and finds her pen on the till. 'Just follow the main road round the corner to your left. You'll see a big old stand same side as the river.'

At the end of the main street, he turns left and walks along the tourist trail until he can see the ground from the top of the riverbank: a huge oval picketed by giant gums, the grandstand on its far side two storeys high. Schoolchildren are playing kick-to-kick while their PE teacher stands watch. He walks around the back of the wooden spectator seats concreted to the ground as the children's voices catch and fly on the afternoon wind.

The clubhouse is open. There's a group of older women inside, football mothers and grandmothers by the looks of them, arranging club sandwiches and biscuits on trestle tables. As he expected, there are player and team photos on the walls, a trophy cabinet, and pennants along the ceiling's rafters. The Echuca Central Magpies, they're called. Honour boards list the club leaders from 1922 until 1993. He skims through the names until the 1960s, and from there onwards reads each row—club president, club secretary, captain, best-and-fairest winner. Michael Casey is listed twice as a best-and-fairest winner, in 1968 and 1972.

'Help you there, love?' one of the women asks him. Her clipped tone—easy but abrupt, as though she's too busy to bother with introductions—says she's a club volunteer, same as Meryl or Jess at the Redbacks.

'No. Thank you.'

'Are you okay?'

'Yes.'

She looks him over again, just to be certain.

'Thanks,' he says.

'You looking for someone?'

He breathes in. 'No.'

'How'd you like a sandwich? You look like a man who could use a sandwich.'

'No, thank you.'

'Sure you're okay?'

'Thank you.' He drops his head and makes his way to the door.

The post office is a block further along the main street from the café, past another two pubs and a youth hostel he could have stayed in for free if he'd planned ahead, if he'd thought for maybe ten more minutes about what he was doing instead of jumping on the first bus here. The man behind the post office desk looks close to retirement age. His thin silvering hair and sideburns are cut in an old-fashioned style, and nothing in the brisk way he sorts the packages by the scales says he'll be interested in helping.

'I need to look up someone,' Jason says. 'You got a white pages or something?'

The older man points to the shelf below the steamboat postcards where the directories have been wedged. 'Best I can do, son.'

Jason flicks through the regional directory to the letter C. There are two listings for Case and another for Castles but no Casey between them. He closes the directory and puts it back.

'Any luck?'

'No.' It's a long shot. 'You wouldn't know of a bloke from here named Mick Casey, would you?'

'Mick Casey? No.'

'Right.'

The older man blinks at him. 'You're a relative?'

'I think so.'

'You think so?'

'My mum came from here.'

'Best bet's the electoral office then.' The man punches open the cash register, prints a short receipt, and disappears into his office. Jason waits. The man seems to be working to his own time. Eventually he reappears and unfolds a town map from the plastic display rack in front of the cash register. 'We're here, swimming pool's there. You'll see an ugly brown office with a sign above the door, and you'll probably have to wake up the bloke inside.'

'Thanks.'

The wire fence around the swimming pool has rust patterned through it, and the brick change rooms behind the diving boards are decades old. She would have swum here, probably, with radio playing on the PA speakers just as it used to when he and Hayden were swimming at the Harold Holt. His mental image of her as a teenager churning up and down one of the lanes is so sharp and sudden that he stops to listen to the glassy water lapping against the pool's edges.

The electoral office is across the road, its sign as old as those around the pool. Inside is a clerk reading a novel as thick as the ones Erin likes so much. He keeps reading until Jason places his hands on the counter.

'Excuse me. The bloke at the post office said I can look up an address here?'

'Correct.' The clerk reaches for a ledger beneath his computer, yawning from the exertion. 'Just need your ID and autograph, brother.'

'Where do I look?'

'We go by elections. Most recent was '93, and we've still got the '87 and '84 as well, if you need to go back that far.'

'All of them, I guess.'

The 1993 electoral roll has the same listings for Case and Castles as the regional directory. As he flips through it, Jason concentrates on keeping his fingers steady on the lines of names. No Caseys, again. The 1987 roll lists a Carey and a Casell. He closes the roll, both dejected and relieved. What was the likelihood, anyway, of Mick staying in the same town for twenty-two years after what he'd done? He chides himself for imagining that things would ever work out so easily. Dumb anger had brought him here, the same dumb anger he'd always listened to instead of just accepting things and moving on.

In the 1984 roll, under Casell, is a listing for Casey, M., of Hodge Street, Echuca. As he looks at that name, all he feels is a cold anxious silence. It couldn't be any other person. The name on the honour board at the football club was proof. A moment later he trusts his voice again. 'Pen and paper, mate?'

The passing cars on the street outside come too fast. According to the clerk, Hodge Street is at the intersection past the cinema and the hardware store. A bluestone pub on the way is busy serving lunch to local office workers, suited men and women in nicer clothes than the customers in the Murray Hotel. On the other side of the road is a travel agency, a Brashs, a hair salon. You could live your whole life here without needing to go anywhere else. While she was growing up, places like Melbourne and Sydney would have been just pictures in the news.

He should have packed his Walkman today, some mix tapes to keep out the fear.

Hodge Street is as wide as the residential streets in Carlton but more ordered, its gutters without leaves, its careful lawns ending in rosebushes and upright fences. He follows the descending house numbers towards the primary school, hotly aware of the looks he must be getting, alone in the afternoon neighbourhood, his face unshaven and unfamiliar. A weatherboard he passes has a neighbourhood safety icon above its doorknocker and another has a boat on a trailer in its driveway. No junk furniture on the verandahs, no bars over the windows, the sky a dome unbroken by apartment buildings. He could have been born here.

Within a block of Mick's address he crosses to the other side of the road. In the bus from Melbourne, with his face against the window and the roadside tree shadows playing across his closed eyes, he had been able to see himself as far as Mick's open door. He had been able to make Mick appear, a blank-faced man of Arnie's size, and had been able to fell him with two words: Christine Dalton. Mick would falter at hearing them, his pretend world of twenty-two years fractured forever. But this street is real, and so are the numbers on each of the letterboxes, and so are the front doors of each house, and so are the people inside them. He comes to a halt, the ache in his stomach intense.

If his counting is right, number twelve should be three houses along.

The for sale sign attached to the fence of number twelve has photos of the rooms inside. It describes the six brand-new self-contained retire-ment units on the property: central heating, on-site gardening, shower and toilet railings, an emergency alarm phone. Completely drained, he stands at the front of the driveway looking at the roller-door garages next to the curtained lounge rooms and at the small purple flowers in each of the garden plots. He leans against the bank of letterboxes, his legs empty pipes. This is 1994. Echuca has moved on from 1972. Wake up, idiot.

Later he finds himself on the riverbank a block from the Murray Hotel, alone, a pie from the local bakery gone lukewarm in its white paper bag beside him. The river's green-brown surface shivers with the ripples from local riverboats tied to their moorings. For what feels like a long time he watches two enormous ants in the fleshy dirt. He takes three bites from his pie, puts it down, and dozes against his knees. With his eyes closed he can hear the river moving.

Training with the Redbacks is in an hour. Ned, Woosh and Leon will be the first to notice he isn't there. If Maddox asks why, they won't even look at each other. Out on the track they'll joke and laugh with the other blokes, and they'll get their rub-down and go home. They'll store the girl, Alex, in a box in their heads where she won't get in the way, just like some of the other blokes can lock up thoughts of their girlfriends whenever it suits them. Just another stupid night, they'll tell themselves. She wanted to be there.

Upstairs in the Murray Hotel he changes into fresh clothes. When he comes downstairs, the girl from the night before is behind the bar again. Her ponytail and the way she smiles is so familiar, like those of a dozen girls he knew at school. He orders a beer and she sashays to the taps as if she's working for the fun of it.

'Listen.' As he watches her feed his money into the till, the words he'd thought of upstairs still sound like good ones. 'I'm looking for a guy who used to play footy for Echuca. I've got a rello in Melbourne who knows him.'

'I'm from Moama.'

'Right.'

'But if you hang around—Cuz, the manager, he might know. He'll be on the bistro at seven. He's lived here all his life.'

Jason orders steak and chips and settles in one of the bistro's booths. Monday night is one-dollar-pots night. By seven-thirty the front bar is crowded with locals his age. A group of five of them are wearing black and white football guernseys. At seven o'clock a middle-aged man wearing glasses and a plain blue tie emerges from the office behind the bistro bar. In 1972, Jason calculates, he would have been twenty-something. Jason mutters his lines one more time into his remaining pot and meets the man who must be Cuz at the bar.

'The girl in the front bar said you'd be a good person to talk to. I'm looking for a bloke who used to play footy up here.'

'What's his name?'

'Mick Casey.'

'Right.' The manager seems to make a decision. 'Just a moment.' He steps around the corner to serve a throng of teenage girls signalling for more pots. Jason sips his beer, not looking at the other customers who probably overheard him.

When the manager appears again he looks busy. 'Yeah, Mick was a full-forward back in the day. Good player. What did you say your name was?'

'Jason Dalton.'

'You a relative?'

'From Melbourne.'

'Well, I couldn't tell you where Mick is these days, mate. We're going back twenty, twenty-five years here. People come and go, you know?'

Jason's resolve fades. 'Thanks anyway.'

The same mixture of dejection and relief comes over him as he had felt at the electoral office. He stands among the revellers in the front bar. Someone has put 'Daughter' on the jukebox and the footballers behind him raise their beers to the song's jangling intro. Eddie Vedder's voice is a comfort: a long calm lament that says he understands what feeling broken is like.

The young bartender puts down her break-time cigarette to serve him. 'Cuz helped you find that bloke you were looking for?'

'The bloke . . . He was from a long time ago—the sixties and seventies.'

'Piercey,' she hollers over his head. 'Magpies got a function tonight?'

'The old-timers, yeah,' one of the footballers shouts back.

'Should head down there.' She winks with the professional charm that Zoe had, a reminder of the other feelings waiting for him in Melbourne. 'Bound to be someone who knows who you're talking about.'

'Tonight?'

'I reckon, if you hurry. Bedtime's early up here.'

He leaves her a five-dollar tip. Outside, the main street is so quiet he can hear the bugs spiralling into the streetlamp at the next corner. It feels like midnight, not dinnertime. Birds screech in the river trees as he follows the tourist trail back to the football ground. The evening silence in Belgrave had always been peaceful but up here it just seems empty, stifling. You'd want to get away from it, like those drinkers in the pub.

The clubhouse's lights are on. As many cars are in the car park as are at the Redbacks' ground on match day. The four grey-haired men smoking outside the clubhouse doors take note of him when he steps into the light, but not enough to interrupt their conversation.

The women he'd seen in the clubhouse earlier in the day must have worked through the afternoon. Tables of premiership cups and team photos have been set out adjacent to the buffet, and two numbered, lace-up guernseys have been pinned to the wall behind them. Dinner is over, but most of the ex-players sitting in the fold-out chairs, talking with their mates, have still got food on their paper plates. One older man has ventured out on his own to mop up the remains of the roast trays. He's still wearing a full suit, unlike the smokers in front of the clubhouse and the drinkers now relaxing in the chairs behind him.

Jason crosses to him. 'Excuse me.'

The man glances at him and sidles along to the roast vegetables, his plate already crowded. 'You're a bit young for our mob, mate. You Thommo Henderson's boy?'

'No, I'm—'

'You look a bit like him.'

'My name's Jason.'

'Well, if you're looking for a feed, I've cleaned us out. Should've elbowed me out of the way when you had the chance.'

'I just came in. I know you've got a night on here. I was hoping you could help me out.'

'No, you're welcome, mate. Good for you to come in and see a bit of the history. You had a look at the guernsey here? We actually played in those. That's the real thing. Morrie Taylor brought it in.'

'Sorry.' Jason follows him along the trays. 'I'm not actually from here. I'm trying to find out about a bloke. Mick Casey.'

'Shit, mate. I thought you were one of the new blokes. You look like you play.' Once he's finished piling his plate the man finally turns to face him. He's tall, over six feet, though his belly makes him look shorter. 'Mick, yeah. I know him. I mean, I don't know him now, but I saw him play. What are you, a cousin or something?'

'A rello, yeah.' Saying it, he can't get used to the thought, and doesn't want to. 'I'm interested in the history.'

'Good for you, mate. I reckon you younger blokes could really get something out of learning it. We don't do it enough, mate. You look around the room, at a joint done up like this. People forget, don't they? I'm talking about the wider club. You see the names on the boards, but if you were to talk to some of these blokes—the stories we've got. Walk around and have a listen. People talk a lot of shit about tradition, but this is it, isn't it? Fair dinkum.' He forks a potato into his mouth, happy for the audience. 'No, he was a good player, Mick. Never actually played with him. He was after our time. Here, I'll show you what I'm talking about.' Halfway across the room he offers his hand. 'Barry Swan, by the way.'

The trophy table has three pictures of the same football team in front of the three premiership cups on display, one for each year: 1951, 1953 and 1954. Barry points to himself in the front row of the 1953 side, his arms bunched beneath a soldier's stare. 'Most of us are here tonight, if you look around. We don't look like it now, but we were one of the top country sides in the state. I reckon four, five of us could have played VFL if we'd gone to Melbourne.'

'When did Mick start playing?'

'Mick?' Barry looks back across the room to where their conversation had started. 'Oh, years after, mate. Late sixties, early seventies. As I said, he was after my time. His name's up on the board over there. Have a squiz.'

'But you saw him.'

'Plenty of times, yeah. He was a full-forward. But what I'm saying is, mate, you should walk around and talk to some of these blokes if you're interested in the history. People forget, you didn't straightaway go down to the VFL if you were a good player. Some of us blokes, if we'd gone and trained with a VFL club at the time, we would've been signed on the spot. Who do you follow?'

'Hawthorn.' Jason glances around at the other men in the room, but they look like they're doing the same thing: reminding one another of what they were. 'More when I was a kid.'

'Case in point. Hawthorn were a nothing team back then. But if they'd had the pick of the country leagues like your AFL clubs do today . . .' Barry looks again at the photos on the table. 'A bloke like Clancy Glendenning, our ruckman. Superstar. Runs a farm down in Kyabram. Could've gone to Melbourne, probably, but he had a wife and kid.'

'What happened to Mick?'

Barry shakes his head. 'Like I say, I only saw him play. But he was another one. Every week he got his six or seven goals. He used to get a little cheer squad behind him, same as Clancy did back in our day. Might have had a few beers with him, come to think of it. That's the other great thing about country footy. You wouldn't know it down in Melbourne. We used to have a beer with the supporters afterwards. They'd follow us week to week, home and away. Especially if we were playing Rochester. You'd have people coming up to you in the street, signs in the butcher's wishing us luck, everything.'

'What was he like?'

'Mick? Regular bloke.' Barry winks at him. 'If you could get past his women. Used to follow him from town to town. Some of us have got it, some don't. I remember that about him.'

The image of Mick being followed by a pack of girls hits Jason hard. Had his mum thought she was lucky, going out with him that night?

He stares at Barry until the older man stops forking his food around his plate and notices. 'Fuck off,' Jason says, before leaving.

He walks through the car park and out onto the pathway. Where had Mick taken her? Somewhere out into darkness like this while the rest of the town was asleep? Somewhere he knew three mates could hold her down and no-one would hear the screams? Jason shudders, his mind filling with images he struggles to repel.

• • •

More drinkers are in the Murray Hotel's front bar than when he left. He walks through them on the way to his room. There are as many girls as guys. Cigarettes and jugs of beer float among them. The guys standing in an open circle in the corner remind him of his teammates at the Redbacks. Is this how it happened—at a pub night?

Their laughter reaches up through the floorboards of his room. He lies awake, the lightbulb above him an eye. His spit is paste. Rolling onto his side and curling into a ball doesn't help. Each time he lets go of a breath he trembles. Later, the sound of the bolts falling on the hotel's front door jolt him awake and he sits up, clammy and panicked in his clothes. He wraps himself in his blankets to ward off the silence.

The next morning he surfaces from sleep at nine o'clock, unable to remember his dreams. He parts the curtains at his window and looks out over the main street, the tang of his sweat sour in his tee-shirt and jeans. His fury at Barry has settled as resignation in his stomach, a crumbled weight. He won't find Mick, and he won't get any answers. That had been a stupid fantasy. In the shower he sits on the floor, lost. The afternoon bus will get him into the city by six o'clock. At home there'll be messages waiting for him on the machine: work and the Redbacks wanting answers. But Erin will be there. Hopefully, she still feels like seeing him, even if he deserves otherwise.

There's still the morning to fill. He tries to remember if his mum
had told him anything else about Echuca. So many Christmases, so
many birthdays. Something about where she lived, near the river. It
comes to him: she'd lived on the same street as her school, on the opposite side of the road. She'd told stories about what it was like to be able
to see her house from her classroom. Echuca Secondary. Finding it and
seeing it with her eyes would be something good to remember—that
and the pool, if nothing else.

After breakfast, he follows the trail outside the steamboat wharf to
the riverbank. According to the town map he still hasn't seen the golf
course, the BMX track, the fire station or the distillery. This is the kind
of place she must have sat in the afternoons, with a magazine, feeding
the ducks on the water.

Around the corner from the Murray Hotel is the police station and,
past it, the high school. He walks there slowly. Most of the houses
along the way are on blocks of land as big as her new place in Belgrave. Their picket fences, front yards and verandahs are spotless. They
wouldn't have changed in fifty years. Her parents, she'd said, had run a
newsagency and had spent their whole lives here. Every day the same
neighbours on the street and, at work, the same customers.

The high school is the size of Burnley Secondary. There's no date
above the entrance, but it looks as old as the rest of the neighbourhood.
Red brick from the floor to the top of the second storey. Two girls in
chequered brown uniforms cross the balcony above the gravel yard.
When they see him, they laugh. So many girls at school had driven him
crazy by laughing that way.

A residential street runs along the school's left side. Its weatherboard
houses are smaller than the ones off the main road and are in view of
the second-storey classrooms. It must have been her street. In one of the
neater gardens a woman much older than his mum is pulling up weeds
and dropping them in a wheelbarrow. The street finishes in trees. He

PAUL D. CARTER

wishes he'd brought a camera. Having some photos might really mean something to his mum. He turns and walks back, slowing outside each of the three houses that are within sight of the classrooms.

'Morning,' says the old woman. 'You'd be one of the Daltons, right?'

'Sorry?'

'I said are you one of the Daltons?' She circles the air in front of her face with one gloved finger. 'Don't mind me. I just looked up and thought, "Hang on, I know that mug."'

'Yeah, I'm Jason Dalton.'

She sits on her haunches, the sleeves of her men's shirt rolled up. 'Yes, you look a lot like old Hugh, especially across the shoulders.'

'You knew my mum?'

'You're Christine's kid, are you? How about that.' She takes off her gloves, grinning, and wipes her hands on her jeans. 'I haven't even introduced myself. I'm Marie. I knew your mum's family when they were two doors down.'

'Right.'

'Staying in town, are you?'

'A hotel, yeah.'

'Mum with you?'

He pauses. 'I'm on a footy trip, me and my team—East Brunswick.'

'How is Chrissy?' It's hard to tell from her expression how much she knows.

'Good. She's down in Belgrave.'

'She a doctor yet?'

'I don't get you.'

'It's what she used to talk about doing, that's all. Maybe I'm confused.' Marie looks across at the school. The sun lines around her squint are as thick as pieces of string. 'She and her school friends used to come past of a morning. I could hear them from the other side of the house.' Her golden hair is shorter than his but looks just as badly kept, curling in clumps around the collar of her polo shirt. 'I taught there myself, once upon a time. Just before your mum was at school.'

He looks down the street again at the house his mum must have lived in, the one with the green letterbox. 'You knew her folks?'

'I used to bowl with Estelle.' She holds her hand up to her brow. 'I wish I had a picture to show you. Especially of Hugh. By gee, standing side by side, you could be brothers.'

'I never met him.'

She puts her gloves back on in a thoughtful way that makes him wish he'd lied.

He looks back at the school, imagining his mum sneaking through the front gates at lunchtime with her friends to raid the fridge in her dad's garage, another story she'd told over the years. 'Any of her friends still around?' He checks his tone. 'I should have got some names before I left.'

'Well, let's see.' Marie's eyes travel to the same place where she had recalled his mum and her school friends moments before. 'We're talking twenty years ago now. You'll have to let me think for a second.' Her tongue works over her stained teeth. 'Joyce Devine. She's the vet up the road. Chrissy would have to have told you about her, I'm sure.'

'Joyce.'

'They used to be bread and butter, the two of them.'

The scrapbook, the *Echuca News* articles. 'Something about Joyce and the RSL. Mum mentioned the story, once,' he lies.

'The Rotary Club, that's it. Joyce went on exchange to Italy when she was at uni. Yes, she's a smart cookie, Joycie. Almost as smart as your mum.'

'She's a vet now?'

'The vet's up next to the swimming pool.'

'Thanks.'

'Give my love to Chrissy. I'm glad to hear she's still up and about.'

On the main street, the lunch crowds have appeared. The town looks as if it could be changing soon: among the antique shops and embroidery stores, three surf shops have opened, and the McDonald's on the corner has the most crowded car park on the street. The fire station is a hundred metres further down the road, the ancient water tower above it like a museum exhibit. Opposite is a small collection of Victorian houses where the vet must be.

He stops in a bakery. A middle-aged woman in an old boxing-kangaroo jumper is running it, but she doesn't move from her portable radio until he's at the counter. He buys a Coke and takes a seat.

'Can I get you anything else, hon?'

'I'm happy for the moment.' He looks at her, waiting. 'Actually, can I have the biggest salad sandwich you can make?'

'You betcha.'

Half an hour later he stands up from the table, stiff. Outside, the day's best light seems to have come and gone, though it's only midafternoon. His bristled, tired face floats beside him in the next shop window. Calling ahead from the pub would have been the smart thing to do, he tells himself. A lot of things would have been the smart thing to do.

. . .

Joyce's name is on the wooden sign outside the second of the Victorian houses, before a line of university letters. The waiting room inside has polished floorboards and smells disinfected. He sits in one of the chairs by the window. A dog barks in the next room, sounding shrill and impatient, like Dundee used to be each time they reached the park. He runs his hands over his jeans. Soon a door opens and he hears the dog and its owner leaving, the man's farewell as relaxed as if he's leaving a bar.

The girl on reception picks up the phone. 'There's a man here, Jason

Dalton. He hasn't got an appointment but he says he wants to see you.
Dalton, D-A-L-T-O-N. He's here now, yes. Okay. Okay.'

A woman who must be Joyce walks into the waiting room a minute
or so later. She's taller than he expected and her hair's ash-blonde, not
dark as it was in her newspaper photo. She stoops a little when she
offers her hand. 'Hi, Jason. Christine's son?'

'Yeah.'

'Your face!'

'I know.'

'Do you want to come in?'

The furniture in her surgery is simple, except for the steel bench in
the centre of the room and the boxes of wrapped medical supplies on her
sink. She offers him a stool. Her white denim shirt and jeans could have
come from the same store as his mum's house clothes. 'Is mum with you?'

'No, I'm up here on a trip.' The lie feels childish in the privacy of her
house. 'On my mum's old street, one of the neighbours . . . I forget her
name—an older lady.'

'Marie?'

'She said this is where you worked.'

'Has something happened?'

'No.'

Her face is as lined as his mum's. But instead of sadness, the lines
show strength, especially when she smiles. 'I never thought I'd see you.'

'You know about me?'

'Of course.' She nods, waiting. Her silence is easy. She must be used
to spending a lot of her time listening. 'But I haven't heard from your
mum since you were born. How is she now?'

'Better.' For a second he thinks to say more, but summing up his
mum's story in a few sentences wouldn't be right—would lessen her,
somehow. 'She had your name in a book at home. There was an article
in the paper about the exchange you did.'

'She saw that.'

'She kept it.'

Joyce nods. Strange, how calm she is, as if she already knew he was in town. 'And how about work? What does she do?'

'She's been a nurse all my life.'

'I studied with her at the nursing college in Bendigo.' She waits for him to respond. Whatever he shares, he judges she wouldn't repeat it. 'You're clearing the air.'

He nods.

'Mick.'

'I saw his name on the board at the club.'

She lowers herself onto a stool, puts her elbows on the bench and her mouth behind her hands. Her wrists are as thick as his, her forearms ropey and sun-damaged. Finally, she says, 'Growing up, did you know about him?'

'No.'

'What were you going to do?'

'I don't know. I don't know why I came, really. This whole trip . . .' He stops, lost. 'I wanted to sort out a few things. But now that I'm here, it doesn't seem like it's working.'

'But you're here, though.'

'Yeah.' He looks at his hands. Something about her calmness, the way she doesn't say anything to try to make him feel better, makes the words come easier. 'Mum wrote me a letter once, when I was living up in Queensland, explaining about Mick.' He clears his throat. 'I know he's my dad. I know why.'

'I can't speak for your mum. It's hard. I'm forty-three now.' She looks at him carefully before speaking again. 'He was four years older than us. He and his mates played for one of the local clubs. We didn't know them then. I didn't get to know him afterwards, either.'

'You were there.'

'We were in the pub when Mick and his mates came through.' She draws breath as if she's about to continue, then stops herself.

For a while it's better just to sit with her.

He says, 'Can I get a glass of water?'

A washed mug is upside down in her surgery sink. She fills it and brings it back to the bench. She sits like a younger person, her hands on the front of her stool. She seems good at waiting, too.

'Thanks.'

'Take your time.'

After finishing the mug he says, 'Did he know Mum was pregnant before she left?'

'He couldn't have, no.'

'But people knew.'

'People like to talk.'

'What about her mum and dad?'

'They were hard people. But I didn't really know them, either—I was a kid.'

'You stayed, though. You've been here your whole life.'

'I could never live anywhere else. It doesn't leave you, this place.'

He looks out her window at her rectangle of yard and the shadows pushing towards her verandah. The awnings are as old as the ones on his mum's street. Is this the house she grew up in? 'Thanks for talking to me.'

'When you went to the club, you asked about Mick.'

'I looked him up. He's not around.'

'He is.' Joyce looks saddened. Jason feels his stomach drop. 'No-one talked about it with you, though. About ten, maybe fifteen years ago now there was an accident, a car accident. Out on the Murray Valley Highway. He survived, but just barely. He's in supported accommodation now.'

'What's that?' His voice sounds as if it's coming out of a well.

'He suffered a head injury. They moved him in there after he came out of intensive care.'

'A hospital.'

'Like a hospital. More a home.' Finding the right words is hard for her, too. 'When people have accidents up here, you hear about it. But maybe you don't talk about them with people you don't know.' She waits for him to nod. 'I can't imagine the men here would have been keen to talk about it.'

'How much do they know?'

'Not what I know. Not directly.' Her face hardens. 'But enough.'

The anger in his chest feels close. He stands up and circles his stool. When the worst of it is over he looks at her. 'How old is he?'

'Forty-six.'

He sits down again and lets himself be silent. That's it then. No other ending presents itself. Today or tomorrow he'll still have to board the bus to Melbourne, still call the Redbacks to quit, still go back to work. 'I want to see where he lives.'

'Jason, I've seen Mick since the accident. I don't think you should visit him. I don't think there's anything for you in going there. I don't even know if Chrissy knows.'

'Do you have the address?'

'Are you a cruel person, Jason?'

'No.'

She takes his mug of water to the sink and refills it for herself. Facing away from him, she pushes her hair off her face. 'It's called the Meyer Cottage. Where are you staying?'

'The Murray Hotel.'

'Here.' She reaches for a business card from her top drawer. 'I'll write you my after-hours number. I hope . . . I hope you're okay. I hated him, Jason. I hated him harder, even, than your mum did. I'm not sorry for what happened to him.'

Outside, cars growl at low speed along the main street then rev out of town onto the highway. Some of the café owners have begun to pack away their outdoor chairs and sandwich boards. It's going to be a cold night.

He walks to the Murray Hotel, checking his wallet. Just enough for another counter meal. When he arrives, the hotel's front bar is crowding up with smokers. He orders a pot from the narrow-shouldered balding man behind the bar. Some of the locals look his way and raise their glasses demurely. He sees his reflection in the hotel's darkening window. Dark hair, a thin nose, small ears—Christine.

That night he lies in bed and lets his mind churn. He sees the street where his mum grew up, the trees and the schoolyard. He sees flashes of Alex's face, her terror, and hears her shrieking. He sees his mum, lying exhausted across the couch after work. Absent-mindedly, he rubs his face with his left hand, trying to settle. What kind of state had Mick been left in? Was he sitting and rotting in a nursing home because of what he did?

'Hi, I'm Jason,' he says to the darkness. 'Do you know you have a son?'

The next morning, he hands his room key to the girl at the bar. Some men have already started drinking, though the trots are yet to start. He slips onto the street. The morning sun is bright on the windows of the passing cars, and the cafés and the local delicatessen are busy with late breakfasters. At the ATM at the end of the block he checks his bank balance. No pay yet. Hopefully, Erin will already have done the week's shopping when he gets home.

There are no buses in the depot when he arrives. According to the timetable in his bag, the next is scheduled to leave at three-thirty. Buying a ticket leaves only silver coins in his wallet.

He sits on the bench in front of the main street newsagency. Two girls his age pass, wearing surf jumpers and pushing prams. He watches them roll down the street and into the chemist. He's exhausted. He shakes his hands out, but they don't stop quivering. In frustration, he tucks them under his thighs. If he went to the cottages now he could still see Mick. There would still be time before the bus. He could still get answers, if he could think of the questions.

At the nearest phone booth, he takes Joyce's business card from his wallet and dials her number. Her secretary answers, the same girl from the day before.

'Hi, it's Jason Dalton again,' he says. 'Would it be possible to see Joyce again in the next hour? I have something to give her.'

'Let me check.'

He waits, looking at the number she'd written on the back.

'She said that's fine. Just come to the front desk.'

'Thanks.'

He hurries to her surgery and her secretary greets him at the door, smiling in a way she hadn't the day before. 'I'll tell her you're here now, Jason. She won't be long.'

Two patients are making noise in her waiting room—a fluffy cat in a travel cage and a Great Dane on a leash. Jason sits down. It's good to be back, it feels as if she's on his side.

A cat in a cage comes mewling out of Joyce's rooms under the arm of a young man. Except for her black shirt, Joyce's outfit is the same as the day before. 'I'll just be a tick, Susan,' she says to the owner of the cat. 'Jason, do you want to come in?'

He follows her into the surgery and she closes the door behind him.

'I haven't got a lot of time at the moment,' she begins. 'But I was thinking, if you're free for dinner—'

'I have a bus to catch.'

'You're going home?'

'Yeah.'

'I had quite a night last night.' She gestures to the door on the other side of the room which must lead to the back of her house. 'I dug up some photos. I didn't realise I had so many. I don't want to keep you waiting. But can you hang on a moment?'

He sits on the stool, looking at his watch. It would have been good to talk with her properly and learn more about her. It's funny how familiar she seems already. Using the pen and notepad beside the sink, he writes his mum's name and phone number for her and hands it to her when she comes back into the room.

'I should have asked for this yesterday,' she says.

'You might get the answering machine a few times. She can be lousy at returning calls.'

'Here.' She hands him an envelope-size photo. 'You can keep this.'

The picture is slightly pale with age. In it, Joyce is almost the same age she was in her newspaper photo. Beside her stands his mum. 'Oh,' he says. They're standing in front of the river on what looks like a summer's day, hugging each other. Their dresses are the same style. His mum has let her hat fall on its drawstring onto her shoulders. He turns the photo over. *April '70*, it says, in light pencil.

. . .

The cottage is across the train line and towards the telephone towers on the western lip of the town. The street looks poorer than the one Mick's old house was on. A lot of the porches are wooden and their driveways have weeds growing through cracks in the asphalt.

He sits in the gutter opposite the cottage, watching. No signage anywhere says what it is. It could be a regular home, except for the minibus parked out front and the hospital white of its window curtains. A gardener must spend time looking after the lawn. Behind the front rooms must be more units, and beside the screen door, he notices, is an intercom, where he'd have to say his name before they'd let him in.

He lies back on the nature strip and, shrinking as low as he can in his bomber jacket, shields his eyes with both forearms. Crying would be better than this hollow calm, or anger—something to carry him forward, through the door, into the room, same as it had carried him here from Melbourne. But rolling over and sitting up again is about all he can manage.

The front door of the main building opens. A middle-aged man, stooped and pale, appears from behind the screen and pushes it aside heavily. Bracing himself against the morning chill, he digs around in his pocket and finds a single cigarette. The cuffs of his pyjamas are showing beneath his bathrobe. His hair is receding. As he raises his cigarette he glances across the road and locks eyes with Jason. His hand freezes at his lips.

The man might be forty-six, if his injury has aged him. He might be the right height, though it's hard to tell because of his posture. He looks unsteady on his feet, and it's hard to imagine him ever being young or agile. But it could be him, Jason thinks. It could be him, just a raised voice's distance across the street.

The man breaks his stare, takes a long drag on his cigarette and stubs it out, shuffling back inside as the clouds start to obscure the last of the sunshine.

Mick, in his mind, had always been a bigger man, stronger. Whoever lives in that place is some other man named Mick Casey, who grew up here, in a house on the street he'd seen yesterday, a man in his forties now and in care. Some guy who never really mattered outside of his home town. He's in there, through that door. Jason scrapes his hand against the jagged gravel at the edge of the gutter and then presses his palm into it, hard. When he looks at it, pinpricks of blood appear in his skin.

Erin's voice inside him is clearer than his own: 'Small-minded fuckers, Jason. And it's not even a community—it's just who's still there.' He remembers Barry in the club, scarfing down as much of the leftovers as he could get. A whole team had been there with him, living in the past, trying to make it matter more than it did.

He stands up and faces back down the street. Walking is difficult at first, his feet cold, his limbs stiff. Each of the houses heading away from the cottage is nine steps wide. He runs his hand along the tops of their fences: slate, brick, pickets, air.

· · ·

Erin's red umbrella is open and drying on the landing outside their apartment door when he gets home. He shakes it out. Its generous size and vintage handle make it good enough to steal. She forgets what people are like.

When he enters the lounge room she turns from the documentary she's watching and looks at him. He grimaces against his exhaustion, but gives in and lets his shoulders go. With the hand not holding her mug of coffee she holds out one arm for him to join her. He lowers his head onto her lap.

'You're okay.' Her hand on his head dissolves some of the sad weight inside him. In his mind, the two nights he'd spent in Echuca have already spiralled together. Just telling her about them won't make sense. He'll have to start with Hawthorn.

epilogue

North Fitzroy in the murk before sunrise is shrouded in elms, their autumn leaves skittering down the street as loud as the passing vans.

Trish from the kiosk has already opened up the Brunswick Street Oval change rooms when he gets there. He sweeps them out before filling the water bottles. Round four has the Cubs playing the Coburg Bombers at home. His clipboard is in his bag. The first aid kit, stop-watches and footballs are in the strappers' room. But the team still needs a goal umpire, a runner and a timekeeper. The morning's paper had forecast rain. If player attendance is like last week, getting a full side on the park will be touch and go.

Michelle is the first of the Cubs to arrive. 'Hi, Jason.' She keeps her boots in her Northcote Primary schoolbag. Her older brothers play Under-Seventeens for the Lions and she always sticks around to cheer them on. She's such a self-reliant kid. This could be her last season—the Under-Thirteens are boys-only—which is a shame. Already, she knows to handball into space, not at the player.

As the rest of the Cubs arrive the team manager, Beth, Flynn's mum, marks them off her roll. 'Eighteen. Thank Christ.' Her schoolteacher rule of not swearing in front of juniors doesn't apply on weekends. 'Anton's got Saturday-morning flu again but I've got Robby and his brother back from basketball. I'll do the paperwork on them after the game. Their dad's happy for them both to play,' she savours his words, "as long as they get a chance to kick a goal".'

'Everyone gets a run,' Jason says.

'That's what I told him.'

Before the game starts he lets the Cubs drill to get a feel for the ball in their hands. 'Don't worry about the score,' he tells them at the huddle. 'I want to see improvement. Last week, five of our goals came from you working together. So look for the handpass.' For now, at least, their eyes are on him. They'll forget his instructions five minutes after they start, but it's not the advice that counts. As Arnie says, it's about believing in them and making a demand out of your belief.

The autumn clouds that had been glowering behind the city sky-line on his way to the ground bring their rain halfway through the Cubs' second quarter. Many of the cars sloshing up the Brunswick Street tramline alongside them have turned on their headlights. It's too big a ground for Under-Elevens, even with traffic cones to narrow the boundaries. Whenever play gets bogged on the ground's far side, half of the Cubs backline sit in the mud.

Nineteen ninety-five won't be their season. Three games in, their lowest losing margin has been six goals. Half of them look like Under-Tens. Their only advantage is their six-foot ruckman, Isaiah, and the opposition know to target him. The rest of the team are underdogs. Keeping their spirits up is going to be hard. Training slogans look good on walls, he knows, but winning is still what gets them running into the huddle and not dawdling as if they're on their way to school.

The Cubs are thirty-four points down when Trish sounds the siren. Jason crosses the boundary line with Erin's red umbrella above his head, though the rain has passed, and stands far enough from the parents on the fence to prevent them from interfering. His backline are muddy on the wrong side of their guernseys and their faces say how lame this is, getting up at seven-thirty on a Saturday morning to get rained on in the back-pocket and watch other guys kick goals.

The team swarms on Erin's quartered oranges. The looks they'd given him when he'd told them she was just his housemate. Every orange peel has to go back in the bag. Every player has to say something good about a teammate before he'll speak to them as one.

He moves among them using the same low voice Arnie had. 'Keep protecting one another,' he says. 'Those buggers are big. Good players, they're always thinking the same thing. What's my team need? Where's my team need me to be? Michelle, you've been doing it all day. That shepherd you put on for Dylan out here on the wing? Champion.'

Isaiah is still fuming from the hits he's been taking. When the Cubs spread to their positions Jason motions him to stay behind. Be what you want the kid to be. If he's quiet, give him a rev with the big voice. If he's fiery, breathe. 'Isaiah, mate. You're ready to throw one. What's up?'

'Dickhead got me in the ribs.' Isaiah's voice strains against his need to cry. His dad's Datsun is in the car park, in the same spot every game. 'He's holding my jumper every time I go for the ball. Ump's too shit to see it.'

'You're gonna let him get you that way, or are you gonna run off him, kick five goals, show him those?'

'He's a cheat.'

'And you're a bloody good footballer who won't stoop to that. Beat him with your brain, mate. Wayne Carey does it every week.'

Isaiah throws a look downfield and kicks at the grass. His tight-shouldered jog back to the middle of the ground is a bad sign. When he stops, his hands are on his hips and his head is down. Jason tries to make eye contact again. Isaiah's stubbornness is good on the track—he doesn't know how to quit—but it becomes an obstacle when things turn against him. Channelling his energy the right way is something he has to learn. The siren sounds.

acknowledgements

To Mum and Dad, thank you for your unending support and encouragement; to Justina, Charlotte and Marcus, thank you for your belief that I would get this book finished, and for the laughs and beers along the way.

To Lynne and Stan, for your generosity, I am forever grateful.

To the team at Allen & Unwin—Clara Finlay, Ali Lavau, Siobhán Cantrill and Annette Barlow—thank you for your time, advice and belief in my book.

To Gaylene Perry and Stephen Alomes, thank you for your expert guidance and incredibly valuable feedback. I would also like to thank the late Peter Davis, a wonderful storyteller and teacher; and Deakin University for its financial support during the novel's initial writing stages.

To Kate, thank you always for your love, inspiration and grace. Still a revelation.

And to Napoleon, for your benevolence and fearless leadership. I am forever indebted.